BRIDLES LANE

WEST COUNTRY TRILOGY
BOOK ONE

BY THE SAME AUTHOR

NOVELS

Forgotten Places

The Devil and the Deep Blue Sea

Music From Standing Waves

SHORT STORIES

Moonshine (West Country Trilogy Prequel)

Goldfields: A Ghost Story

The Dutchman

Afterlife

BRIDLES LANE

WEST COUNTRY TRILOGY
BOOK ONE

JOHANNA CRAVEN

CONTENTS

"These superstitions have their origin in the purest feelings of the heart… They are the shadowings forth of love, tinctured with the melancholy dyes of that fear which is born of mystery."

Robert Hunt

Popular Romances of the West of England

DEAD WRECK

Cornwall, England.
1740

Three gunshots.

Ship in the bay.

A woman crouches in the churchyard. She grips a lantern and peers over the cliff at the sea thrashing the headland. Behind her, a little to the right, her family lies; their coffins crumbling and their bones becoming earth.

But there is a living brother, in a whisky-laden lugger, past where her eyes can reach. Scarlett Bailey has tossed a bunch of heather down to the sea spirits.

Bring him safely home.

She has been waiting here since dusk; signalling lantern in hand. A bundle of furze sits at her side, ready to set be ablaze if riding officers appear.

A flash of the lamp for an empty beach. Fire for prying eyes and revenue men.

ld
ach.
the
nen,
xes.

one. There'll be
ge the wreck; tear
eir goods with such

n to the beach is steep
and   her fist and runs it with
the certain

The ship plun   s strike the headland, hull
into rock. Mast lamps u   ldly; one plunging into the
sea.

No shouts. No cries for help. No-one struggling for
escape. The strange stillness makes Scarlett's breathing
quicken.

Men launch themselves into the sea. A whaleboat pulls
towards the brig's starboard side. Men working for Charles
Reuben, Scarlett is sure. Following orders while Reuben
stands on the cliff and counts his fortune.

The ship writhes against the land like a wounded beast.
Scarlett tucks her skirts up and clambers over the rocks at the
edge of the beach. She will board the ship from her port side
and get her hands to a little of the cargo.

Look what I found, she will tell Isaac. *Are you proud of
me?*

The cold sea steals her breath. She lurches towards the
ship's ladder, a sudden swell slamming her legs. She

snatches the rungs and pulls herself from the water. Climbs tentatively over the gunwale.

The wreck is dark. Spars groan and glass shatters. Lifeboats sway on their davits. The boats look untouched. No attempt made to use them.

In the moonlight, Scarlett sees dark beads staining the boards. Blood? Perhaps.

Dark blood.

Old blood.

It leads from the hatch to the gunwale and disappears into the sea.

She ought to leave.

No. She cannot go to Isaac empty-handed. To hell if she will let Reuben's men take everything.

The hatch opens with a creak. She climbs below and feels her way, sightless, through the dark passage.

There is no sound of life here in the crew's quarters. But nor is there anything in the darkness to hint at the presence of the dead.

She feels an indentation beneath her hand. Traces a finger along the carving in the bulkhead. A crooked crucifix is scrawled into the wood.

She can hear Reuben's men raiding the hold. She can't hope to compete with them. But she will find plenty in the captain's quarters. Trinkets and navigation tools, no doubt. Coin if she is lucky. Enough to put food on their table for a few nights at least.

The ship groans. The sea thunders into a distant cavity.

Scarlett stumbles down the passage, water at her ankles. She shoves open the door of the captain's cabin. The sea swirls around her knees. Lamplight from shore glows through the shattered porthole.

She wades towards the desk and tugs open the drawers.

Empty.

No trinkets, no tools, no coin.

She goes to the cupboard in the corner of the cabin.

Empty.

Dead wreck, they call the ships that are flung onto their shores with no living soul left aboard. But here is a skeleton; a wreck already plundered.

Lifeboats untouched.

Scarlett's mind goes to freak waves, to sirens, to hidden monsters and mutinies.

The rising water chases her from the cabin. Soon this ship will rot on the floor of their bay. She hurries back to the deck, clutching the corner of the pilot house to keep her balance.

She hears movement, groaning. She crouches, reaching into the dark. Her fingers find something hot and wet. Blood.

And this dead wreck, she realises, is still breathing.

He feels fingers work across his neck, searching for a pulse. Sharp pain at the side of his head. Blood runs over his ear.

He makes out the shape of the person leaning over him. A young woman.

Her hand on his forearm eases him into sitting. Nausea turns his stomach. He hears the sea battering into unwelcome places.

He shifts, his hand finding the pool of blood on the pilot house floor.

The woman tears at her underskirt and presses the fabric against the cut on his scalp. "Listen." Her voice is a sharp whisper. "There are men plundering your ship. They'll want this to be a dead wreck so they can legally claim her cargo. If they see you, they'll want you killed."

Asher stands, stumbles. He hears voices and footsteps. Life. But these voices are unfamiliar.

"Nothing down there but a few ankers," a man says.

"Take them ashore."

The woman darts out of the pilot house, leaving Asher alone in the darkness.

"What are you doing here, girl?" says a gravelly voice on the other side of the door.

"I thought to bring something back before you get your greedy hands to everything." Fear shakes her words. "You found cargo?"

"A little. Half the hold is underwater."

"The rest of the ship is empty," she says. "Was this Reuben's doing?"

A laugh. "Not everything untoward is Reuben's doing." She snorts.

"Get off the ship, Miss Bailey. We're setting her alight before the riding officers find her."

The men's footsteps disappear.

The woman throws open the door. "Come with me," she tells Asher.

He grips the bulkhead to keep his balance. "What's your name?"

She glances over her shoulder. "Is it important?" A flash of light illuminates her face. Thin and pale, dominated by large charcoal eyes. Tangled black hair clings to her cheeks.

"Your name." Urgency in his voice.

"Scarlett. Scarlett Bailey."

Asher's heart quickens at the impossibility of it. He says nothing.

She clamps a hand around the top of his arm. "Come on now. Lean on me." She crouches, edging her way across the violent slope of the deck. The sea swells over the gunwale and the ship's ladder vanishes.

Asher grapples with the deck's smooth surface. Finds nothing to steady himself. He reaches instinctively for a fistful of Scarlett's dress.

Her eyes scan the sea for a path back to the rocks. "This way."

Dark water sweeps over the deck, licking Asher's boots. He breathes hard, tightens his handful of her skirts.

"Can you swim?" he asks, his mouth dry.

"Ayes. I can swim. But the water's shallow. We'll not need to."

With a deep, undersea groan, the deck shifts further. Scarlett pulls her skirts free from Asher's grip and laces her fingers through his. She moves with sudden urgency towards the shore. He stumbles behind, blood running into his eye.

And the ship is gone from beneath his feet. Water on all sides. He panics, thrashes until his toes find the rocky sea bed. Scarlett looks back at him, gripping his hand tightly. Water swells around their shoulders. Asher feels the sea tug him back towards the wreck. He keeps wading, keeps stumbling. Finally, the water becomes shallow and he drops to his knees on the rocky outcrop beside the beach.

Orange light flares on the edge of his vision. He glances over his shoulder to see flames shooting up the limp, tangled sails. Smoke plumes, melting into the blue dawn.

A crowd is gathered on the sand. Their murmurs carry on the cold air.

An empty wreck?

The boats untouched.

"Stay back," Scarlett hisses. "Don't let them see you."

Ghost ship.

A sight he must be with his matted hair and his shirt black with blood.

Keeping his back pressed to the cliffs, he edges around the point behind Scarlett. At the top of the hill, a church spire is silhouetted against the lightening sky.

Talland.

Oh, this village. How he despises it. And yet what twisted joy he feels to have been flung onto her shore.

Scarlett follows his gaze. "You can't go to the church. No one there will help you. Come with me." She leads him up the steep path from the beach. By the first bend in the road sits a dark stone building.

She thumps on the door. "Flora! Quickly! Let us in!"

And then there is a woman in the doorway; pale hair falling over her shoulders and lamplight flickering on her cheeks. Her eyebrows shoot up as she takes in Asher's bloodied clothes, Scarlett's wet skirts. She takes his other arm and leads him into a world of shadows and flickering orange light.

He is in the village tavern, Asher realises. A dark wooded room lit only by the lamp in the blonde woman's hand. The bar is empty of both people and liquor. Crooked shelves, stacked stools, tables lined up against the wall. A great black hearth sits cold and empty.

The noise from the beach has disappeared, replaced by the loud, fast thud of his heart beating in his ears. His legs give way. The dark closes in.

BELL HOUSE

'My dear brother Dodge,

I have ventured to trouble you, at the earnest request of the people of my parish with a matter which ... is causing much terror in my neighbourhood.'

Taken from a letter to Rev. Richard Dodge from Mr Gryllis,
Rector of Lanreath
1725

Isaac Bailey trudges up the hill to the church, legs weighted with exhaustion. The service is filling. He slips onto the end of a pew.

How glad he is to see them; Caroline with her brilliant gold-flecked eyes, Mary wriggling in her mother's arms, Gabriel marching toy soldiers across his knees.

His wife eyes him.

He's a mess. He smells of sweat and sea. His hair is dishevelled, his greatcoat flecked with salt. He has left a trail of wet footprints down the aisle. He pushes dark strands of hair behind his ears and rubs his eyes.

Caroline twitches her lips, considering. "Has something happened?"

He reaches for her hand. "A late night is all."

Gabriel lurches across his mother's lap. "Tasik, did you bring us a gift from the ship?" He grins and Isaac sees himself thirty years ago.

A quick smile. "Hush, boy. A good sailor knows when to keep things to himself."

They had returned to Talland with a lugger full of French whisky. Fresh from the hold of a merchant moored in the Channel. Give us your best price.

Isaac had not seen the wrecked ship until he was about to enter the bay. A brig, dancing like a madman. He'd had no doubt it would be wrecked. Had cursed at missed opportunities. A wreck about to be handed to them and he'd been stuck at sea with a lugger full of contraband. There would be no landing in Talland that night. The wreck would bring a crowd. A circus of treasure hunters and paupers. Revenue men perhaps.

Isaac had taken his load to Polperro and unloaded in the caves that burrow into the cliffs.

Scarlett slides into the pew behind him and pokes her head over his shoulder. "Did you see it? The wreck?"

Isaac nods. "From a distance."

"I went aboard. Tried to get my hands on something before Reuben's men got to it all. But it were the strangest thing. The ship was near empty."

Isaac turns to face his sister. "You went aboard? Alone?"

"Did you not hear what I said? The ship was empty. No crew. No bodies. Reuben's men found a few ankers of brandy in the hold but the rest of the cargo was gone."

"Lifeboats?"

"Not been touched."

Talk of the ship is everywhere, Isaac realises.

A dead wreck, say the villagers; shoulder to shoulder in the pews.

A twisted gift from the sea spirits.

No bodies.

How does a ship sail the seas without a man on board?

Lord protect us. For we all know a wreck brings a curse.

The vicar shuffles towards the pulpit, spine bowed with age. The black sleeves of his gown stream behind him, face weathered beneath his powdered white wig.

Reverend Dodge has inhabited this church for as long as Isaac can remember. He had listened to the vicar's sermons as a boy; lectures of ghosts and demons and otherworlds. Back then, Dodge's words had been truth, told in candlelight and gloom as the wind tore across the clifftop. Isaac had only been able to see the vicar's eccentricities once his travels had returned him to Talland with adult eyes.

Dodge leans forward, hunching over the pulpit. Caterpillar brows obscure his eyes. A hush falls.

"Let us pray."

The prayer echoes in the candlelit church. A hymn swells; fervent, nervous voices.

"Many of you have come to me afeared," says Dodge. "Afeared of the ghostly ship washed up upon our shore last night. Afeared this community has been ill-wished."

A murmur ripples through the congregation.

Isaac swaps a smile of amusement with Caroline.

11

Such is the value of eccentricity, he thinks. Tell tall stories with conviction and breed believers.

Caroline pockets Gabriel's toy soldiers that have walked their way to the top of the pew. The baby fidgets and gurgles. Isaac blinks, fighting off a wave of exhaustion.

"I remind you in times like this of what we hear in Corinthians, chapter four, verse four: 'In whom the god of this world hath blinded the minds of them which believe not, lest the light of the glorious gospel of Christ, who is the image of God, should shine unto them'." He leans forward, wiry, speckled hands gripping the pulpit. "We have been tested before. And now the devil is testing us again by bringing this phantom ship to our shores." Dodge's voice rises as he gathers momentum. "But have no fear, good people. We will remain believers. Have faith in the Lord and He will deliver you from the evil around us."

Charles Reuben waits outside the church, arms folded across his thick chest. In his powdered wig and crimson justacorps, he is a sight among the sea-stained greatcoats of Talland. When he sees Isaac, he raises his eyebrows expectantly. "Where are the goods?"

"In the cave at Polperro."

"Everything?"

Isaac nods. "They'll be brought to the church tonight."

"Any water damage will be taken from your cut."

Scarlett huffs loudly behind them. Isaac hadn't realised she was there.

"Water damage," she snaps. "How was he to land with half the county on the beach last night?"

Reuben ignores her. Scarlett's eyes flash and harden at the sleight.

12

When he was twenty-one, Isaac had come home to
Talland for the first time in four years. His merchant voyages
had shown him Europe, then taken him to the East Indies,
where the air was damp and fragrant and England was easily
forgotten.

He walked the cliff path from Polperro with a pack on his
back, waiting to see his parents' faces when he burst through
the door.

The house was swathed in cobwebs and dust. A strange
stillness about the place.

He couldn't make sense of it. The place felt odd, like he'd
stepped off the ship at the wrong port and this village just
bore a passing resemblance to his childhood home.

He went to see Martha Francis who lived in the
neighbouring cottage.

"Oh." She looked at her feet. "Isaac."

Their graves were in the churchyard, she said. Isaac
realised he must have walked past them minutes earlier. A
shipwreck. An illness. Both taken within months of each
other.

He looked over his shoulder at the empty cottage, unsure
what to do. His parents had been dead for almost two years.
It seemed too late for goodbyes. He stood staring at the
house until Martha said:

"And there's Scarlett, of course."

Scarlett was not an *of course*. She was a distant,
supporting character in Isaac's life. He'd left home when he
was seventeen; his sister all of three.

There had been other siblings that had come and gone as
he had grown up. An ever-expanding row of headstones like
crooked teeth in that graveyard atop the cliff. Isaac had given
little thought to Scarlett, assuming perhaps, that the same

fate would befall her. She was a stranger. Little more than a name and a fading, outdated image. But an outdated image, he learned, who was waiting for him at the children's home in Polperro.

He ought to leave. There was nothing for him here. Scarlett could stay at the children's home. She was an orphan now. It was where she belonged.

He began to walk through the drizzle, climbing higher and higher up the cliff path until the expanse of white sky was matched by a churning grey sea. Isaac kept walking. He was heading for the harbour, he realised. Board the first ship leaving for who cared where. But he found himself knocking on the children's home door.

"Yes, yes, Mr Bailey. Scarlett will be so excited to see you."

Isaac followed the woman down the hall, their footsteps echoing in the cavernous passage. Children peered at him with vague, saucer eyes. Children everywhere; tangled hair and snotty noses. Mouths gawping like they had questions to ask but couldn't find the words. Which of these children was he to take with him? He had no idea which was his sister. He tried to swallow, but his mouth was dry.

The woman pointed to a girl kneeling by the window. Her back was to them as she crouched over a pile of jacks.

"That's her?" Isaac asked throatily.

"Ayes, that's her." The woman padded over to the girl. She bent and put a gentle hand on her shoulder.

He ought to leave. His sister would be better off here. The woman caring for her seemed loving and kind. More of a parent than he would ever be.

Scarlett rose from the floor and turned to face him. She was small and dirty, clad in a blue pinafore that had slipped off one shoulder. Her black hair hung loose past her shoulders. Eyes dark like his own. Isaac saw their mother in Scarlett's high cheekbones and sharp chin. His stomach twisted.

"Are you Isaac?" she asked.

He nodded.

What did she see in him, he wondered? Was she disappointed in this tatty, sea-hardened man who had come to claim her? Had she been expecting something better?

Her lips curled up. "Are we going home now?"

He managed a nod. "Get your things."

She grinned and disappeared down the hall.

The gravity of the situation swung at him suddenly. He was a sailor. How was he to earn a living now he was shackled to the land by this pitiful creature? He had a sudden urge to throw himself at the woman with the kind eyes.

Help me.

"I don't know how to care for her," he said huskily. "I can barely care for myself."

The woman reached up and held his shoulders. "I know you'll do right. It's the best thing for her to be around her family."

"Family." He exhaled sharply. "She don't know me from the next man."

The woman smiled gently. "She will."

They walked back along the cliff path, Scarlett clutching her cloak and a chipped wooden court doll. Isaac's mind raced. He had no food or clothing for her. Little money. He'd not even thought to explore the house before he'd plucked her from the children's home. Were there any bedclothes? Firewood? Pots and pans? Hell, even if there were, his cooking skills extended as far as opening a jar of pickled fish.

He realised he wasn't breathing.

He felt her hand at his wrist. She smiled up at him. Giant eyes. "Do you want to hear a story?"

And among the cobwebs that had taken over the house after their parents' deaths, they began to cobble together a life.

Each morning, a walk across the cliffs to Polperro. Isaac would sail into the Channel with the fishermen. Scarlett; walk to the charity school with the court doll tucked beneath her arm. After her lessons, she would wait with the women of the pilchard palace, learning to salt and press. Practice her crooked letters in the mud.

There was strength in his sister, Isaac realised. Resilience. He was a terrible parent, but Scarlett would not curl up and die from a diet of salted fish. Wouldn't crumble when the world shook beneath her.

Sometimes she'd look to him like he were her father.

Yes, bedtime. Agreed.

Other times they'd fight like the siblings they were, the fourteen years between them insignificant.

She was full of stories, this little creature who had upturned his world.

Giants and fairies and merrymaids.

The chirruping bird who had accompanied their mother to Heaven.

Tales to placate the horrors that had filled her seven years of life.

Were the horrors to blame for her temper? Isaac couldn't be sure.

Wild, unpredictable rage would seize her without warning. A poison that crept up from behind. It would steal the stories and the smiles and the warm-hearted sister he was coming to know.

The first time, it was cold stew. Scarlett leapt from her chair and hurled the tin plate against the wall, contents splattering. She screeched, unintelligible. Her eyes shone wild in the lamplight. Who was this child, Isaac wondered? Where had she been hiding? She kicked, pulled at her hair. Knocked over the chair and tore at her clothes like something savage had crawled inside her.

He blew out the lamp. Didn't know why. Just felt, somehow, that the darkness would soothe her. He crouched on the floor. Said nothing. Watched as that rage disappeared with the light. Watched as his sunny sister returned to him.

Scarlett sat as his side, breathing hard.

He looked through the darkness to find her eyes. "What's this about then?"

She peered back at him, confused. Trying to place her anger? Trying to remember it? She opened her mouth to speak but said nothing.

Isaac lit the lamp. Nodded to the stew running down the wall. "Clean it."

She nodded. Cleaned. Bewildered.

He came to see they were both survivors. Saw why they had not been buried among their other siblings in the graveyard on the cliff.

They'd been together a week when Charles Reuben appeared at the door.

"Ah, the young Mr Bailey. I'm most happy to see you." His smile reached his eyes, but the sting of it made Isaac wary.

"Who are you?"

And there on the doorstep, Reuben proceeded to tell the whole miserable story.

A smuggling run to Guernsey. Reuben's cutter captained by Isaac's father, Jacob. With the ship full of French tobacco, the cutter had detoured to Saint Helier. A sly, secret journey.

Jacob Bailey had made free trading contacts of his own. An agent starting out in the business. Jacob had invested his own money, arranged his own buyers. Loaded Reuben's ship with additional contraband until the bulkheads groaned.

Overloaded and unbalanced, the cutter had rolled; the ship and her cargo sucked into the whirlpooling sea. Jacob had crawled into a lifeboat and watched his dreams of wealth disappear. Fishermen had ferried he and the crew back to Talland and the critical eyes of Charles Reuben.

Less than two years later, Jacob had been wrecked again. This time there had been no fishermen to save him and he had faced the critical eyes of God.

Reuben handed Isaac a scrawled ledger. "I paid for that vessel out of my own pocket. Her cargo too, of course. I expect repayment."

Isaac glanced at the ledger. His hand clenched around the door frame. "Does it look like I've that sort of money?" He screwed up the page and tossed it in the mud.

Reuben smiled, unperturbed by the rain drizzling down his collar. "I'm quite sure you don't. You'll work for me. You're a sailor, I hear. Just the man I need to captain a lugger to Saint Peter Port once a month. I put up the capital and liaise with my agent. You get the lugger there and back. Complete the transactions. I'll provide you with enough of the profits to keep you and your sister clothed and fed. The rest of your cut will go towards paying off your father's debts, and the interest accumulated."

Isaac's stomach tightened. The world seemed to lose its colour. "This is criminal."

"It's not criminal. It's business. The repayment plan was drawn up by my banker. You'll find it a fair deal, I'm sure."

"Go to hell," Isaac spat. "I left this place so I'd not get caught up in free trade."

Reuben smiled thinly. "A shame your father didn't have your sense."

"Your business was with Jacob, not me. I'm not willing to take on his debts."

"But you're willing to take on his property, his land. I'm sorry, Mr Bailey, but this isn't your choice."

Isaac closed his eyes. "Take the house and the land. Leave us be."

"A sailor is of far more value to me. I'm glad you turned up when you did. I was beginning to think I'd have to have your little sister hawk for us."

Isaac felt suddenly, fiercely protective. "Stay the hell away from Scarlett."

Reuben plucked the ledger from the mud and shoved it against Isaac's chest. "I've made arrangements with my agent for you to be in Saint Peter Port in a week."

Isaac clenched his jaw. "I've no boat."

"Lucky for you, I'm in a generous mood. I've recently taken ownership of a new lugger. Purpose-built out of Mevagissey. In the right hands, she can cross the Channel in eight hours. You'll meet me at Polperro harbour tomorrow morning. Get to know your new vessel."

That night, Isaac stuffed their few belongings into a pack and bundled Scarlett's cloak around her shoulders. They made it as far as the landing beach before the smugglers' banker found them and put a gun to their heads. Reuben had eyes all over the village, Isaac realised. To try and leave would be the end of them.

He had never been close to his father. Even as a boy, he had seen something in Jacob that had made him wary. His sailing lessons had been interspersed with tours of cliffs and coves; this beach good for a landing in low tide, that cave a perfect hideout. Instructions on how to rope up the barrels and hide them in shallow water. How to use a grappling hook to haul them from the sea.

He was determined that this would not be his life; this endless, oppressive crawl beneath the revenue men's eyes.

There was an entire world out there, beyond the village, beyond the Channel. A world of which Isaac knew nothing, but of which he longed to know everything. The urge to leave was overpowering.

He packed his bags the day after his seventeenth birthday, desperate to escape the pull of Jacob's smuggling ring.

His father stood at the front door with his arms folded across his chest. Watched Isaac kiss his mother's cheek. Watched him swing his pack onto his back with poorly hidden enthusiasm.

"So this is your choice then."

"Ayes, this is my choice. Forgive me, Tas."

His father didn't speak again, just pulled the door closed with a dejected sigh.

In the end, Jacob had gotten what he wanted; his son following in his footsteps.

His legacy is heavy on Isaac's shoulders. Captain of a smuggling lugger. Errand boy for the wealthy landowner who controls the region's free trade.

It has been fourteen years since Reuben had appeared at their door. Fourteen years since Isaac had stood in the rain and listened to the story of his father and the lost cutter.

He feels this will be his entire life.

Charles Reuben is past fifty, but he is a wealthy man with high-placed connections. Could find himself a wife without trouble. Produce an heir to hold the debt over Isaac's family for another generation.

No. He won't- can't- let such a thing happen. Can't give his children the life his father had given him.

"Has the vicar been informed you will be loading the church tonight?" Reuben asks.

"He's been informed." Isaac touches Scarlett's elbow, ushering her towards the gate. "I'm sure the spirits are trembling as we speak."

SAILOR

Asher opens his eyes. Candlelight flickers over the cellar walls. He smells earth and clay. He lies on his side with a flimsy cushion beneath his head, a blanket tossed over him. His legs and head ache. Tight strapping around his skull. His hair feels matted and brittle. His breeches are stiff with salt and blood, chest bare.

He looks around for his coat. Finds it draped across a barrel in the corner of the cellar. His bloodstained shirt is nowhere to be seen. He crawls towards the coat. Checks the inner pocket. The letter is there, sodden, but intact. He shoves it into the pocket of his breeches.

He hears footsteps and the creak of stairs. Shuffles back to his makeshift bed. His blurred vision makes out two women; one dark, one fair. The blonde woman carries a lantern and a bottle.

"He's awake," she says.

The dark-haired girl comes towards him. Scarlett. She is younger than the other; barely twenty, perhaps. Dishevelled, but faintly pretty with high cheekbones and pale skin. Wildness at her edges.

She had been a child when last he had set foot in this village. Asher had been the age Scarlett is now. Had brimmed with similar impulsiveness.

She kneels. Tilts her head so their eyes meet at the same angle. She takes the bottle from the blonde woman and holds it to Asher's lips. He gulps the water as it drizzles down his cheek. He sits, head thumping.

Scarlett lifts the strapping around his head and peers at the wound. "Bleeding's stopped." She jabs his skull.

"Don't go poking the poor fellow, Scarlett. He's not a pudding." The blonde woman's voice is lyrical, gentle. She winds the strapping around his head again. "How do you feel?"

Feel? He feels a constant prickling beneath his skin at being in this place again. Feels impatient, wary, frustrated by his injuries.

He squints. The woman's face is familiar. Her hair is eerily, unnaturally pale. So blonde it is almost without colour. Her eyes blaze deep sea blue.

He hopes she has no recollection of him.

"Where am I?" he asks.

"In the cellar of the Mariner's Arms," says Scarlett. "Flora's inn."

She sits close. She has questions for him. And Asher answers, because of who she is and what she might know.

Yes, the wrecked *Avalon* was a merchant ship. London to Penzance. A cargo of liquor and lace embroidered with gold anchors.

A tragedy, yes. No, I remember little.

23

"The ship was empty but for you and a few ankers of brandy," Scarlett tells him. "We found no bodies. The lifeboats were still aboard. The village is in a panic because they've never seen such a thing. A ghost ship washed up on our very shore. They fear it has cursed us."

He chuckles to himself. Fools.

He tries to stand.

Flora's hand shoots out and finds his arm. "Stay down. You need to recover. I'm sorry for such miserable lodgings, but it's important no one sees you. If customs see fit to investigate, the men who plundered your ship will ensure it was a dead wreck."

Investigate? He almost laughs. There will be no investigation. The ship has been burned. And this is Charles Reuben's trading territory. Asher is sure they have the protection of the revenue men. How deep does the rot go, he wonders? Has Scarlett Bailey taken up the family business?

She pokes and preens, easing him back to the bed of blankets. They have cheese for him. Tea, stale bread.

He takes the food. Eats.

"I'll stay with him," Scarlett says, giving Flora a look that clearly says she wants her to leave. And Flora does, letting the door close with a creak and thud.

There is a gaping hole hacked into the wall of the cellar. It has been boarded up with rough planks. He crawls towards it, curious. The planks have been hammered crookedly, hurriedly.

"You can't get out that way," says Scarlett.

"What is it? A smuggling tunnel?"

She straightens his blankets. "What's your name?"

He tells her: "Asher Hales." The name he has adopted. The name the world will one day come to know. He tells her

24

again: "my name is Asher Hales." He likes the sound his new name makes as it rolls off his tongue.

Asher Hales is a shipwreck survivor. He is a man who prospers when life hands him a rough deal. A man who rises above the rest.

Scarlett smiles. "A pleasure to meet you, Mr Hales."

He takes her outstretched hand. Squeezes it gently and looks into her eyes until her cheeks flush and she pulls away. He allows himself a faint smile.

Asher Hales recognises opportunity. When he is pulled from a sinking ship by Jacob Bailey's daughter, he will draw her close and not let go.

EXORCISM

*'I will ... recount to you the whole of this strange story as it
has reached my ears, for as yet I have not satisfied my eyes
of its truth. It has been told me by men of honest and good
report ... with such strong assurances that it behoves us to
look more closely into the matter.'*

Taken from a letter to Rev. Richard Dodge from Mr Gryllis,
Rector of Lanreath
1725

The vicar paces, a whip in his fist. A lamp hangs by the
door of the church. It sways in the wind, making shadows
dance.

A laying of the spirits. Behold the great ghost hunter,
Reverend Dodge.

Onlookers huddle at the edge of the lane. Women
entangle themselves in shawls while men pace, trying to hide

their unease. Whispering, peering, shuffling. Residents of the surrounding villages braving the darkness and demons to witness a spectacle.

"You ought not be here!" Dodge tells the crowd.

Flora snorts. Heaven forbid the vicar's theatrics go unobserved.

In the cove below, the boats of Isaac's landing party pull towards the shore. Flora hears faint voices floating up to the clifftop, the sigh of oars in sea.

She ushers her daughter, Bessie, towards the church. "Go on now. I'll not be long."

Bessie clutches a book to her chest and scurries through the crooked gravestones.

"We have again been challenged by evil," Dodge booms. "A ghost ship washed up upon our shore. But we will not let Satan defeat us, will we, Mrs Kelly?" He whirls around to face Flora.

"No," she mumbles. "We will not let Satan defeat us."

A woman grabs her husband's arm and tugs him back up the lane. The rest of the pack draws closer.

Dodge paces across the churchyard, hurling the whip into the darkness.

Crack and the onlookers jump. Huddle closer.

Crack. Can you see the demons hiding in the dark?

Out onto Bridles Lane. *Crack.*

"The holy water, Mrs Kelly."

Flora hands Dodge the bowl.

He circles the cemetery again, droplets of water flying from his fingertips.

A final word to God.

"Amen," Flora echoes. The insincerity in her voice is so blatant she is sure the crowd can sense it.

She has done this with Dodge; this sham, a thousand times.

A solemn prayer, a flick of his wrists and Bridles Lane will be clear of prying eyes. Free for the landing party to carry their haul to the church.

The vicar had singled Flora out, asking for her assistance long before she'd married Jack. An extra voice to send away the demons. An extra set of eyes to keep the curious away from the Bridles Lane deliveries. No, she had told Dodge firmly. She'd not involve herself in free trade.

But then there was Jack Kelly, the sailor with a laugh that made Flora's heart skip. Arrived from upcountry and joined the Polperro fishing fleet. He had hair the colour of autumn leaves and eyes full of light. Had been snatched up by the free traders before his first month was through, but Flora had loved him in spite of it.

Married to Jack, there were long, sleepless nights. Nights she lay in bed staring into the dark, her stomach turning over with worry. She became gripped with fear that he would fall into the hands of the revenue men. She needed to be involved, she realised. Needed to be the eyes Dodge had asked her to be.

As a love-drunk young wife, hunting ghosts with the vicar had been a thrill. A joke. She'd cast out the spirits with Dodge, then drink away the night with the traders once the haul was safely stored in the church.

Two years after Jack's death, she is still here. Still traipsing after Dodge on his otherworldly adventures. Here for the paltry pennies the vicar pays for her services. A pittance, of course, when Reuben hands Dodge such a large percentage of the profits from the sales of the contraband.

She has come to hate the scam, the dishonesty. Distilling fear into the villagers for the sake of greed.

He is full of stories, this vicar. A headless horseman banished from Blackadown Moor. The demons of Bridles Lane.

True? Of course they are true.

Yes, yes, Flora says, whenever wide-eyed spectators ask. *I saw that horseman with my own eyes. I saw Reverend Dodge send it back to Hell.*

The tales grow legs. Fairy tales become truths. A haunted coast, the people say. Men refuse to ride Bridles Lane at night. Richard Dodge has become a legend. And Reuben's pockets have grown heavy with smuggling riches.

The vicar watches as the last of the onlookers disappear into the night. "Signal the men," he instructs Flora. "Tell them the lane is clear."

She takes the lamp to the edge of the cliff. Moonlight spills across the sea. The charred skeleton of the *Avalon* juts from the water.

She shines the light to the men below. Bring up your goods. Fill our bell house with liquor.

She pulls her shawl tight around her shoulders. Opens the church door and finds Bessie in a pew at the back of the nave. The girl hunches over a candle, the book in her lap. Her blonde hair glows in the candlelight.

"Come, *cheel-vean*. Time to go."

Bessie blows out the candle and plunges the church into darkness. Her footsteps patter on the flagstones. Hand in hand, she and Flora hurry towards the gate. They keep their heads down, avoiding the vicar.

Flora unlocks the creaking front door of the inn. She lights the lamps and sends Bessie to bed.

She finds Scarlett in the cellar, watching over the shipwrecked sailor. He sleeps on his side in the pile of blankets. She dozes, sitting up against the wall.

Flora shakes her shoulder. "Go home, Scarlett. Get a little sleep. I'll take care of him."

Scarlett hesitates. She glances at the sailor, then at Flora. Finally, she nods and makes her way sleepily up the cellar stairs.

When Scarlett is gone, Flora walks slowly through the empty bar. It creaks and groans like the hull of a ship.

With the money she has earned tonight, she can afford fresh paint for the window sills. She will be able to open the inn's doors again soon. No more exorcising the demons of Dodge's imagination. She'll extract herself from the vicar's grasp. And once the Mariner's Arms is open, she'll keep her feet firmly planted in the land of the living.

The building is old and crooked; a relic from the turn of the previous century. The ceilings are low, lined with beams hauled from faraway forests. The great black hearth gapes and wind whistles down the chimney. The windows are thick, speckled with salt. Even on the brightest days, the Mariner's Arms is a place of candlelight and shadow.

Upstairs, the rooms are dusty and neglected, silent with the voices of guests who had never arrived.

Flora's memory is filled with countless games of hide and seek. First as a daughter, then a mother. Climbing over rickety furniture, hiding in cupboards. Don't sneeze from the dust.

Bessie, I hear you breathing.

One day, she will empty these rooms. Send guests up there to make their own memories. But for now, opening the bar consumes her.

Flora's family had owned the tavern, though it has not been a public house since her grandfather had closed its doors some forty years earlier. For all Flora's life, the tables have been nothing more than dust collectors, the cellar cluttered with broken furniture. Neither of her parents had had any interest in bringing the tavern back to life.

But this place had been Jack's dream. On the death of Flora's mother, three years ago, he had inherited the property. Had struggled to hide his excitement beneath the obligatory grief over his mother-in-law's passing.

He'd taken Flora by the hand and walked her through the building.

The bar here, guest rooms there, a rocking horse for Bessie and a great curtained bed for us. Fit for a king and queen.

Flora is determined to see his dream come to life.

She brings out a pot of beeswax from beneath the bar and dips in a rag. She polishes until her arms ache and the counter begins to shine.

Soon people will sit at this bar and speak of hurling matches. Speak of changing winds and stolen kisses. They'll spill ale on the counter and never notice how much it shines.

She can't wait for it.

A knock at the door makes her start. There is Isaac, the wind whipping his dark hair around stubbled cheeks. Dawn is creeping over the horizon.

"I saw the lamp lit," he says.

Flora ushers him inside. She gestures to the polish. "I'll sleep once the inn is open."

Isaac digs into his pocket. A seashell. Pink and white and perfect. "I found it in the cave. Thought it a good fit for your collection."

Flora takes the shell and turns it over in her hands. She runs a finger over its pearly surface. "It's beautiful." She places it among the shells that sit upon the window ledge. "Thank you."

Isaac runs a hand across the polished surface of the bar. He looks up at the shelves behind the counter. One has worked free from the wall and slopes like a see-saw. "You need help with that?"

"I can manage. I don't want to make trouble."

"You know it's no trouble." He grins. "I'll come by tomorrow."

SEASHELLS

Isaac walks the length of the bar, floorboards creaking beneath his boots. Sun struggles through the windows. The inn has been swept free of its eternal layer of dust. The tables are planed and polished, the enormous hearth blacked. New stools are stacked in the corner of the room.

"The place looks grand," he tells Flora. He tilts his head, considering the crooked shelves. "Better way they come down. Start again, I'd say."

"Whatever you think best."

He pulls a hammer from his satchel and sets to work attacking the rotting wood.

Flora watches. Watches him flick his hair from his eyes. Watches his muscles tense beneath rolled-up shirtsleeves. And for a moment, it is Jack with the hammer in hand, his rust-coloured hair as bright as Isaac's is dark.

Her chest tightens.

A delivery tomorrow, he tells her between his hammering. Half the whisky brought in from the run.

"You've buyers already?" Flora asks, attacking the tables with the beeswax polish.

"Ayes. Customs House."

She laughs. "What?"

"I'm to plant the ankers on the moor. Then pay customs a visit. Let them know I found a haul of contraband while I was out riding. Collect a handsome reward." There is light in his eyes.

She gives him a crooked smile. "Your idea, I'm sure. Reuben would never have come up with such a plan."

He chuckles. "And he's to pay me well for my brilliance. Thirty percent. A decent cut for once."

"Seems a bargain for your brains."

He has always been this way; sharp witted and clever. As children, Isaac had been the one full of ideas. Build a raft to sail to the eastern beach. Supper of blackberries from the bushes behind the bell house. A lantern-lit parade into the cave at Polperro to find the ghost of poor drowned Willie Wilcox. Flora had trailed along with her skirts at her knees, doe-eyed and doting.

Even as a boy, Isaac had had an air about him. A dark magnetism that set Flora on edge.

She had been thirteen years old when he had gone to sea. Had thrown her arms around him, then turned away quickly so he wouldn't see her cry. She watched out the parlour window as he disappeared over the clifftops.

She'd been sure then that he had a great life ahead of him. He would see the world, make his fortune. Return to Talland as a sea captain.

But not like this. Not captain of a smuggling lugger whose strings are pulled by another man. The injustice of it burns inside her.

He hammers in the final nails. Steps back to admire his work. "What do you think?"

Flora tosses down her polishing rag. "It's perfect. Thank you."

He presses a hand to her arm; warm and solid. "You'll tell us if you need more help. You're not alone, you know."

"Of course I'm not. I have Bessie." She closes her eyes, instantly regretting her sharpness.

Isaac tucks his tools back into his satchel and wipes his dusty hands on his breeches. "And you've Caroline and I. And Scarlett."

Flora nods stiffly. She can't bear to be seen as the needy widow. Especially not to Isaac and Caroline. "I'm sorry. I didn't mean to be so curt."

His eyes meet hers.

She flushes, ashamed. "The seashells," she manages. "They'll fit perfectly on the top shelf."

Isaac smiles. "I'm glad of it."

She walks him to the door. "You'll be watchful tomorrow night, won't you. You've a fine plan, but it's a dangerous one. I hope you're as careful as you are clever."

"Nothing dangerous about it. Customs are nothing but a bunch of understrappers."

She jabs a finger under his nose. "It's talk like that that'll have you in trouble."

He catches her outstretched finger and gives it a quick squeeze. "We'll watch ourselves. I swear it."

THE HEALING WOMAN

'There is in this neighbourhood a barren bit of moor which had no owner. ... The lords of the adjoining manors debated its ownership between themselves, ... both determined to take it from the other. ... The two litigants contested it with much violence and ... it is said to have hastened [one's] death. If current reports are worthy of credit ... at night-time his apparition is seen on the moor to the great fright of the neighbouring villagers.'

Taken from a letter to Rev. Richard Dodge from Mr Gryllis,
Rector of Lanreath
1725

"Corpse candles," says Isaac's spotsman.

The two men are high on the shadow-bathed moor, the road a narrow ribbon through snarls of gorse. Their wagon creaks beneath the weight of the whisky ankers. Ahead, the sea and sky melt into one another. Specks of blue light glitter on the horizon.

"You see them? The lights?" Isaac's spotsman, George Gibson is a weathered, grey bear of a man. A sailor with a healthy fear of the sea and the spirits who inhabit it.

Corpse candles. Isaac remembers the stories. Told by his father who had lived with one foot in a world of fantasy. The corpse candles were the souls of the dead, Jacob Bailey had said. Ghosts of drowned sailors.

Gibson breathes hard and fast. "They appear right after that cursed ship washes up on our beach. Tell me it don't mean something."

"Forget that ship. It's the best thing for all of us."

"You think it that easy?" Gibson wraps his arms around himself. Stares at the hovering lights. "You know what they say about the corpse candles, ayes? Death is coming for whoever sees them."

Isaac snorts. "You've been listening to too many of the vicar's stories."

While his father had believed wholeheartedly in such things, Isaac sees them for what they are; stories, superstitions. His travels have shown him an enlightened world; a place of reason and rationality where nature lives by laws and the dead stay in their graves. But this county refuses to let go of its ancestors' legends. It has lived in ignorance for far too long. As far as Isaac is concerned, the sooner Cornwall comes to agree with the rest of the country, the better.

"Enough of this," he says. "Help me get these ankers hidden." He leaps from the wagon and tosses aside the thin layer of kelp hiding the whisky. He heaves out the first of the barrels and shoves it into the tangled scrub.

Gibson hides the ankers without speaking; his eyes darting from the wagon to the lights on the horizon.

He will go to the vicar, he announces as they conceal the last of the whisky. Leaps into the box seat and snatches the reins.

Isaac chuckles. "Dodge? What's that mad bastard going to do?"

"Send these spirits away, can't he. We've all seen it. Rid us of the very devil, so he did."

Gibson goads the horse into a trot. The corpse candles disappear behind the curve of the hills.

Isaac lurches for the reins. "You can't go to Dodge. I've to be at Customs House in Fowey in a few hours. Tell them about this whisky."

Gibson tenses. "Stop the wagon. I need to see the vicar. If you'll not take me back, I'll bloody well walk."

"Come," says Dodge. "We've people to see."

Flora grips the doorframe and tugs her shawl around her shoulders. "It's barely dawn. My daughter is sleeping."

"She can sleep in the carriage. George Gibson has requested my help. It seems we were plagued by corpse candles tonight. The man is most unsettled." Dodge shifts impatiently. "Please, Mrs Kelly. We must make haste."

Flora clenches her teeth and hurries upstairs.

Damn George Gibson and his feverish faith. For a man who has spent years loading Dodge's bell house with contraband, he is easily swayed by the vicar's ghost stories.

She pulls on her dress and cloak, then scoops Bessie out of bed, wrapping a blanket around her limp body. She follows Dodge out to the carriage.

The driver pulls away from the inn and they wind up the narrow path towards the top of the hill. The houses lining the road are lightless, lifeless.

"Really Father? Is such a thing necessary at this hour?"

Dodge smiles. "The Lord will protect you, Mrs Kelly. You know that."

"I'm not afraid. I just… I suppose I don't see the point."

Dodge raises his woolly eyebrows. "My people have come to me for help. What kind of man would I be if I did not follow up on their claims?"

The driver stops the carriage and tethers the horse to a tree. Flora follows Dodge into the orange dawn. They have left the road behind and the carriage stands in the farmland that sprawls across the clifftop. Far below, the sea is agitated and grey.

On the cliff edge, Flora can make out the figures of Gibson and several other men from Isaac's crew, pacing edgily. There are a few others; women from the charity school and an elderly couple wrapped in enormous brown greatcoats.

Flora squints into the rising sun. "I don't see the corpse candles."

"They are there," Gibson says darkly. "That ship brought them with her, I know it. They left with the dawn. But they'll be back."

"We saw them too," the old woman pipes up. "Clear as day. Lost souls, Father. You must cast them out before they bring ill-luck to this village."

Dodge squeezes the woman's hands. "I will speak with these uneasy spirits. Draw from them the dread secrets that trouble them." He walks to the edge of the cliff and closes his eyes. Begins to rock back and forth as though entranced.

Flora feels ill.

What is this, this theatrical swaying and murmuring? These prayers howled to the wind? What is it but trickery?

"You have nothing to fear if you put your faith in the Lord," Dodge says finally. People cluster around him, clutching at his gnarled hands.

Flora follows him back to the carriage. "That couple was in the churchyard two nights ago. They watched you cast the demons out of Bridles Lane."

"Indeed. No doubt that is why they have sought my counsel."

"Your exorcisms are beginning to frighten people."

"As well they should! Only a foolish man would not fear the devil!"

"Father, you and I both know these tales of ghosts and demons are a sham to keep the lane clear for the traders."

For several moments, Dodge doesn't reply. "These strange lights," he says finally. "What do you believe them to be?"

"I didn't see any lights."

"Do you think these people lying?"

Flora sighs. "I don't know what these people saw. But I don't believe lights on the horizon are to be feared. And after this wreck…" She pauses. "Perhaps validating the villagers' worries by traipsing out to the clifftops at first light is not in their best interest."

Dodge purses his lips. For a moment, Flora is a child again, cowering in a pew while the vicar pelts out a sermon.

"We will go where we are asked to go. These people need to have faith in their vicar. And faith in the Lord." He looks at Flora pointedly. "As do you, Mrs Kelly. I am surprised to find your mind so closed to the divine. I admit I am shaken by it."

"I'm no fool, Father. Your exorcisms are based on trickery and greed. I'll not be a part of it any longer."

Dodge's eyebrows shoot up. "You cannot just walk away."

"Of course I can. I'll have the inn to run soon. I can't be spending my evenings gallivanting about the clifftops." She glances down at Bessie. "And I want more for my daughter than sleeping in the back of a carriage while her mother chases ghosts."

"Instead she is to sleep above a public house while her mother plies the village with liquor?"

Flora grits her teeth. "Find someone else to accompany you. Any fool could hand you holy water and carry a signalling lantern."

"No. It must be you. It is of utmost importance that I keep you on the path of God."

She sighs. "This is about my mother."

"Yes," Dodge admits. "Your mother darkened her soul by dabbling in witchcraft."

Flora laughs humourlessly. "My mother did nothing more than offer a few herbal remedies. She was just a healing woman. And a mediocre one at that."

"She was a practitioner of dark magic. I tried to bring her back to God, but I failed in my attempts. It is my duty to ensure you do not follow the same path."

"That's what this has been about? That's why you asked for my help? To try and prove God's power to me so I didn't stray?"

"I've proved God's power to you a hundred times over."

"Is that so?"

"How can you be so dismissive after all you've seen?"

"After all I've seen? I've seen nothing. Just you waving your arms about on the clifftops while the smugglers load their haul into your church."

"Perhaps there were a few theatrics for the benefit of the traders. But my exorcisms are based in truth. Evil is all around us, Mrs Kelly. We must be vigilant."

Flora snorts. "You've fallen for your own sham. Stop the coach," she calls to the driver. "I can walk the rest of the way."

Dodge waves a bony finger in her face as she pushes open the door. "You'll come to me when your soul is darkened by your mother's legacy. You'll come begging for redemption. You shall see."

Flora hauls Bessie from the carriage and slings her over her shoulder. "I've no intention of darkening my soul, Father. But my days of chasing demons are through."

SEA SPIRITS

The men talk of corpse candles as they sail out of the harbour. George Gibson speaks of Dodge's performance on the clifftops. A banishing of lost souls. A counter to the ill luck cast over the village.

Ill luck? Isaac doesn't see it. He'd made five pounds that morning.

He had led the customs officers out to the moor and watched as his whisky had been hauled from the undergrowth.

Thank you for your vigilance, Mr Bailey. And he'd left with a pocket full of coin.

Much of the money will go to Charles Reuben, another slice divided up between the crew. But there will be a sizeable chunk left in Isaac's hands.

He ought to put the money towards his debts, of course. Chip away at a little of that ugly figure. But he can't help thinking of the things that money could buy. A spinning top for Gabriel. New shawl for Caroline. A boost for Scarlett's paltry dowry.

He smiles to himself.

Today they are honest fishermen, scooping pilchards from the sea. Isaac sails his lugger with Gibson and John Baker, the other boats of the fishing fleet filled with men from his trading ring.

The day is grey and heavy. Isaac is glad to be on the water. Glad for open space and clean air. He does his best to stay away from the men and their endless parade of horror stories.

A shout comes from the huers standing by the watch houses on the cliff.

Pilchard shoals.

The huers wave their sticks, directing the boats towards the dark masses of fish. The men are tiny on the cliff; Gabriel's toy soldiers.

Nets are cast into the water, strung between the three boats. Pilchards swarm beneath them. The fish are hauled aboard, silver and squirming.

Another shoal. Another shout. Another net of fish.

They float now on the edge of the Channel. Polperro has disappeared. There is a dampness about everything. The clouds are low, melting thick and grey into the sea. The boat is heavy with pilchards.

Turn back. Home.

As they come about, the wind blows up, squally and fierce. The swell climbs. The sky blackens.

Isaac buttons his tarred greatcoat, hair whipping around his cheeks. He grabs at the line above his head as the lugger pitches wildly. He peers into the bank of cloud, seeking out the lights of the village. Sees nothing through the wall of mist.

The sky opens. Fat rain blackens the deck and runs down the back of Isaac's neck. The deck seesaws. He glances upwards at the single, shortened sail. Furl it and they'll be swept back into the Channel. Continue to sail and they risk rolling on this wild sea.

He looks to the men. "Hand her in." His shout is swallowed by the roar of water.

The sail thunders as it's furled. The sea curls into mountains. Water sweeps across the deck.

Ocean waves. A deep sea storm.

Isaac has never seen conditions like this; not here on the fringes of the Channel.

He stumbles towards the hatch, water streaming from his coat. They have little choice but to huddle below deck and let themselves be flung about like a cork. Wait for the sea to settle.

He does not even see the wave coming. He feels the deck fly beneath him. Snatches at the gunwale. The baskets of fish tumble; thousands of silver bodies swept back into the ocean. The bare masts arc through the air, lurching until they are horizontal, lying against the sea.

For a moment, Isaac feels the stillness. The ship hanging, hull to the sky. His knuckles whiten. Nothing beneath his feet but air and sea.

No thoughts. Just *hold on*. And *survive*.

And then from deep in his mind come a thousand stories. Angered sea spirits and cursed ships. Ill-wishing and omens of death. The names of drowned sailors hummed in the wind.

The lugger rolls back, righting herself. The masts rise from the waves and reel against the grey sky.

Isaac scrambles to his feet. He is dizzy with something. Is it fear? Relief? His breath is hard and fast. His world solid again. No longer filled with tales told by desperate men.

He says nothing to Scarlett about the knockdown. Underplays the loss of the fish when she runs from the pilchard palace asking questions.

An accident. Clumsiness.

There's an uneasiness in her, he knows. A respect for the sea that borders on fear. Her vivid imagination has populated the ocean floor with monsters. Catch hold of Gibson's *curse* and *lost souls* and she'll be tossing sleepless in her bed for weeks.

She grips his arm tightly as they follow the cliff path back to Talland. Walks pressed to his side until the path becomes too narrow to walk together.

Isaac shivers in his wet clothes. Doesn't let himself think of how close he had come to drowning. Tries not to picture his own memorial stone standing in the churchyard beside his father's.

It's late when the men come to the house. Scarlett has disappeared to Flora's inn and Caroline sits at the table with a needle and thread. Isaac stands close to the fire, his blood cold and fingers stiff.

Gibson knocks loudly and lets himself inside, the other members of Isaac's crew trailing.

Caroline lowers the shift she is hemming. She glances at the men's muddy boots. "Do come in. Make yourselves at home."

Gibson lowers his eyes. "I beg your pardon, Mrs Bailey." He takes off his knitted cap and bundles it into his fist.

He is afeared, he tells Isaac. The men are afeared. Death is coming for them. His speech is garbled and punctuated with phrases like *corpse candles* and *curse*.

But his meaning is clear. The men will not return to sea.

"Don't be so foolish!" Isaac demands. "You can't leave me stranded like this! We've a run to Falmouth in a week. Guernsey in a fortnight. How do you imagine Reuben will react if we don't make it?"

The men won't look at him. Won't look at Caroline. Their eyes are on the fire, on the floor. Reuben is Isaac's concern, of course. How he will react is of little bother to the other men.

"How are we to make a living if you'll not go to sea?" he asks tautly.

"I'll not die in pursuit of making a living," Gibson says. "We could well have drowned today. The corpse candles, you know they foretell death. It nearly were ours."

"And yet here we are."

"I daresay we was only spared because of the fish."

"The fish?"

"We lost them all. Sea spirits took them as a sacrifice. So they let us live."

Isaac curses under his breath. "You're my spotsman, George. You know I need you."

Gibson says nothing.

"I'll increase your cut. Fifteen percent."

"This isn't about money. We value our lives too much. There are mysteries out there, Isaac. You're a fool if you don't respect the sea."

Caroline snorts. "You come in here with these fanciful tales and have the nerve to call my husband a fool?"

"With respect, Mrs Bailey," Gibson says carefully, "you don't come from these parts. We'd not expect a foreigner to understand."

Caroline's eyebrows shoot up. *Foreigner* is barbed after her twelve years in the west country.

Isaac steps towards Gibson threateningly. "I'm no foreigner," he says. "And Caroline is right. You'd do far better if you kept your feet planted in the real world."

HENRY AVERY

Scarlett reports. No word of an investigation. And no one suspects the *Avalon* was anything but a dead wreck. Asher is free to leave.

He sits. The cut on his head is tender, but the searing pain is gone.

"I am a mess," he tells Scarlett.

Her eyes brighten. Clean clothes, yes of course. Boots too, perhaps she can find boots.

"A razor," says Asher.

She hurries from the cellar. Returns with her arms full. She hands him a clean shirt and coat. Breeches. No boots. She is sorry.

She turns her back as he peels off his filthy clothes. He slides the letter into the pocket of the greatcoat. The clothing Scarlett has brought smells musty and neglected. She looks back to see him brushing a layer of dust from the coat's sleeves.

"I'm sorry," she says. "They belonged to Flora's husband. He's not been with us for several years. I'm afraid his things have seen little daylight." She has placed a water bowl and razor on the floor by the lamp. "Sit."

He kneels in front of her. She grips the razor.

"Let me," says Asher.

She shakes her head. "Please."

She has saved him. Nursed him. Wants to see him clean and shorn before she sends him back out into the world. There is something mildly touching about it.

And so he sits motionless and lets her run the blade over the pale stubble on his cheeks. Her strokes are careful, precise. A crease appears between her eyes as she frowns in concentration. Tenderness in her touch.

This girl needs a dog. Or a husband.

She leans close, tilts her head. Trying to place his age, perhaps. His hair is thick and sandy, eyes blue and bright. The creases in his face tell of a difficult life, but not a long one. Her father's age, no. Closer to her brother's.

And what is that look? That light in her eyes? Desire?

Little Scarlett Bailey. What would your father think?

He remembers her. A black-haired child building castles on the beach. Little legs powering up the hill to keep pace with her striding father.

She continues to shave. "George Gibson saw the corpse candles. They say they are the souls of your crew—" She stops. "Forgive me. I'm sure it is difficult to speak of them."

Asher says nothing.

Easy for these people to believe in tales of lost souls. Look at the depth of the darkness. Listen to the shriek as the wind makes twisted wrecks of trees.

Their stories make sense of a wild world. They give these people a beacon in the night.

Corpse candles. Asher had heard of them when he had arrived in Cornwall as a young man. Floating lights, displaced souls. Spoken of in whispers, among words of prayer.

And what might they be, he had wondered, filtering the stories through a mind that had grown up reading Newton, Kepler, Galileo.

The lights had appeared on the edge of the graveyard, following the burial of a local man in Looe. The town became gripped with terror. An omen of death, they said between mumbled prayers.

Asher had walked the abandoned cemetery, seeking answers to satisfy his curious mind.

Blue lights hovering inches above the ground, close to the grave of a newly buried man. A flash of energy, perhaps? A fragment of the dead man's escaping soul? Each time he grew close, the lights would melt into the atmosphere.

Asher had been born to a struggling family in Bristol. His father had spent every penny on educating his son and Asher was determined to make the most of his opportunity. He dreamed with an expansiveness far greater than his station in life. Between endless hours of hauling fishing nets, he consumed as many books as he could manage. His mind was torn open by the riddles of science. Invisible life writhing beneath the glass of a microscope. That unfathomable chain of distant planets and moons.

Why turn to myth when the natural world held so much magic and mystery?

He found himself drawn to the work of the animists and their fascination with the human soul. What was it that separated the living from the inanimate? What was this inexplicable life force? A great, intangible mystery. A mystery Asher wanted solved.

The animists' ideas were controversial. Groundbreaking.

A soul is overactive and illness results. The soul chooses to leave the body and a man will die.

The idea obsessed him.

This would be his life, he decided. He had been blessed with an inquiring mind and he wanted all the world to know he was better than the rest. He would rise above the salt-stained filth of his fishing boots. Somehow, some day, he would make it to university. Study alongside those who shared his passion for knowledge. Seek answers to the questions that puzzled humankind.

For a pilchard fisherman, a university degree was as distant as the moon. But Asher held tight to his dream. One day he would make it reality. He felt certain of it, even if he had no clue as to how he would make it so.

There had to be a solid, scientific explanation to the corpse candles. He wanted to solve the mysteries of the natural world and he would begin with the riddles of the Cornish myths. But his hunt for the solution led him down the same blind alley as so many of his searches in this place. A futile hunt for answers. A quest for evidence where there was none to be found.

"There." Scarlett puts down the razor and wipes his cheeks with a fresh cloth. "You are most handsome."

Asher runs a hand over his smooth cheek. He feels more like a man and less like something the sea coughed up.

His lifts his chin. Presses his shoulders back.

Behave, they say, like the man you wish to be.

"Take the lane up the hill," Scarlett tells him as they climb from the cellar. The tavern above is empty and dark. "Once you're out of the village you can follow the path into Killigarth or Polperro. Perhaps you'll find someone willing to give you work. Earn enough for passage to Penzance. Or back to London."

He hears sadness in her voice. Aiding his recovery has been her mission. She is not ready to let him go. Perhaps she imagines saving his life might fetter them together for eternity. And that, thinks Asher, would be serve him well.

"The thing is, Miss Bailey," he says, leaning towards her conspiratorially. "I don't want to leave Talland. I'm looking for something. And I believe it to be in these parts."

She leans closer. "Looking for what?"

He has her. "Have you ever heard of Henry Avery?"

"The pirate."

"Yes."

Excitement in her voice. "Of course. He plundered the Grand Moghul ships. Commanded a whole fleet of pirates. Biggest haul ever taken." Her eyes shine. "Hid his jewels somewhere on this coast, so they say." She steps closer. "Is that why you planned to come to Cornwall, Mr Hales? Are you looking for Avery's haul?"

He chuckles. She has been told a glorified version of the tale, he is sure. No word of the torture and rape Avery had inflicted on his victims. No word of the women who had flung themselves into the Persian Sea to avoid his crew's attentions.

Asher keeps the details to himself. Scarlett has fantasised about that hidden haul; he can see it in her face. She has dreamt of stumbling across jewels in the sand. Has glanced into rock pools in case something glittered beneath the surface.

"You think Avery's haul is real?" she asks.

"Far more real than the ghost ship that has your village so afeared." Asher gives a short smile. "Do I believe Avery buried a treasure chest in your landing beach? Of course not. Why would any man be foolish enough to do that? But I have reason to believe a little of that haul made it to these parts."

"What reason?"

"You have an interest in this, I see. Perhaps you might help me with my search."

"Ayes. Of course." She catches his eye. "In exchange for compensation should you find it."

Perhaps her head is not as full of air as he had first thought. He is coming to like this girl, in spite of her father's blood. "Compensation, of course. Perhaps you might start by relaying the stories you heard as a child. It would be a great help to hear these tales as they were told by local men."

Her smile widens. "It would be a pleasure. My father was most intrigued by Henry Avery. We used to dig in the sand and pretend we were looking for his treasure."

Good. Jacob had shared his fascination with Avery with his daughter. Perhaps he had also shared information.

Asher leans close; close enough to smell her honey soap and the salt on her skirts. He says: "this will be our secret, of course."

The rest is easy. He needs a place to sleep. Does she think the innkeeper will mind him curling up on her cellar floor while he begins his search?

"Oh no," says Scarlett. "You cannot stay down there."

And she leads him by the arm, up the hill to the candlelit cottage once owned by Jacob Bailey.

1724

Five men, pipe smoke and brandy. Could have been any night at sea.

Polperro to Saint Peter Port. Round trip, sixteen hours in good conditions.

Asher had completed the voyage several times. Each time, he'd tell himself it would be his last. He was an honest, hardworking fisherman. Soon an honest, hardworking surgeon. Not a man who dirtied his hands with moonshine.

The Cornish, they saw nobility in their free trade. A service that made lives better. But Asher had been born the wrong side of the Tamar to see greatness in the tax evasion and midnight rendezvous. Saw free trade as no more than theft.

But there was money to be made in smuggling. Plenty of it. Asher had dreams of greatness that a life hauling pilchards could not hope to fulfil. And so when Jacob Bailey had sat him down in the Ship Inn and spoken of a free trading run, Asher had listened.

Yes, yes sir, I can sail a cutter. Channel Islands?

A challenging voyage to be certain, but his hands were callused and his sea legs sure. He would make a challenging voyage a hundred times over if it saw his pockets filled with the enticing sum Jacob had promised.

The cutter was owned by the great Charles Reuben, so Jacob said. To Asher, Reuben was no more than a name, a myth. The man who would fill their pockets when the voyage was complete.

His ship held five men and their tankards comfortably when a black-glass Channel had them marooned in their own saloon.

With each emptied glass, the stories grew wilder.

Murmurs of a capsized ship. A debt that would fetter Jacob to Reuben until death.

And then; Henry Avery. Moghuls, pirate fleets, vanished jewels.

Asher snorted into his brandy. The story-teller, Albert Davey, had no family and few friends. A prime candidate for a man loose with the truth.

"I was there," Albert said.

Laughter.

Jacob leant forward. "You're a liar."

"I never lie. I was there, on the *Fancy* with Avery himself. I helped take the *Gunsway* from those Moghul bastards."

"You're a liar," Jacob said again. But Asher could see something behind his eyes. Challenge.

"They say that haul was hidden at Lizard Point," said Asher. "Men went searching for it a few years past. Said they had a letter from Avery himself saying it were hidden in the dunes. Didn't find a thing."

Albert snorted. "Of course they didn't. That letter was a fake. Avery was far too intelligent to hide his fortune in the sand."

"Then where is it?"

"Divided among his men, as the ship's articles dictated."

When the others were snoring around them, Jacob said: "They say it was the richest haul ever taken. If you've a share of it, why do you spend your days free trading for other men?"

"Because the sea is in my blood." Albert reached into his pack. He opened his fist. "My good luck charm."

The coin was rugged and silver; illegible, alien writing spun across its surface. Jacob took it from Albert and held it to the candlelight. Asher reached for it, but Jacob pushed his hand away. Gave Albert a crooked smile.

"Is there more?"

"Of course."

"Where?"

He laughed. "Why should I tell you?"

Neither man said more. But Asher saw something flicker behind Jacob's eyes.

THE MAN FROM THE SEA

She brings home the man from the wreck like a child presenting a crab she'd fished from a rock pool. There is no back slapping, no congratulations, no *well done, Scarlett, for saving a man's life*.

Caroline looks at Asher as though he were dripping with plague. "He cannot stay here," she says with dagger eyes. "We don't know a thing about him. Besides, how are we to feed another mouth?" She paces, slinging the baby from one hip to the other. "Isaac, tell this man to leave at once."

Scarlett feels something sink inside her. She has saved a man's life. Worth a little recognition, surely?

She has always been the one who has needed saving, feeding, scooping from the children's home. Always the burden, never the protector. She had assumed her gallant rescue might warrant at least a smile of approval.

She looks at Isaac, trying for some acknowledgement. He is uncorking a brandy bottle with a level of concentration Scarlett is sure isn't necessary.

"Forgive me, Mrs Bailey," Asher says in a velvety voice, his eyes following Caroline across the room. "I would hate to cause you trouble."

She doesn't look at him.

Finally, Isaac speaks. He has filled a glass and is swirling it in his hand. He stares into the whirlpool of liquid. "You found this man on the wreck? The ship was empty." Amber drops slosh over the side of his glass. "You told everyone it was a dead wreck, Scarlett. Why?"

"I thought it best to keep it a secret," she says. "Keep Mr Hales safe from Reuben."

"Why didn't you tell *me*?"

Why not? Because of the criticism she can see in his eyes. Because of *that was foolish, Scarlett.* And because of the distrust she can see he has for Asher. He is never trusting, her brother. Always waiting to be deceived and double-crossed. Guard always up. He will see a man's faults before he sees goodness.

She is sure he is looking now, wondering if the sailor from the ghost ship has dared touch his sister. And whether his sister has been bold and mad enough to touch the man from the ghost ship.

"We don't keep secrets," Isaac says finally.

Scarlett feels anger stir inside her.

It comes from nowhere, this rage in her blood. The Wild, she calls it. The wild thing that takes her over. Naming it makes it easier. Makes it a thing separate from herself.

It has been with her as long as she can remember. The sudden swings of anger, the blinding rage. Sometimes warranted, sometimes irrational.

When the Wild takes over, she feels she is watching herself from afar. Watches herself scream and curse and destroy. Watches thoughts fly through her head that do not belong to her.

But today she is determined not to let her anger out. Not in front of Asher. She closes her eyes. Inhales until she feels the dark thing within her lose its shape.

"I'm sorry," she tells Isaac, calmly, evenly. "You're right. We don't keep secrets." But the knowledge of Asher's search swirls warmly inside her.

What a thrill it is to be sharing a confidence with the mysterious man from the wreck. The men in her life are sea-stained and rough around the edges. Asher Hales shines among them. She sees an intelligence behind his eyes. The man come to Cornwall to unearth hidden riches.

Sharing his secret, she thinks, sliding the coat from his shoulders, is made even more appealing by the unwelcome reception her heroics have earned from her family.

Isaac empties his glass. Caroline looks at Asher, the extra mouth to feed. Her eyes blaze. She herds Gabriel into the bedroom, the baby warbling beneath her arm. The door slams.

Isaac watches Caroline disappear. He rubs the dark stubble on his chin. Brow creased in thought. He paces. Paces. Paces until Scarlett is mad with it.

"Mr Hales, please, you will take my room," she says, deciding her brother is not going to speak.

"I'll not take your bed. A blanket by the fire will be plenty."

"Please. I insist. You are still injured. I'll be quite fine by the fire. This way." She ushers him towards the bedroom, liking the feel of his arm beneath her fingers. She waits for Isaac to stop her.

"Sailor," he calls. "Can you handle a lugger?"

THE HOUSE ON THE HILL

Flora peers into the mirror and straightens her bonnet. The straw is coming loose in places, ribbons frayed at the edges. Every penny has gone into the Mariner's Arms. No time or money for hats and ribbons.

She straightens her back and lifts her chin. She might not look a successful business owner, but she can damn well act as one.

Charles Reuben's house is a sprawling brick monstrosity overlooking Polperro harbour. The building is cluttered with windows and chimneys, a ridiculous mock turret cobbled to one wall. Wealth, Flora realises, has little bearing on good taste.

Reuben's maid ushers Flora and Bessie into the parlour. The room glitters with gilded mirrors and polished tables. The windows are bathed in crimson curtains.

So this is what Isaac's ventures are funding.

Reuben's boots click against the flagstones. "Good afternoon, Mrs Kelly." He smiles warmly and eases himself into an armchair. "To what do I owe this pleasure?"

"I'm here on business."

"I see."

A black and white dog scurries into the room, its claws tapping rhythmically. Bessie grins and flings herself towards it.

"Bessie! Behave."

Reuben chuckles. "Take him outside, my dear. He could use a good run."

Bessie grins and hurries out to the garden, the dog trotting beside her.

Reuben gestures to an armchair so elaborately embroidered Flora is embarrassed to sit on it. "Please. We'll talk business over a cup of tea."

"I don't plan on staying long."

"Humour me."

She sits reluctantly. Takes off her bonnet and squeezes it between her hands. A clock on the mantle ticks away the seconds.

"I plan to open the Mariner's Arms," she begins.

"So I hear."

"You've a store of liquor in the bell house."

He nods.

"Do you have buyers?"

"Of course," says Reuben. "But that doesn't mean I can't spare enough to get your doors open. Will the Mariner's Arms be a licensed property?"

Flora's mouth is suddenly dry. "I have an ale licence. But as for the liquor…" She looks down, irrationally ashamed.

"Well, perhaps in the future I will be able to do things lawfully…"

"So you also want my protection from the excisemen."

"I'm not asking for anything from you other than a sale. I'm willing to take my chances with the excisemen."

Reuben smiles. He laces his hands over his thick, waistcoated middle. "I'll see they don't come near you. If you wish to purchase liquor from me, it's in my best interests to keep your doors open."

The maid returns with a tea tray and pours two cups.

"How much were you hoping to purchase? I've deliveries of whisky going to the Three Pilchards and the Ship Inn." Reuben brings the cup to his lips. "But then there's the brandy from the wreck that unexpectedly fell into my hands the other night. I'm sure we can put some aside for you." He smiles. "That's if you don't mind taking goods from a ship many believe has brought a curse. To be honest, I've had trouble shifting the stuff."

"Then you'll give me a good price."

He chuckles. "Indeed. How much will you take?"

"I've ten pounds." A pitiful sum. Flora reddens.

"Then you'll take all twenty ankers. It's fine stuff. Cognac, I believe."

"I can't take that much. You're selling it to me far too cheaply."

"You can't very well run a public house with less."

Flora hesitates. Bessie flies past the window with the dog, her blonde hair streaming out behind her.

Reuben's cup clinks as he places it on the saucer. "You don't want to be indebted to me like your friend Mr Bailey."

Flora says nothing.

"You'll not owe me a thing, I assure you. Consider it a gift."

"I no more want to accept a gift from you," she says stiffly.

"I simply want to see the Mariner's Arms open, Mrs Kelly. The good people of Talland can't be traipsing over the clifftops every time they want a drink." He runs a finger through his beard. "My footmen will bring the goods to the inn this afternoon. You'll have the money for them then."

FAR-FETCHED TALES

Scarlett can tell her father's stories are useless. *Hmmm,* says Asher as she garbles through tales of lost gold and sword-fights too dashing to be true. *I see.*

These are bedtime stories, she realises. Far-fetched tales Jacob had told while she peeked out from beneath her blankets. Whatever her father had known about Henry Avery, he had smoothed the edges for his five-year-old daughter.

The house is quiet. Close to midnight. Tomorrow, they will trade with an East India merchant in Falmouth. Isaac sleeps. Caroline has barely left her bedroom since Asher appeared at the door.

Scarlett pushes the pie she has baked across the table. "Eat. Please." If she cannot aid Asher's search, she can at least feed him. She passes him a fork. Asher Hales, she is sure, is not a man who eats with his hands.

He eyes the pilchard heads poking from the pastry. Then he digs in his fork. Chews slowly. "It's good. You're not eating?"

"You have it. You need a good feed more than I do."

He pushes the plate into the middle of the table. "We'll share. I insist."

Scarlett hesitates. Then, her hunger getting the better of her, she pulls a small piece from the edge of the pie. Asher digs in his fork again. Swallows the fish head-first.

"What are you doing?" she cries. "Eat that way and you'll turn the fish away from our coast. Tail first, if you please."

Asher gives a snort of laughter. But, Scarlett notices, he is careful to eat the tail of the next fish first.

When she has finished her mouthful, she says: "My stories are of no help."

Asher chuckles to himself. "Your stories are useless."

Her cheeks flush with embarrassment. "What will you do next? Where will you look? You must have your reasons for believing the haul is in this village."

"There was a man," he says, "who once showed me a piece of Avery's silver. A man from these parts. Said there was more. Said he had it well hidden."

"What man?"

"A former crewman of mine. And of Avery's. He died alone, very suddenly. Wherever he hid his wealth, I'll warrant it's still there."

"And if you find it? You will just take it?"

Asher leans close. She sees the faint lines around his eyes, the freckle beside his nose. "It's not theft, Miss Bailey. It's resourcefulness. It's how you rise to the top in this beastly world." He sits back in his chair and folds his arms. "Being a part of the convoy that captured the Moghul ships was this man's greatest achievement. He would have told others of the money. Perhaps hinted at where it was hidden. There may be people in this place who know something."

She will ask, Scarlett tells him. Seek out the wrinkled faces and gnarled hands and old minds who will remember the stories of a man who brought jewels to their shore. If the haul is here, she tells Asher, she will find it. She punctuates her announcement by slamming her tankard onto the table.

"Hush," he hisses, his eyes light with amusement. "You want to wake the witch your brother has married?"

Scarlett laughs.

He leans close. "Forgive me. I have judged her hurriedly."

"You have judged her well." Scarlett grins, buoyed by his nearness. She lowers her voice. "When my father died, he left us in great debt to Charles Reuben. It is a hard thing for Caroline. It is wearing her down after so many years."

"What kind of woman marries into a family with such a debt hanging over them?"

"The money, it never mattered to her. She and Isaac love each other. My brother is a good man, Mr Hales. He would do anything for his family. Caroline is lucky to have him."

For a long time, Asher says nothing. Finally: "Your father left you in quite the position."

Scarlett nods. "I know he couldn't bear it if he knew the life he'd left for us. Sometimes I fear he's not at rest at all."

Asher's eyes fall to the cracked hearth stones, the threadbare curtains. What must he think of this shabby, grey existence?

He points to the brass quadrant that sits on the shelf above the range. "Was that his?"

Scarlett nods. "An offering from a wreck."

"Your father was a wrecker?"

She feels a sudden flush of anger. Pushes it away. "No. My father was a good man. He'd never see a ship wrecked for his own gain. Wrecks happen in these waters, Mr Hales. The shores are rugged and the weather can change in an instant. We treat the ships that come to us as gifts. The food that washes up on our beaches keeps us fed. The wool keeps us warm."

"And what of my ship? What did that bring you?"

"Well." She smiles. "That depends who you ask. My father used to say a wreck would see a place haunted. He was very superstitious. Not that it helped him in the end."

"He was drowned?"

She nods. "He went out fishing in a dory one morning and never came home."

"And your mother?"

"She died not long after my father. Went to sleep one night and never woke up. I suppose she tried to live without him and couldn't. After that it was just me and Isaac." She picks at the pie crust. "The villagers speak of the corpse candles. They believe we have been cursed by the souls of your lost crew. I can tell you have no such beliefs. What do you think happened on your ship?"

Asher slides his chair back from the table. "Let's not speak of it."

"Why not?"

He folds his hands. "Those men were murdered," he says finally.

"Murdered?" Scarlett's stomach turns over.

"My crew were involved in the trade," says Asher. "The night of the wreck they were engaged with smugglers.

Selling our cargo for a price. And they paid dearly for involving themselves with such men."

Scarlett shakes her head. "The free traders in these parts are fair men. Not killers."

Asher snorts. "I know of many free traders with blood on their hands."

"You're mistaken. I'm sure of it."

Asher pushes back the sweep of sandy hair that hangs over his eyes. The cut beneath it is still red and raw. He leans towards Scarlett. "This wound was not caused by the wreck. I was struck when I tried to fight the smugglers who boarded our ship. Knocked unconscious."

Scarlett raises her eyebrows. "Why fight them?"

"Because I believed the *Avalon* was a fine British merchant. She deserved better than to be caught up in the trade."

He sits back and ties his hair neatly at his neck. "Once, I was foolish enough to involve myself in smuggling. It near ruined my life. I'd never have signed aboard the *Avalon* if I'd known the sole purpose of the voyage was free trade." His voice hardens. "The men were blatantly flouting the hovering act. Had we been caught, I'd have been as guilty as the rest. I was not willing to risk conviction for something I didn't believe in. I was alone in my protests, of course. I was overpowered and knocked out. When I regained consciousness, I found the smugglers gone and my crew dead."

Scarlett sits back from the table. The pie feels heavy in her stomach. "Why were you spared?"

"Perhaps they believed me already dead."

She clasps her hands tightly in her lap. Asher's story feels cold and raw. "These men. What did they look like? Did you see their ship?"

"I'm sorry. I remember little. But I know I'm lucky to be alive."

Scarlett busies herself carrying the dishes back to the kitchen. "If you despise free trade so, why are you willing to come to Falmouth tomorrow?"

Asher catches hold of her wrist as she passes. Pulls her close. Her heart leaps into her throat. "You are to help me with my search," he says, his fingers moving on her wrist. "It's only fair I help you make your run, wouldn't you agree?"

"Ayes," she mumbles. "I suppose it only fair." She sits back at the table, entwining her fingers in her shawl. "We need to tell Isaac what happened to your crew. If you truly believe they were murdered, he needs to know there are traders out there willing to kill."

"No. You're not to tell anyone. I don't know who I can trust."

"You can trust Isaac."

"I don't know that."

"You trust me, don't you?"

"Yes."

"Then believe me when I say you can trust my brother."

Asher covers her hand with his. Squeezes tightly. Scarlett's heart shoots into her throat.

"This is between you and I. Promise me."

SEA MONSTERS

Here he is, tangled again in free trade. This time, under the command of Jacob's son. The irony is not lost on him.

"I want a guarantee," Asher says to Isaac. "If we're caught, you'll tell the revenue men I was forced into this. I'm willing to help you, but I'll not risk conviction."

Isaac nods faintly. "Ayes. A guarantee."

"And payment, of course. For this voyage and the run to Guernsey. Enough to see me out of this wretched place."

It is late afternoon when they slide out of the harbour towards Falmouth. The sun is dull and low, the sea leathery. A bunch of withered heather floats on the surface; Scarlett's sacrifice to the sea spirits.

Asher says little. He follows instructions, proves himself a knowledgeable sailor.

When the lugger is careening rhythmically along the coast, Scarlett hands him a mug of tea and sits beside him on the afterdeck.

"You know how to sail," he says.

"That surprises you."

"Most women I know would turn green if they even looked at a ship."

"You must know some right boring women." She is dressed in breeches, cinched alluringly at her narrow waist. She wears tall black riding boots, her hair bundled into a knot at her neck. "I've been sailing since I could walk. My father didn't believe I ought to be stuck at home with a needle and thread." She wraps narrow fingers around her mug; fingers Asher is sure have never once held a needle and thread. He can't deny she is intriguing.

Is it worth it, this gamble? His smooth-talking infiltration of the Baileys' world?

Perhaps not. One look at that rickety cottage had told him they had not a scrap of wealth. If Jacob had found the haul, he'd not shared it with his children.

And the stories? He'd been hoping for some clue, some fragment that might point him in the right direction. Jacob had had information about the haul's whereabouts, Asher is sure. But Scarlett's tales had been full of froth and fantasy.

Nevertheless, her trust is a valuable thing.

She will ask the villagers. Dig for tales and clues among those old enough to remember. And those wrinkled faces will look at her and see that poor, innocent maid whose family died around her and they will give up their secrets.

So, in the name of trust, he'd begun to toss out scraps of the story. A most unsettling, pitiable story of murder on the sea.

He had thought of telling Scarlett that he'd known the father she idolises. Thought fleetingly of telling her that first night, when she'd plucked him from the rising water.

But no. If he begins to tell the story of his time with Jacob, he might be unable to stop. She can't know things yet. Not until the desire in her eyes has her clinging on to every word he says.

This game, this girl must be played with care.

His story, of course, will sully her memories of a heroic father with the truth of who Jacob was. The picture of the caring family man she paints is very different from the Jacob Bailey Asher had known. How would she react if she found out the truth, he wonders? How *will* she react? It will be a fine thing to see. But not yet.

Patience.

He'd not even been twenty when he'd stepped aboard Jacob's smuggling cutter. Had become drunk on dreams of the wealth that would see him become an educated, enlightened man.

Within months, his life was destroyed.

He was captured, convicted. Sold to a merchant as an indentured servant and hauled out to New England. Where there had once been reading and learning, there was digging, hauling, building. A decade of exile.

Asher blames it all on Jacob Bailey.

He takes a long mouthful of tea. His insides are shaken. He hates this backward, windblown land. Even at sea, this place is oppressive. A warren of narrow lanes and cramped harbours. Just being in the place, his breathing feels constricted. And yet that hollow promise of riches has drawn him back, as surely as if he were caught on the tide.

He glances sideways at Scarlett. Providence has served him well by wrecking him at her feet.

Seize the opportunity.

When Isaac has disappeared below deck, Asher reaches out and pushes back the strand of hair that has fallen across her eyes. She smiles crookedly, cheeks flushed.

Drawing her close will be easy. And, he thinks, his insides warm from the rare human contact, perhaps he might even enjoy it.

They reach the anchored merchant vessel by dusk. Scarlett stands at the wheel while Isaac climbs aboard the ship, Reuben's ledger in his pocket.

Her eyes are on the horizon. The corpse candles have not been seen in days, but she has no trust for the ocean. She scans the purple expanse of sea and sky.

The men of Isaac's crew are right to be afraid. Scarlett feels it too; an uneasiness inside her as they rise and fall with the sway of the sea. She feels the invisible presence of lost souls and water spirits. Imagines unseen monsters gliding beneath the ship.

The ocean had taken her father. His dory swallowed, body never recovered.

She had been seven years old when Isaac had sat her down and told her he too was to sail to Guernsey. She had been gripped with fear. The sea had taken her father and then, in its own twisted way, her mother. She couldn't bear for it to take her brother too.

No choice, Isaac had said. *Be brave.*

She had clung to his neck. Wrapped her legs around him tightly so she might tether herself to him. She didn't want to be brave. She had had enough of bravery.

Be brave, as she had farewelled her father, then her mother. As Dodge carted her over the cliff to the children's home.

Always, *be brave.*

Isaac's voice was muffled by her hair. "I'll be back soon, I promise."

He couldn't make such promises. Not really. Scarlett was a child, but she knew. Knew a man could promise and plan and pray all he wanted, but the sea chose at will who it would allow home again.

But she recognised sorrow in her brother's eyes as he said: "I'm sorry, Scarlett. I've no choice."

And so she unfurled her arms and legs and let him go.

Be brave, she had thought, when Isaac had told her Gibson and the other men had refused to come to sea.

He had secured Asher's services, but the lugger could not be sailed and loaded with less than three.

"The landing party?" Scarlett had suggested. But no, they were farmers, miners. No use past the bay. And so she said: "I can come with you."

Isaac raised his eyebrows. "I thought you'd be as taken with these ghost stories as the rest of them."

Scarlett laughed it off. Corpse candles? She'd rather deal with phantom lights than the anger of Charles Reuben. "Let me come, Isaac, please. I want to help. You know I can handle the lugger. Besides, I'm good in the dark. I can act as spotsman."

And so, here she is with a cold sky pressing down on her and merrymaids beneath her feet. Perhaps out here there is even a ship full of smugglers who would kill an entire crew.

She can't think of it. Monsters hiding at the bottom of the sea she can handle. But a murderous crew is far too real.

Isaac climbs back aboard the lugger. He and Asher shoulder the crates and barrels passed down from the merchant ship. Whisky, tobacco, tea. A roll of silk the colour of fresh blood. All carried below and hidden beneath the fake bottom of the lugger.

A passenger craft, they will say if customs comes prowling.

Ahead of them, the merchant slides into the dark.

Asher and Isaac heave the lugger's halyards and the sails spill noisily.

Isaac looks at Scarlett across the deck. *All right?*

She nods. She feels emboldened by the knowledge that she is of use. A help, not a hindrance. Today her brother will look at her and see more than the thing that has tied him to Talland and a life under the control of Charles Reuben.

A light on the sea. Her heart jumps— *corpse candles?* — but this is just a ship. "Light," she calls. "Three points to port."

Isaac lifts the spying glass. "It's Tom Leach."

"Revenue men?" Asher's voice is taut.

"They're free traders out of Polruan," Scarlett tells him, marching onto the foredeck. She squints, trying to make out the ship. Leach has decked out his cutter with a black hull and sails to slide undetected into the estuary. "They're thieves and liars. Bring a bad name to the trade." She looks at Isaac. "Should we let them catch us?"

He shakes his head. "Whatever they want I'm not interested."

A voice from Leach's speaking trumpet: "Isaac Bailey! We need to speak."

Isaac keeps the lugger steady. Gives no response. A gunshot splinters the stillness. He shoves Scarlett aside as a bullet flies across their foredeck. "The dogs," he hisses. "Let them catch us."

He stands at the bow as Leach's ship draws closer. Scarlett hovers at his shoulder, bolstered her brother's nearness.

"That how you're doing things now, Leach?" says Isaac. "A trigger-happy rifleman on your watch?"

Their captain chuckles. "Only way to get your attention." Leach is tall and thin, a dirty black greatcoat hanging from his shoulders and a grey-streaked beard hanging from his chin. His narrow eyes make heat shoot down Scarlett's spine.

Isaac folds his arms. "What do you want?"

"You took the silk from the East India brig." Leach shakes the parchment in his fist. "Our agent placed an order for it. We already got buyers."

"Shame it's in my hold then."

Leach's eyes dart between Asher and Scarlett. "This the only rabble you can get to sail with you these days?"

"Indeed," says Isaac. "And I've still beaten you to the prize."

"Rabble?" Scarlett hisses, rage flaring suddenly.

"Stop," Isaac murmurs.

She grits her teeth. The muscles in her stomach tighten.

"Where are Gibson and the rest of your lot then?" Leach asks. "They been scared off by that wreck that washed up on your beach last week?"

Isaac says nothing.

A chuckle ripples through Leach's crew. Scarlett glances at the pistol in her brother's belt. What a satisfying thing it would be to pull the trigger and see Leach's blood stain his own deck. The vicious thought makes her breath catch. She shoves it away.

"The silk," says Leach. "Give it to me."

"Reuben placed an order for it," Isaac tells him. "If you've a problem, take it up with him. I'm just the runner."

"Ayes. Reuben's errand boy. Always will be."

"You know nothing, Leach!" Scarlett yells suddenly. "Shut your filthy mouth!"

Isaac snatches her wrist. "Enough." He looks over his shoulder at Asher. "Come about." He marches Scarlett towards the hatch. "Get below," he hisses. "Now."

She climbs down into the darkness. Crouches in the saloon with her knees to her chest. Forces herself to breathe deeply.

Somehow, the Wild is afraid of the dark. Somehow, when the light is gone, it takes the rest of the world with it. It takes Leach and the pistol. Takes cold stew, torn stockings, lying men. Takes the anger back to its hiding place. For all the ghosts that wait in the dark, Scarlett fears who she would be without it.

She feels the ship turn, carving its way towards home. Her breathing begins to slow. The violent thoughts fade into the blackness. But she finds herself thinking of wolf-eyed Tom Leach and the wreck coughed up upon their shore.

Dodge has heard the whispers.
Charlatan. Fraud.

He is grateful for the darkness. He can let anger crease his brow and make knots of his fists. More than thirty years he has been vicar of this scrappy parish. More than thirty years of soothing nightmares. Of reminding his people that power lies with God; the hand behind the natural world. And now, at the flickering of lights on the horizon; *charlatan, fraud.*

He had stood upon the clifftops at dawn for these people. Sent away the spirits that haunt them. But George Gibson had returned from his ill-fated fishing trip garbling of bad luck and omens of death. He has stirred up a panic. Cast doubt over the vicar's abilities.

From the cliff, he sees a flash of blue light shoot up from the sea. An empty pistol fired from Isaac Bailey's ship, alerting his men of his arrival. From the cliff at the edge of the churchyard, the lander responds with a flash of his lantern. The path to the church is clear.

Slowly, the landing party trudges up the hill; a paltry cluster of miners and farmers. Some little more than boys. Hunched under the weight of the ankers on their backs, they file into the churchyard and pile their goods into the vestry.

Charles Reuben watches, order papers crammed into his fist. Hidden in the shadows and dressed in his customary black, Dodge feels pleasantly invisible.

Footsteps up the lane. The Baileys have moored their ship and returned to Talland.

"Reuben's here," the girl hisses. "I've got to keep Mr Hales out of sight."

The vicar shifts curiously. He sees Isaac approach Reuben. Sees nothing of the girl, or the stranger of which she speaks.

"Take twelve ankers to the Ship Inn," Reuben tells the men. "Keep the rest in the church for later distribution." He hands Isaac the papers. "I trust you can take care of things here." And he is gone.

Dodge weaves through the crooked headstones. The girl hovers by the gate, a tall, thin man beside her. There is a disturbing, haughty air about the way he lifts his chin. A vague familiarity to him. Dodge cannot place it. Too many people have passed through this place in his time.

"Who is this?" he demands.

The girl starts. "It's no one, Father."

"No one?"

Her brother appears behind them. "He's an extra pair of hands, Father. Nothing more."

"An extra pair of hands from where?"

"It's not important."

Dodge clamps wiry fingers around the top of Isaac's arm. It will do a rattled community no good to find an unfamiliar face hiding among their graves. "Where did this man come from, Mr Bailey? Tell me."

Isaac sighs. "My sister found him on the wreck." He looks the vicar in the eye. "I trust you'll protect a man's life and not tell Reuben."

"Your crew won't like that. They are convinced that ship was cursed. They'll not welcome a man who came from it."

"My crew have given me little choice in the matter." He eyes the vicar. "Is it not your job to allay their fears, Father? They came to you for help and reassurance. And yet they're still afraid."

Dodge pushes away his anger. Anger is not what these people need. "I have asked the Lord's help to cleanse our village of the ill luck that came to us with this ship. And help will come. Perhaps your men would feel more at ease if they remembered that God works in His own time."

"Perhaps the men would feel more at ease if you didn't fill their heads with ghost stories each Sunday." Isaac turns away. Conversation over. "We've enough hands," he tells his sister. "Take Mr Hales back to the house."

THE GIRL WITH THE WHITE RIBBON

It is close to dawn when Isaac returns to the cottage. Light pushes beneath the door of his bedroom. Caroline is perched on the edge of the bed, buttoned into her cloak and riding boots. A worn wooden trunk sits at her feet.

"I can't do this anymore, Isaac," she says. "I can't live this way. Let's just go. Get as far away as we can."

He sits beside her. "Has something happened?"

A cold laugh. "Has something happened? The last decade has happened! All these years of handing everything over to Reuben. And now Scarlett brings home this jetsam from the wreck…" She rubs her forehead in frustration.

Isaac presses a hand to her knee. "I've tried leaving before. You know that. Reuben, he has eyes everywhere."

"That was a lifetime ago. You've been loyal to the man for fourteen years. Surely you've built up enough trust that he no longer has men spying on you in the night."

"How can we risk that? How can we put our children in that kind of danger?"

The children weigh on him heavily. A desperate, unconditional love, of course, but a constant, vague sickness in the pit of his stomach. Bringing children into this life? What had he been thinking?

Sometimes, gripped with anxiety, he watches them in their sleep. Gabriel's grubby half-moon fingernails. The veins in Mary's paper-thin eyelids. How can such innocence exist in this world of corruption?

Already, he can see so much of himself in his eight-year-old son. The crooked smile, the dark ribbon of hair tied at his neck. It's his need to see the world he wants to pass on to Gabriel. His need for adventure, for knowledge.

Not his debts.

And rosy, fragile Mary. Will she grow up creeping about in the moonlight like her aunt?

Isaac has already failed to keep Scarlett from dirtying her hands with free trade. The moment he'd begun working for Reuben, she'd had bladders of moonshine quilted into her skirts. He'll die before he sees the same thing happen to his daughter. But he will not risk her life by trying to flee without proper means of escape.

Caroline's cheeks are hot and pink, her eyes glowing. Her hand tightens around his. There is desperation in her touch. Anger.

How blessed Isaac had been to find her. A woman willing to marry into a life of debt to Charles Reuben. Into instant motherhood to a nine-year-old spitfire.

With Scarlett latched to him, Isaac had resigned himself to unmarried life. But then there was Caroline; lighting up the Ship Inn with her bell of a laugh and making Isaac's day hauling fishing nets seem a distant memory.

She sidled up to the bar and stood close enough for her shoulder to graze his. "Buy me a drink," she said, the gold flecks in her eyes lighting as she smiled.

Isaac grinned at her boldness. "How can I turn down such a request?"

"Well. You look a man who has little time for games." Her words were neat and polished beside his own clipped speech.

She wore skirts the colour of daisies; her dark hair tied with a thin white ribbon. Arrived in Polperro from the east, she said. No family. Twenty-one and left to make her own way in the world.

Isaac was taken by her optimism, her bravery. He told her of his own trials and felt not a scrap of shame. Her face was even as she listened without judgement or pity. She stirred in him some long-abandoned hope.

They escaped to a corner of the tavern and sat with their heads bent towards each other to keep out the rest of the world. Told tales of their lives and drank mahogany, until Isaac remembered he'd left Scarlett with a packer from the pilchard palace.

They were married by Dodge two months later; forty ankers of smuggled whisky in the vestry behind them.

She knew it all, of course. The debt, Isaac's role in the smuggling syndicate. Knew he had nothing to give her but love.

That was enough, she'd said. How could she want more?

Before Gabriel had arrived, she had joined him on his voyages to Guernsey. She would stand at the bow with her hair flying and her cheeks pink. Sprawl over his bunk like a siren, her skirts tossed to the floor.

Suddenly, with Caroline, there was hope. There was fireside conversation, arms around him at night. There was more on the supper table than sailors' rations; scraps of vegetables magicked into pies. There was someone to steer Scarlett away from the rudderless life he was providing.

But Caroline's optimism has faded. The spark behind her eyes is gone. How can he blame her? The pressure of debt, the bleakness of their future is enough to extinguish any light.

Isaac aches for her laughter, for her fingers pressing into his arm as the wind sweeps through their hair. He longs for her skirts on the floor of his cabin, her naked body in his bunk. Longs for that distant time when loving her was enough.

"There has to be an end to it." A waver in her voice. "If we take the lugger—"

"Steal Reuben's ship? We'll be at the mercy of the authorities. They'll hang me if we're caught. In all likelihood, they'll hang you too."

"We need to start taking risks. You say you don't want to put the children in danger by trying to leave, but can't you see it's just as unsafe for them here?"

"Why?" he hisses. "I'd never see any harm come to them."

"But you're willing for them to have the same life you and Scarlett have had?"

"Of course not. But what can I to do? Go behind Reuben's back? Deceive him and earn money on the side like my father tried to do?"

"Yes!" Caroline pulls him towards her. New lines around her eyes. New threads of grey at her temples. "What loyalty do you owe him? What decency? We both know your father's debt will never paid off. Reuben designed it that way. Deceiving him is the only way we will be free of him." She squeezes his hand, too tightly. "You're an intelligent man, Isaac. Hiding that whisky was clever. You've a resourcefulness in you that Reuben doesn't have. You've got to use that."

They've made these plans before. Complete runs behind Reuben's back. Earn enough for passage out of Cornwall. Tickets for a voyage to Scotland, Ireland, anywhere far from Reuben's watchful eyes. For fourteen years, Isaac has plotted and dreamed of ways to free his family. And each of those fourteen years, escape has seemed more distant. The drive to succeed has faded. Because the reality is always there, staring him down.

Once, his father had tried to deceive Charles Reuben. And the world had fallen down around him.

And so he climbs into bed, stepping over his wife's packed trunk. He hears himself mumble his apologies.

Caroline remains perched on the edge of the bed in her cloak and boots. Her eyes are hard in the candlelight. "You're a resourceful man, Isaac," she says finally. "But to hell if you're not full of excuses."

MARINER'S ARMS

'The appearance is said to be that of a man habited in black,
driving a carriage drawn by headless horses. This is, I know,
very marvellous to believe, but it has had so much credible
testimony in my parish that some steps seem necessary to
allay the excitement it causes. I have been applied to for this
purpose, and my present business is to ask your assistance.'

Taken from a letter to Rev. Richard Dodge from Mr Gryllis,
Rector of Lanreath
1725

A creak of the door and the Mariner's Arms is open. An
occasion worthy of the hike from Polperro.

By six, the tavern brims with laughter, chatter, ale-fuelled
cursing. Glasses filled with brandy hauled from the ghostly
Avalon.

George Gibson puts down his cup and scowls at Scarlett. "You're just trying to bait me, maid. This didn't come from that cursed ship."

"Flora says otherwise." Scarlett leans close. "Drink it. Feel the darkness flowing through your veins."

A curse? Perhaps. She's heard of stranger things. Either way, it's a pleasure to stir up grizzly George Gibson. A welcome distraction from Asher's tales of killers in the bay.

Gibson looks across the bar to Flora. "This true, Mrs Kelly? You serving the brandy Reuben's men brought ashore from the wreck?"

Flora plants a hand on her hip. "If you've a problem with it, don't drink it."

"I'm surprised at you, Miss Bailey," he says loudly. "Working for a landlady who's been dealing with Charles Reuben."

Scarlett glances at Flora. She had mentioned nothing of her business with Reuben. Still, Scarlett can hardly claim to be surprised. She shrugs. "A person wants to open a tavern in these parts they've little choice but to deal with Reuben."

Gibson snorts. "And what's he gone and done? Sold her brandy from a cursed wreck."

"What's this about a wreck?" This is Bobby Carter, sidling to the bar with a dimpled grin. He wears the brass buttons of the revenue men and the loose morals of the free traders. Pockets full of smuggling riches in exchange for protection.

Men like Bobby are hauled out of the preventative service regularly. Strung up to cries of *corruption* and *shame*. But Bobby has a decency Scarlett has seen in few men from either side.

"One day, Scarlett Bailey," he'd told her, swanning around the Ship Inn in his blue and yellow uniform, "I'm going to make an honest woman of you."

She had laughed and snatched his glass. Emptied it in one mouthful. "You'll have to make an honest man of yourself first. Weren't it Reuben's money that bought this whisky?"

Bobby winks at Scarlett, his cheeks round and pink. "Never heard of no wreck."

She grins. Pours him a glass from the kettle beneath the bar in which Flora has hidden the liquor. "Indeed you haven't. And that's why we love you."

He tosses back the brandy, blue eyes sparkling. "I can feel the darkness in me already."

She laughs. When Bobby is around, ghost ships and curses fade away.

"You're both asking for trouble," says Gibson. "Making light of such things. The vicar ought to have a word in your ears."

"Thought you'd lost faith in the vicar," says Scarlett.

"I was a fool. God works in His own time, so he does. Dodge will rid us of the lights. He's always come through for us in the past."

"The man's a fraud," Bobby snorts. "Laying ghosts and demons not a soul can see."

Gibson bristles. "Dodge laid the ghosts on Blackadown Moor. There were plenty of souls saw that carriage. Headless horses and all, so they say."

"So they say." Flora smiles crookedly. "Did you see this ghostly carriage, Mr Gibson?"

He slides from his stool. "You don't need to see a thing to know it's real."

"There are no demons in Cornwall," says Flora. "They're too afraid they'll be made into a pie."

Scarlett laughs.

Gibson jabs a finger at her. "Your father knew better." He disappears out the door, leaving his brandy untouched.

Bobby slides onto the vacated stool. He leans across the bar so his face is close to Scarlett's. "They say you're keeping a man from that wreck for your own purposes."

Her cheeks flush. "They're lying."

Bobby tugs at the strand of hair hanging over her cheek. "I hope so. Or I fear my poor heart would break."

Scarlett's eyebrows shoot up as two riding officers walk through the door. "What are you doing bringing the cavalry?" she hisses at Bobby.

"Calm yourself. They're here for a drink, is all. They don't want no trouble." He grins at Flora. "Give them all a serve of shipwrecked brandy."

She empties Gibson's glass and nudges the kettle further beneath the bar. "As far as they're concerned I'm nothing but an alehouse." She fills three glasses from the anker of spiced ale and lines them up along the counter for the riding officers. "Try the lambswool, gentlemen. Specialty of the house."

And here is Charles Reuben, swanning in, nodding to the officers.

Bobby flashes Scarlett a grin. "See? We're all friends here."

Scarlett narrows her eyes at Reuben. "What do you want?"

"Nice to see you making an honest woman of yourself, Miss Bailey." He smiles, more to himself than Scarlett. "Ale, if you please."

She hesitates. Reuben is a man with eyes everywhere. If there is information to be known about the wreck of the *Avalon*, he will have it. She has promised Asher her silence, but the thought of the murders gnaw at her constantly.

She lowers her voice. "What do you know about the crew of that wreck?"

"I asked for an ale," says Reuben. "Fetch it for me, then perhaps I'll answer your question."

Scarlett fills a tankard and tops it with a glob of spittle.

Flora sighs. Takes the glass from Scarlett and empties it into the trough. Gives her a fresh tankard and a warning look.

Scarlett dumps the ale on the bar in front of Reuben. "Tell me what you know."

He sips slowly. "What makes you think I know anything?"

"Because whenever there's something untoward, you've always got your hands in it."

Reuben chuckles. "I've always liked you. That sharp tongue of yours keeps things interesting."

She narrows her eyes. "An entire crew vanished from that ship." Careful words. Nothing that might give away Asher's presence, Asher's theory. "These are free trading waters. Perhaps they were involved in smuggling."

"Very likely. But I can't tell you what happened to those men. If that curious mind of yours is seeking answers, you'll have to look elsewhere."

She eyes him. "Are you lying?"

"You know I don't lie. And you know I've never given you any reason not to trust me. Besides, I don't know why you're asking me. You'd never catch me out at sea. Speak to your brother. Perhaps he's come across some unsavoury creatures in his travels."

"My brother does not associate with unsavoury creatures. He is a good man."

"Just like your father, is that right?" Reuben chuckles. "Ah, Miss Bailey. It never ceases to amaze me you can be so deep in free trade yet see such goodness all around you."

She folds her arms. "I don't see goodness in you."

The lights of the Mariner's Arms glitter in the bend of the road.

The grand opening.

Isaac is glad of it. He needs a drink.

Needs to see Flora.

No, needs a drink.

He'd met with the traders' banker in Polperro. "I want the conditions of my arrangement with Charles Reuben to be rewritten."

"You'll need to speak to Mr Reuben himself."

"You think I've not tried?" Isaac hissed, stifled by the curtain of pipe smoke in the banker's office. "He'll not see me. Told me to speak with you."

He'd take the moral approach, he'd told himself. Going behind Reuben's back was trouble. "I've been loyal to the man for fourteen years. I want terms that will allow my father's debt to repaid. A reduction in interest."

"The terms of repayment were signed by your father before his death. I'm afraid there's little room for negotiation."

Isaac shoves open the door of the inn. Inside is hot and noisy. Traders share tables with revenue men. Bobby Carter playing both sides. Reuben in animated conversation with Scarlett.

Bastard. Rather spend his time drinking than be bothered giving his captain an hour of his time. Isaac marches towards him, simmering with frustration.

Flora catches his eye across the room. Her face lights. Isaac feels his anger dissipate. He'll not confront Reuben. Not now. He's too happy for Flora.

He returns her smile and slides onto a stool.

She darts back behind the bar, blue skirts swilling. She is striking; her cheeks pink and eyes alight. Blonde hair swept into a neat knot on top of her head. Isaac finds it hard to look away.

"You made it," she smiles.

"Of course." He leans over the bar to kiss her cheek. "Jack would be very proud."

"Thank you, Isaac. I couldn't have done it without your help." She drops her voice. "Your meeting. Was it a success?"

He glances across the room at Reuben. "Let's not speak of it here."

The door creaks. In come Tom Leach and three of his men. Isaac watches Reuben's face darken.

"Who brought these dogs?" Scarlett says brassily.

Flora leans close to Isaac. "Who are they?"

"Tom Leach and his men. From Polruan."

"Traders?"

He nods. "Ayes. Been making trouble for us."

Scarlett moves towards them, but Isaac grabs her wrist. "Leave him."

"I'll not make trouble," she whispers. "Just want to find out why they're here."

He sighs.

Flora hands him a glass. "She just wants to impress you. You know that, don't you."

He smiles wryly. Holds out a penny.

Flora shakes her head. "Put it away."

Scarlett sashays across the bar towards the men. "Don't you have your own taverns to destroy?"

Leach grins. "We've come all this way just to see you, dearest."

"Are you planning on ordering a drink? If not, you can bloody well get out."

"You hear that, innkeeper?" calls Leach. "Your bar wench is threatening to throw us out on the street!"

Flora raises her eyebrows. "It seems my bar wench is a good judge of character."

Isaac hides a smile.

"Don't you go making out you're the innocent ones," Leach tells Scarlett. "Your brother over there took that French silk we had our names on."

"I'm sorry," she says. "It would have looked most becoming on you."

Leach glares. "This has happened too many times."

"Your issue is with Reuben and his agent. Not with Isaac. Or are you too stupid to know how this game is played?"

He lurches towards her. Isaac leaps from his stool, but Reuben steps in front of Scarlett, pressing a firm hand to Leach's chest.

"She's right," he says. "Your issue is with me. We can discuss it further if you wish."

Leach hovers. Considers further discussion. Then one of the other men pulls him away.

"The bastard ain't worth it," he hisses.

Reuben runs a hand over his bald head. Watches them leave. "You ought to be careful who you let through these doors, Mrs Kelly."

Flora shrugs. "Their coin is as good as anyone's."

"They're trouble."

"I can handle them."

"Yes," says Reuben. "I don't doubt that."

Light and laughter spills from the inn. Asher keeps walking. The church is dark and empty. He tries the vicarage.

"Oh no," says the young woman who answers the door. "The reverend doesn't take lodgings here." She points him up the winding hill towards Killigarth.

Asher follows the woman's directions to a manor house on the edge of the village. Knocks. "I need to see the vicar."

The maid leads him into a lamp-lit parlour. Dodge is reclined in an armchair, his stockinged feet stretched towards the fire and a glass of brandy pressed to his chest. Without his wig, thin white hair rises from his head like wisps of smoke. He looks up as Asher approaches. "You're the man from the wreck."

"Yes."

The vicar rubs his chin, considering. After a moment, he gestures to the armchair beside him. Asher perches on the edge.

"Is it your lost crewmates that bring you to me?"

Asher smiles crookedly. His lost crewmates? Those bastards can stay hidden at the back of his mind until time removes them completely. "I need information," he says. "About a man from this area."

Dodge drums his fingers against his glass. "Which man?"

"Albert Davey."

The vicar makes a noise from the back of his throat. He empties his glass and sets it on the side table. "Why do you seek information on poor Albert Davey?"

"That is my own business."

Dodge's voice darkens. "Leave the past where it is, Mr—"

"Hales."

"Mr Hales. I suggest you leave this place. The people believe your ship has cursed the village. If they see you walking the streets, it is hard to say where their fears will lead them."

"Perhaps to the tales of ghosts and demons you are so fond of?"

"Perhaps." Dodge gives a humourless smile.

Asher chuckles. "I am neither ghost nor demon. Any sane man can see that."

Dodge clasps his wiry hands. "This is a village of believers."

"Because you have made it so."

"Yes."

Asher leans forward. A log shifts and crackles in the grate. "And are you a believer too, Father? Do you believe demons walk Bridles Lane? Or do you believe only in the gold Charles Reuben lines your pockets with?"

Dodge's eyes harden.

"How many of your villagers know their church is full of smuggled goods?" Asher keeps his voice even, controlled. "Such a thing would shake their faith, would it not?"

Dodge breathes heavily, noisily. "The people would not believe a word that came from you."

"Are you so certain of that?"

For a long time, the vicar doesn't speak. The fire pops loudly. Finally, he says: "what do you want?"

Asher smiles faintly. "Albert Davey. Tell me where he lived."

Flora heaves closed the door and slides the key into the lock. Drunken voices disappear up the lane.

Scarlett smiles, reaching for a broom. "Congratulations. A success."

Flora pours two cups of brandy from the kettle. *A success.* She allows herself to savour the words. She paces across the bar with the tin cup in her hand and a faint smile on her lips. Runs a finger along one of the seashells on the shelf. "Sit, Scarlett. Drink. We'll clean later."

Scarlett hesitates.

"In a hurry to leave, are you?" says Flora. "Does this have anything to do with your shipwrecked sailor?"

Scarlett's cheeks flush.

Flora sits, sips her drink. The alcohol softens her aching muscles. "Please be careful. None of us know a thing about him." The man from the wreck has a vague familiarity to him; one she has been unable to place. But he is no stranger to Talland; of that she is sure.

"I trust him," Scarlett says defensively. "I don't want to live my life seeing the worst in people as my brother does."

Flora nods. A difficult case to argue. "Go to him if you wish."

"No. We ought to celebrate." Scarlett takes her cup. "Are you worried about Bobby bringing the revenue men?"

Flora shrugs. "They just want a cheap drink like the rest of them."

"And what if the excisemen were to pay you a visit? What if they catch you serving liquor? Ask to see your licence?"

Flora looks down. She feels oddly reluctant to tell Scarlett she has secured Reuben's protection against the excisemen. Accepting so much help from him feels like a betrayal.

"They'll not be bothering us," she says shortly. "They're easily bought. And with this place open, I've had the last of the vicar and his games."

Scarlett rolls the cup between her hands. "Why did Dodge ask for your help with his exorcisms?"

"I suppose he knew I needed the money. Felt sorry for me, perhaps. After Jack."

"No. You were helping him long before Jack died."

Flora glances down. In the corner of her eye, she can see a grin on Scarlett's face.

"My mamm, she used to come to your mamm. When one of us were sick and the like. I remember her boiling herbs on the range. Making teas that smelled of faraway places. She was a healer, wasn't she. A charmer."

Flora nods.

Scarlett peers over the top of her glass. "Is Dodge keeping you close because he fears you have her abilities? Because he fears it ungodly?"

"I have no abilities. Nor did my mother. The graves of your brothers and sisters ought to tell you that."

Scarlett shrugs. "That were God's way." She leans forward. "Do you ever think of it? Doing as your mother did?"

"No." Flora empties her cup and grabs the broom. "Never."

With Scarlett gone, she climbs upstairs, letting the sudden stillness of the inn wash over her.

"I did it, Jack," she murmurs. "Are you proud?"

Silence, of course. Her heart lurches.

She peeks into Bessie's room. Her daughter is asleep on her back, pale hair fanned out across the pillow. Flora pulls the door closed, too overcharged to sleep.

She carries a lamp into the parlour and lights the fire. Perches on the edge of a chair and stares into the flames. If she is honest with herself, excitement over the inn accounts for only half her jittery state. Scarlett's comments have worked their way beneath her skin.

Her mother the healer. Flora remembers people coming to the inn at all hours.

Fix my cough, my cuts, my curse.

Her talents had done little to help the Baileys, but people had kept coming.

Flora has made no attempt to follow her mother's path. She wants the Mariner's Arms to be the thriving business she and Jack had dreamed of, not a wish house for the desperate souls of Talland. And yet there is a restlessness within her, stirred up by Scarlett's prying.

She leaps suddenly from the chair. Paces down the hall.

When her mother had died, Flora had been unable to part with her belongings. But nor could she bear to look at them. Instead, she had piled them into one of the empty guest rooms on the second floor.

The passage is narrow and crooked. Her bedroom and Bessie's at one end, beside the parlour and kitchen. At the other, the three untouched rooms. A room for her mother. Her father. Her husband. Too many rooms that brim with loss. Too many untouched shrines to the dead.

She will open them all. Go through each locked chest. Keep the good memories and dispose of the bad. Now the tavern is open, she has to look forward. And she will start with her mother's room. Tonight.

She turns the handle slowly. The door sticks, creaks. She shines her lamp around the room. Her mother's things are everywhere; ankle boots crammed beneath the wash stand; a pile of books beside the bed, threadbare cloak hanging from the back of the door. Everything is blanketed in dust.

A scratched wooden chest is hidden in the corner. Flora unlatches the lid. Inside is a jumble of glass bottles and wooden boxes. Pouches crammed with dried herbs. A gold-rimmed hand mirror with a painted black surface.

Flora has told no-one of the hours she and her mother had spent among these bottles and herbs. Told no-one of the days she had spent memorising remedies and incantations.

As a child, such things had been lore. But with Jack's arrival, Flora had begun to see the world through adult eyes. Easterner's eyes. Jack had laughed at the rhymes and rituals. Smiled politely at Flora's mother when she spoke of her craft, but there was a humour behind his eyes. Flora had begun to see the humour too. She kept her knowledge of such things a secret from Jack. A fragment of her past she'd become ashamed to admit to.

But Jack is not here to see her now. No one is here to see. She carries the chest back to the parlour and lifts out a tattered cloth bag. The worn fabric in her palms makes her feel suddenly, happily close to her mother. She opens the bag.

A musty floral scent rises into the darkness, plunging Flora into her childhood. The bag is full of dried flowers and herbs. She lifts out the fragile leaves, one by one.

Groundsel, for fever.

Brambles for a burn.

Out with thee fire and in with thee frost.
In the name of the Father, the Son and the Holy Ghost.

The incantation comes to her like a long-forgotten nursery rhyme.

Now the mirror. Firelight flickers across its black surface; a glimmer in a bottomless pond. Flora stares into the dark glass.

How many times had she watched her mother sit with the glass in her lap, eyes growing vacant as she stared into its surface, waiting for images to appear. Pieces of the future, plucked from the depths of the mirror.

Flora smiles wryly to herself.

Pieces of the future. As real as the demons cowering beneath Dodge's whip.

She puts down the mirror.

Her work with the vicar has left her jaded. She sees the irony. Dodge has kept her close so she might embrace the power of God. But instead she has been left with a world unenchanted.

A pouch of herbs, a jar of animal hair. Black mirror. These things are not cures. These things are just trickery. This is nothing but a chest of false hope. A craft built upon trickery and deceit.

Flora shoves the mirror back in the trunk. She will not involve herself in such things. Not after ridding herself of Dodge's games. Her world may be unenchanted but its edges are clear.

She peers into the chest. Sees her own eyes stare back at her from the depths of the mirror. She hurriedly slams the lid.

FALSE HOPE

Everyone has a tale about Henry Avery.

With each story, the haul gets bigger. Mountains of gold, silks and spices. Enough jewels to bathe in.

Everyone has a theory. The haul stolen, spent, divided. Buried in the sand at Lizard Point.

"Lizard Point?" Scarlett says flippantly, swimming through endless cups of sweet tea. "Oh, how interesting."

No, she tells them, she is asking for no reason. Nothing but curiosity.

After winding her way through Polperro and Killigarth, she ends at the door of her neighbour, Martha Francis.

Martha's eyes light up. She tugs Scarlett inside and plies her with saffron cake.

Scarlett sits at the table and eats. For a moment she is a child again, coddled by Martha while Isaac's lugger slides soundlessly to Guernsey.

But: "Henry Avery," Scarlett says and the smile disappears from Martha's lined face.

"Oh Scarlett. There's nothing to those stories."

Scarlett shuffles to the edge of her chair. "Ayes, there is. I can tell by your reaction."

Martha sighs. She looks down, cobwebs of hair falling over her cheeks. "Don't do this, my girl. Your father was convinced that haul was real. For a time, he talked of nothing else. But you can see what it was can't you? It was his way out. He'd find that money and be under Reuben's control no longer." She reaches for Scarlett's hand. "I know things are not easy for you and Isaac. But searching for something that doesn't exist will only bring you disappointment."

"My father believed it was real. Why?"

"It was his desperation talking." Martha squeezes her fingers. "Don't go digging up the past, *cheel-vean.* Please. Don't give yourself false hope."

Scarlett pushes her plate away, her appetite gone.

Martha reaches for her arm as she makes for the door. "Is it true you found a man on the wreck?" Her voice is hushed, though they are the only ones in the house.

"Where did you hear that?"

The old woman shrugs. "Word gets around."

Scarlett sighs. "Dodge."

"Don't be like that. You can trust me. So did he tell you what happened? How did the rest of his crew die? Is there anything strange about him?" Her grey eyes glitter in pitted cheeks.

"The vicar is mistaken. There was no one on that ship. It was a dead wreck." Scarlett feels a pang of guilt at her lies. But there is a wreck in the bay and corpse candles on the horizon. People mumble prayers and speak of approaching death. Every scrap of misfortune is attributed to the curse. Lost cats, burnt bread, broken windows; each the result of the wreck the sea spirits flung upon their shore.

What would the villagers see in the man crawled from the ship? A hint of the devil, perhaps?

There has been talk, of course. In this place, there is always talk. A man from the wreck. A man who had fought off the sea monsters or sirens or the great sweep of the sea. And for such a tale to come from the vicar, well, what can it be but truth?

"No," Scarlett says when people approach her in the street. "The vicar is mistaken."

"Mistaken?" Martha Francis repeats.

Yes, mistaken. She will forget about Avery's haul, she promises, if Martha speaks no more about the man pulled from the sea.

The man pulled from the sea stands outside the house once inhabited by Albert Davey. A pauper's house on the edge of Polperro; cramped and dark, the roof sagging, windows patched. A thin line of smoke rises from the chimney.

Sixteen years, of course, since Davey had lived here, but even without the chipped paint and broken glass, it hardly looks the cottage of a man with a pocket of foreign riches.

Asher peers through the window. The fire is smouldering beneath a black iron pot, underskirts hung over a chair to dry. He feels a faint sinking inside him. No doubt the cottage has been lived in since Davey's death. If he'd hidden his share of the haul here, it would have been found. Still, he has come this far. Prised the information from the vicar. He needs to get inside.

The door is locked. He rattles the wood covering the broken window. It is damp, pliable. Easy to snap.

He glances over his shoulder. The street is empty. He scrambles through the gaping window on his front, landing heavily on his hands. Pain shoots through his wrists. The cut on his head throbs.

He scrambles to his feet. The house smells of wood smoke and wet laundry. The soup pot on the fire is simmering. Whoever lives here could return at any time. Asher glances around. What is he hoping to find?

He thumps on the wall. Solid brick. He walks the length of the room, keeps thumping. Solid brick, solid brick. No hiding places. He tries the floor. Packed earth; dense and unyielding.

He hears voices and footsteps at the back of the house. He scrambles out the window and runs.

When Polperro is behind him, he stops, gasping down his breath. Sweat runs down his back. There is an ache in his knees, reminding him he is no longer the agile teenager he had been last time he'd visited this place.

He sits on the edge of the path and watches the sea roll towards the cliffs. Tries to untangle the emotions swirling inside him.

Disappointment? A little, yes, but he'd known from the beginning that visiting Davey's cottage was unlikely to bring results. He feels strangely invigorated. Perhaps by the charge up the cliff path, or perhaps by the knowledge that he has returned to Albert Davey's world. The knowledge that, although the haul is still hiding, he is closer to it here than he has been for almost two decades.

Or perhaps it is the knowledge that he has Jacob's daughter on his side. He can see now he will need to take his search further afield. Find people from the past, push aside the secrets and lies. How valuable Scarlett will be.

But not yet. She needs to trust. Needs to believe every word carefully chosen word that comes from him. Needs not to let go when he turns her world upside down.

SAINT'S DAY

Caroline has been busy. Isaac finds the house brimming with scents of lamb and plum cake; a lavish Feasten Sunday supper.

Underneath it is another, earthier scent. Plants. Animals.

Caroline leans over the table, spreading a tray with dark, wet leaves. Gabriel kneels up on a chair, watching his mother with interest.

Isaac slides off his coat. "What is this?"

"The tea you landed the other night." Caroline uses her wrist to push a strand of dark hair from her eyes. "I'm making us a little money."

And he realises at once what she is doing. Soak elder leaves in water seeped with dung. Dry them, bake them, crumble to resemble tea. Mix with the real thing. Half the tainted tea back in Dodge's vestry. The rest in their hands.

Caroline smiles out the corner of her mouth. "I'm sure you could find a gentleman or two interested in purchasing a fine French infusion."

"That tea was hidden in the church," says Isaac. "How did you get your hands on it?"

She shrugs. "Town's going mad. The wind blows the wrong way and everything falls to pieces. Your son and I managed to get our hands on the stuff while the vicar was busy consoling Martha Francis."

"Gabriel stole this?" Isaac feels something twist inside him.

The boy grins. "I sneaked in like a mouse, Tasik. The father never knew I was there."

Isaac forces a smile. Runs hand through Gabriel's knotted hair.

Caroline wipes her hands on her apron. "Don't give me that look, Isaac. I'm doing this for the good of our family. I'm going to earn enough for those tickets. I'm going to get us out of this life. As you ought to be doing."

He hears footsteps come towards the door. "Put the tea away. I don't want Scarlett knowing about it."

"I've not dried it yet."

Scarlett lets the door slam. "What's all this?"

Isaac takes the tray of leaves into the bedroom. "Nothing you need to involve yourself with."

Scarlett goes to the table, the man from the wreck trailing. She peers at the spilled leaves, at the bags of tea leaning against the table leg. Hand on hips, accusingly. "Did you steal those from Reuben?"

"You heard your brother," Caroline says sharply. "It's nothing you need to involve yourself with."

109

"We shouldn't keep secrets," says Scarlett, infuriating because she is right.

What is that look in her eyes? Disappointment. It hits Isaac hard.

She has always looked up to him. Respected, listened. Never given him this thinly veiled scorn.

Caroline sweeps the stray leaves onto the floor. She spoons boiled potatoes from a pot on the range and sets the bowl on the table. Looks at Asher, then back to Scarlett. "This man is not welcome at our supper."

"Of course he is."

"The saint's day is a sacred occasion. I don't want a stranger at my table. I don't trust him."

"Sacred occasion," Scarlett snorts. "The house smells of sheep dung."

Gabriel giggles and lurches towards the potato bowl.

Scarlett glares at her brother. "I'm no fool, Isaac. I can see what you're doing. I never took you for a thief." She flings her cloak off dramatically. "Mr Hales will stay."

Caroline's eyes meet Asher's. "You are not welcome here," she says again. "Leave."

Asher smiles slightly.

"Isaac!" Scarlett demands. "This man has agreed to come to Guernsey with you! We'd be lost without him! Are you really going to let your wife cast him out of the house?"

Isaac looks at Caroline. Scarlett is right to be angry, of course. This animosity she has towards the man has come from nowhere. And he needs Hales to make the Guernsey run. But he will not, *cannot* disappoint his wife any longer. "You will do as Caroline has asked."

Scarlett huffs and pulls on her cloak.

"Where are you going?" he demands.

"I'll not stay here."

"Caroline has prepared supper for you."

"And I am to be grateful?"

"Ayes," Isaac says tautly. "You are to be grateful."

Scarlett snorts. Her eyes flash.

Isaac walks away, leaving her fuming in the kitchen. He is no mood to deal with her dark streak. If she is to let loose that temper, she can damn well do it in the street.

Scarlett snatches a brandy bottle from the shelf. "Let's leave," she tells Asher. She looks back at Caroline. "Mr Hales has done nothing to you. What a sad life you must lead to be so untrusting."

Caroline stares after her. "It's time you found that girl a husband. See her settled in a life of her own." She heaves the stew pot from the range. "You've done enough for her, Isaac. It's time you let go a little."

He knows what she really means. Time for them to raise their children without Scarlett's brassy chatter and shipwrecked sailors.

But he finds it hard to let go. Hard to cast his sister out into the world with his questionable parenting behind her. Scarlett has strength, but there is plenty within her that could set her adrift. Her blind naivety. The way she trusts so easily. And that wildness hiding in a corner that twists her into a different woman.

"I promised her she could make her own choice of husband," Isaac tells Caroline.

She laughs coldly. "And look at the choices she's making." She spoons the stew into three bowls. "You're hungry, I hope. No point letting her share go to waste."

"Why not ask Flora and Bess to join us? It seems foolish for us to be celebrating alone."

"The food is on the table, Isaac. I've been cooking all day. I don't want you to eat it cold."

There is more to it, of course. Caroline and Flora barely share a word these days. The four of them had been inseparable when Jack was alive. The men at sea, the women sharing each other's kitchens. Gabriel and Bessie sharing each other's toys.

Now there is guilt, regret. Blame, perhaps.

Caroline had pulled away from Flora after the accident. Couldn't bear to look in her in the eye.

Isaac knows Flora has never held him responsible for Jack's death. But Caroline? Though she has never said a word, Isaac knows there's a part of her that wonders.

"Perhaps it would do you good to see her," he says. "Remember how things were."

Caroline sets his bowl in front of him. "Isaac," she says, "will you say the grace?"

He feels an ache deep inside him. The futility of trying to recapture something that can never be restored.

Asher follows Scarlett out of the cottage and up the hill.

Is she angry on his behalf? Or angry that her heroics have not been properly recognised? The brandy bottle swings in her fist. He hears *Caroline* and cursing.

"Dishonest," she hisses. "That's what this is. Stealing Reuben's tea and tainting it for their own gain. It's dishonest thieving, Mr Hales." She storms past the beach. "My brother is not a dishonest thief."

The tea laced with sheep dung would suggest otherwise, Asher thinks.

"And to throw you from the house after all you've done for us? How dare she? How dare *he*?"

He watches her curiously. Energy is exuding from her. Where is sweet-spoken Scarlett who had baked him pilchard pie?

She leads him to the clifftop. The village below is a wash of lamplight. A crowd follows a piper up the street, the guttural melody floating on the wind.

Asher remembers coming here as a young man. Come to think, reflect, dream.

Scarlett uncorks the brandy. Drinks. Passes him the bottle.

He wants to tell her it doesn't matter. He has no desire to sit down for a Feasten supper with Caroline Bailey and her viper tongue. But he is curious to see where Scarlett's anger will take her. How much of her father's blood is running through her?

He takes a gulp of brandy and hands the bottle back to her.

"The village thinks your haul is a myth," she says finally. "Martha Francis tells me my father's interest came only from his desperation."

Asher makes a noise from the back of his throat.

She turns to face him. The brandy and the charge up the cliffs have flushed her cheeks. Dark hair falls across her face. "But you believe the haul is real. And you're not driven by desperation." She looks at him with hot eyes. "What are you driven by, Mr Hales?"

For a moment, he sees himself through her— an enigmatic man arrived on the tides. Older, wiser. Brimming with secrets.

He likes the way he looks through her eyes.

He tells her the truth. He is driven by a desire for the world to one day know his name.

She edges closer. He smells brandy on her breath. Her hand slides towards his; fingers touching.

What is this, an act of defiance? Or an act of desire?

Asher is not sure he cares.

He wants to be the man she sees; this enigma arrived on the tides. Wants to be looked at with blazing eyes.

And his lips are on hers. Is this his doing? He is unsure. The anger in her, he can feel it. Feel it in the hands pulling at his collar, pulling at his hair. Feels it in the way her mouth opens so willingly beneath his. An act of both defiance and desire.

Asher pulls away.

Control.

His blood is hot, thumping inside him. When had he last felt a woman's hands on his body? A part of him would lift Scarlett's skirts and have her here on the weatherworn cliffs. But Asher Hales is careful, calculating. He needs Scarlett to want more from him. Needs her to keep returning.

She lies on her back, eyes on the stars peeking through the cloud. Her hair spills across the earth. Lips flushed, parted. Her breathing heavy.

She reaches for Asher's fingers and tugs him down beside her. Lifts his hand to her chest. He feels her ribs rise and fall.

Asher Hales is careful and calculating. But he feels a striking, unbidden pleasure at feeling someone else's heart beat beside his own.

STORM WINDS

'To the ignorance of men in our age in this particular and mysterious part of philosophy and religion— namely, the communication between spirits and men, —not one scholar out of ten thousand ... knows anything of it, or the way to manage it. This ignorance breeds fear and abhorrence of that which otherwise might be of incomparable benefit to mankind.'

'An Account of an Apparition'
Rev. William Ruddel, Minister in Launceston
1665

The village crawls out from beneath its unease for the saint's day fair.

As a child, Scarlett had loved the feast day celebration; the gypsies and freak shows, charmers with bottled wares.

Huntsmen gathering at the church with their horses and dogs.

Today, she is restless.

She had crept back to the house with Asher after midnight. The cottage smelled of cold grease and wood smoke. Scarlett found the remains of a bread loaf. Handed half to Asher. She stood close, feeling the heat of his body. Her fingers roamed his chest, his face, his lips.

This man she had saved.

She lifted her face to his, hoping for another kiss. Hoping for more. Daring Caroline to catch her.

Asher took her arm and eased her away from him.

"I wish you could come to the fair tomorrow," she said.

A laugh. "And what would your villagers make of me? The man pulled from the ghostly wreck? I imagine the sight of me might ruin their celebrations." He pecked her cheek and disappeared into the bedroom without waiting for her response.

Scarlett lay by the fire and replayed the night in her mind.

There have been men in the past. Boys. Spotty-cheeked fishermen and sunburnt farmhands. An uninspiring parade of stolen kisses and sweaty hands. Each nothing but a momentary distraction.

But with Asher, there is more. There are secrets in him. Ambition. Passion simmering below his polished surface. She had felt it, fleetingly, when she had curled up beside him on the cliff top.

Is this what is drawing her to him? The lure of what he represents? Has the possibility of finding Avery's lost wealth hooked her the way it had hooked her father?

Perhaps.

But there is more to it, she knows. Asher Hales reminds her that once she had been of value. When she looks in his eyes, touches his skin, tastes his lips, she remembers the night she had dragged him from a sinking ship. Remembers that once she had been a hero.

She trudges past fruit stalls and gypsy wagons. The sky is punctuated with waterlogged ribbons, strung beneath the trees.

She closes her eyes and her hearing sharpens. The world is a dissonance of footsteps and voices and hunting horns. Her restlessness makes her heart quicken. She feels it swim inside her, threatening to become rage.

This wild anger that plagues her, she has always felt it a separate entity. She is light and optimism and trust. A victim of the violent thoughts that seize her without warning.

She opens her eyes. A dog gallops from the hunting party and presses its nose against her palm. *Light*, she tells herself. *Optimism. Trust.*

She makes her way to the wrestling ring and watches two men from the landing party fling each other across the grass. A cheer rises from the crowd.

Bobby Carter squeezes his way to her side, a neat figure in his blue uniform.

Scarlett is glad to see him. "I'm surprised you're not involved in this," she says, twisting the buttons on her cloak.

He laughs. "I've too much class to be seen covered in mud and sweat."

She gives him a short smile. "Is that so?"

The farmers shake hands and clamber from the ring. Isaac makes his way into the centre. He pulls off his shirt and slides on the wrestling jacket. He circles his opponent; eyes dark and serious. There is anger in his movements, tension.

He grabs his opponent's jacket and flings him onto his back. The crowd roars.

"I don't like who my brother is becoming," Scarlett tells Bobby. "He and Caroline have been stealing tea from Reuben. Tainting it."

Bobby chuckles. "They could do plenty worse than steal from Charles Reuben."

"Isaac is not a thief. Something has changed in him lately. He's thinking of escape again, I'm sure of it."

"You don't wish to escape?"

"Of course. But I don't want Isaac to become a thief to do it. He'll come to regret it. I know he will."

Bobby presses a hand to her shoulder. "Perhaps a tussle in the ring will do him good."

A thud as the men's bodies collide. Isaac's black hair has come loose from its queue and is plastered to his neck and shoulders. Beneath the jacket, his bare chest is splattered with mud.

Scarlett's lips curl in distaste. She glances across the ring at Caroline. She watches the wrestling with her hand around Gabriel's wrist, Mary on her hip. Does she find this boorish display from Isaac attractive, Scarlett wonders?

She tugs Bobby's arm. "I want to leave."

They walk towards the beach. Wind whips through the street, rolling apples from tables and making flags dance wildly.

"People claim they've seen this man from the wreck," says Bobby. "It's true, isn't it. He's staying at your cottage."

Scarlett looks at her feet. "I'm sorry. I didn't mean to keep things from you. But the village is unsettled. Knowing there's a man from the wreck among us would do the people no good. I don't want to put him in danger."

"You care for this man."

"I just want to help him find out what happened to his crew."

Bobby tucks a strand of hair beneath her woollen bonnet. "You've a kind heart. I wish you'd give me a piece of it."

Scarlett sighs inwardly. Marriage to Bobby has been tossed about since she was seventeen.

A gentle nudge from Isaac. Comments over the supper table.

He's a good man, that Bobby Carter, or *you could do plenty worse.*

Scarlett had laughed it off. "See me married to the revenue service, will you?" Because, yes, Bobby Carter is a good man, but even before Asher, Scarlett had been sure there was someone out there who would make her heart speed and her cheeks flush.

She has been friends with Bobby since her days at the charity school. After their classes they would escape to the beach and bury themselves in the cave. Tell ghost stories until the tide licked their boots.

Scarlett loves him deeply, desperately. Has even allowed herself to consider being his wife during nights when there seem to be one too many chairs at Isaac and Caroline's supper table. But the thought of climbing into his marriage bed leaves her cold.

A gust of wind sends a vegetable cart tumbling. A dog gallops towards it and sniffs at spilled cabbages. Onions roll down the hill. A crowd descends, snatching armfuls of food. The stall owner shouts, shoves, curses.

Scarlett feels the Wild shift inside her. She squeezes Bobby's arm. "You don't want my heart," she mumbles. "There's darkness inside it."

Unreason works its way into every space, Flora realises, as she watches clouds roll over the fair. Unreason is dark and damaging; water freezing in cracks and fracturing the rock.

She hears whispers pass through the fair.

Do you hear them in the wind? The voices of the dead?

The wind is strong today, but they are perched on a hill with the sea unfolding beneath them. A strong wind is no anomaly. Not a thing to be feared.

Flora shivers. The wind? No, it's the people who unnerve her.

She pulls her cloak around herself tightly. Voices of the dead in the wind. Calling the name of the next to die.

Jack had laughed at such sailor's superstitions. Over time, she had come to agree with him. Come to see life through his critical, well-travelled eyes. It had been his gift to her, Flora thinks. A solid, reliable world where wind is just wind and the dead have no voice.

She had defied tradition by taking a husband from outside the village. Who would she be if she had married a man whose world extended as far as the Polperro taverns? A man whose worldly knowledge was built on the ghost stories spouted by Dodge each Sunday?

She'd be the village charmer, Flora is sure of it. She'd live by the moon and hear the dead in the wind. Whisper prayers to the sea spirits into her shells.

She watches Gabriel pull Bessie up the road in a rickety cart. The wooden wheels clatter and crunch. Wind howls, streaming the children's hair behind them; Bessie's like snow, Gabriel's dark as coal. For a moment Flora is watching herself and Isaac charge up the street.

The two children had once been inseparable; Bessie trailing Gabriel like the older brother she had never had.

Flora glances at Caroline, who watches the children from the opposite side of the road. They meet each other's eyes. Faint nods. Flora turns away uncomfortably. So much had died with Jack.

Another gust and Bessie's shawl flies from her shoulders; dancing kite-like in the sky. The boats in the bay lurch on the swell. Hawsers groan and ratlines clatter.

Now there are more whispers snaking through the fair.

A body, washed up on the landing beach.

People swarm down the hill. Shouting. Frantic footsteps. A dog barks. Men bowl toward the beach, upturning the children's cart. Bessie shrieks and tumbles to the path. Flora glares as the men charge by, oblivious. She helps Bessie climb to her feet and smooths her hair. "You're all right," she says firmly. "Everything is all right."

She will not let her daughter fall to this madness. Her daughter will have strength. Sense. She will see more clearly than the parade of grown men trekking towards the beach, crying desperate prayers and shouting of curses.

A crowd gathers on the sand. Bessie presses herself against her mother.

A man, they say, spat out of the rotting wreck.

A man with a bullet wound in his chest.

There are questions, many questions.

Who killed this man? Where was he hiding?

"The ship was half underwater." Scarlett's explanation is lost beneath the shouting.

Of course they couldn't search the whole ship, she is saying. More bodies? Yes, perhaps there are more bodies. She shoves her way to the top of the beach. Bobby Carter grips her arm, as though protecting her from the barrage of voices. Flora grabs Scarlett's other hand and pulls her through the crowd.

Scarlett scrambles from the beach and looks back at the wild-eyed mob. Her bonnet has slid from her head and hair whips around her cheeks. She clings to Bobby's arm.

Flora lets her hand fall. There is a face in the crowd with a vague familiarity. Dark, narrow eyes. A long beard splattered with grey.

Yes, she remembers. Tom Leach, the trader. Flora eyes him. A strange thing for a Polruan man to bother with another parish's feast day.

She thinks of Asher Hales, the wrecked sailor. Does he know his ship carried a murdered man?

Bessie tries to push her way through the crowd. "I want to see the man on the beach, Mammik."

Flora catches her arm. "No you don't. Let's go." She tugs her daughter back towards the inn. There will be fears to soothe with brandy. Panic to ease with a tankard of ale. If the village is to crumble beneath the weight of its dread, Flora will use it to her advantage.

"Flora."

She turns at the sound of Martha Francis's voice.

"What do you make of all this? Do you believe this talk of a curse?"

"A curse, no." Flora presses a key into Bessie's hand. "Go home, *cheel-vean*. Quick now. I'll not be long."

Martha watches the girl hurry up the path towards the inn. "They are saying the man was murdered."

"So why do we look to evil spirits instead of evil men?"

Martha glances back at the beach. "Reverend Dodge will have you out here tonight, I'm sure of it."

"I've told the vicar I'll involve myself in his theatrics no longer."

"Theatrics? Is that what you believe them to be?"

"Of course. Look where his tales are leading. Are we to become screaming fools each time the wind blows? I'll not be a part of it. And I've no desire to watch this. I've a tavern to run."

Martha flashes her a smile. "Your mother would be proud of you. Even if you've not embraced her way of life." She walks with Flora towards the inn. "Your mother used to give Henry and I a tonic for our joints. Worked a charm." She smiles wistfully. "I do miss her."

Flora looks down.

"You know there are many people who would find great comfort in having a healer in the village again."

Flora glances over her shoulder at the crowd on the beach. Men are wrapping the body in a hessian bag. Dodge hovers over them, head bowed in prayer. Desperate hands grapple at his greatcoat.

"Camomile flowers," says Flora.

"What?"

"That's what my mother would prescribe for aching joints. Seep them in boiling water and add it to your bath."

Martha squeezes her hand. "Bless you."

Dodge dreams of brandy. Bed. A fire.

The allure of normality is intense.

But a man like him has no luxury of normality. There are souls to soothe, to save. Phantom lights to extinguish and howling dead to silence.

None of these things are new. He has been a man of God for too many decades to be surprised by the things life can fling at him.

Corpse candles had been seen above these waters not long after he had arrived in Talland. A curious thing, for certain, light dancing on the edge of the sea. A thing of mystery. Beauty.

But; *souls of the dead,* the people had cried. And souls of the dead they had become.

Dodge had shouted a prayer from the clifftops. Spouted comforting words to his frightened parishioners. The corpse candles had disappeared after a night and never been seen again.

Dodge had taken the credit. As far as his people were concerned, he had sent those wayward souls into the netherworlds, where they would never haunt the living again. *Yes, my children. You can rely on me.*

And rely on him they have; these needy people of Talland. These sorry souls who live on the edge of a restless sea. He has laid the ghosts haunting their dreams. Exorcised the demons of their imagination. And managed to line his pockets with free trading gold in the process.

But he can feel his control slipping.

Lights on the horizon, voices in the wind. Ghost ships and a murdered man. The truth somewhere between nature and the unknown.

He's heard talk.

Camomile flowers.

A strange thing, he thinks with odd detachment, that camomile flowers might strike such fear into his heart.

God is challenging him. Testing his resolve, his influence. He feels the pressure to succeed as a weight upon his chest.

He seeks George Gibson out from the crowd. Bodies are trickling up from the beach, seeking out the illuminated building at the bend in the road.

Gibson is a flushed mess. He clutches at his hair and garbles about the storm winds. "I heard the dead speak my name, Father. The voices in the wind were calling for me. I fear my death is coming."

Death is coming for us all, Dodge wants to say. It is coming faster for a weather-beaten vicar approaching ninety.

Instead, he presses a hand to Gibson's shoulder. The man can be no more than forty, surely, yet his face has become lined and weary in what seems like days.

"These people are making for the Mariner's Arms, are they not?"

Gibson sniffs. "I suspect so, Father."

The Mariner's Arms. Its dark windows and thick stone walls speak of ungodliness. Black mirrors and burning herbs.

"Flora Kelly is offering healing charms to our villagers. What do you make of it?"

Gibson breathes heavily. "It's as you say, Father. The people need God. Not thinly-veiled witchcraft."

Dodge nods. "I wish to speak with her. Fetch her for me."

The vicar paces. Flora slips out of the tavern and folds her arms in greeting.

"You offered herbal charms to Martha Francis," says Dodge.

125

She doesn't reply.

"I don't want this in my village, do you understand? The people need God, not sorcery."

"You can hardly call a few healing herbs sorcery."

She is not as fragile as she looks; this snowy-haired scrap. Dodge had realised this early on. Had watched her grow, as he has so many of these villagers. Watched her change from a blonde twig of a girl to the woman who so resembles her mother. The village charmer.

He feels a surge of old regret at not being able to save the soul of Flora's mother. The physical ills, they are challenges from God. A thing to be endured. But it is the vicar's job to see his parishioners' souls purified.

Flora's mother had died with an adder stone beneath her pillow and weakness in her lungs. Dodge fears where God will send a woman who dies with an adder stone beneath her pillow.

His anger gives way. "Mrs Kelly, it is not too late. Come back and work with me. God is forgiving of those who lose their way."

"No. I'm sorry. You know my thoughts on this business."

"And how many of my parishioners are you going to drag down with you?"

"Please. I offered the woman a few camomile flowers for her joints."

"Camomile flowers today. What tomorrow? Hemlock and blood magic? I will not have it."

Flora raises her eyebrows. "Are you threatening me?"

"You were not in church last Sunday."

"Does that truly surprise you?"

"I fear for your soul if you choose to abandon the church, Mrs Kelly. And the soul of your daughter."

"Leave my daughter out of this." She turns her back. "If you'll excuse me, Father, I've a tavern to run."

Scarlett returns to the cottage after the fair, her cheeks flushed and her hair wild. Her words are a garble. *A body*, she tells Asher. *Murder* and *Leach.*

Calm down. Tell me again.

So it seems the sea is unable to keep secrets. A body washed from the wreck of the *Avalon*. A body with a bullet in the chest.

Confirmation, Scarlett says, of all Asher has claimed. The crew murdered by smugglers.

There is a loud thump at the front door. "Is he there?" Angry, frightened voices. "The sailor from the wreck? Did he kill the man on the beach?"

"Hide." Scarlett ushers Asher into the bedroom. "There is no sailor from the wreck," he hears her hiss through the door. "Leave me in peace."

When the voices are silent, he emerges to find her pacing by the hearth.

Her brother is not safe, she says. She is not safe. None of them are. She has inhaled a little of the crowd's mania. Caught their disease.

"I want to speak to Tom Leach," she announces.

"Leach? The captain who wanted the silk?"

"He and his men were at the fair. They were on the beach when the body was found. Why were they here, Asher? I need to know."

"Don't be foolish. You think to charge up to these men and accuse them of murder?"

"I can't just do nothing!" She paces. "Did you hear the storm winds? They speak the name of the next man to die."

Asher rubs his eyes. She is tiring him.

"What if it's Isaac? What if my brother is the next man to die?"

He grabs her arm to stop her pacing. "We will confront no one. Do you hear me?"

"Why not? Don't you want answers?"

His grip tightens. "Scarlett, you are to tell no one what I told you."

"Tell no one your crew was murdered? I'm sorry, but I don't think that's a secret any longer. Not after your crewmate washes up on our beach with a bullet in his chest."

"My crewmate was foolish enough to engage in free trade. He deserved all that came to him. I've no desire to hunt down his killer."

Scarlett's eyes flash. "You may not want answers, Asher, but I do. The free traders I know have always worked together. The people against the system. If there are traders out there willing to kill, I need to know who they are."

"If you were to tell everyone what I told you, where would that lead? To an investigation. To this village crawling with the authorities. Is that what you want?"

"Of course not."

"No. And nor do I. Because the revenue men will dig, and they will shine a light on you and your brother. You'll be strung up for smuggling and what use will you be to me then?"

"What *use* will I be to you? Is that all I am? A means to finding your precious haul? Why are you even still here?

I've no information for you. No one does." She shoves against his chest. "Leave! Go on! I'm no use to you!"

Oh no, he is far from being done with her. He grabs her wrists.

She says: "Your haul is a myth."

"It's not a myth. I'm sure of it." He holds her until she stills. He stands close, his breath against her ear. "Forgive me," he says smoothly. "You are far more to me than just your father's stories. You are the only goodness in my life. You saved me." And all this, Asher realises, is true.

She pulls away. "Leach and his men took the cliff path to Polperro. I'm going after them." She takes a knife from the kitchen and slides it into her garter.

He watches her go. Watches from the window as she climbs the hill on the men's trail.

Let her go. She is disobedient and rash. Makes his blood heat.

But: *you are more to me than your father's stories*.

Curse on her. He pulls on his coat. Follows her into the village.

Dusk is falling. The whitewashed buildings of Polperro are otherworldly in the lamplight.

Scarlett peers through the window of the Three Pilchards. The tavern is dark and smoky. Leach and his men sit in a corner, talking, laughing, drinks in hand.

She slips inside. Approaches the innkeeper.

He turns away. "I can't be seen talking to you, Miss Bailey. You'd best leave now."

"Can't be seen talking to me? Why not?"

He sighs. "Go home. There's enough trouble about."

"Leach and his men. Have you caught word of what they're saying?"

"Just leave. Please. Those men are dangerous."

"I know they're dangerous. That's why I'm here." She slides onto a chair at Leach's table. "You were in Talland today. Why?"

Leach chuckles, exhaling a cloud of pipe smoke. "Visiting the fair, of course."

Laughter from the men. One pulls his stool closer to Scarlett's. She smells his sweat, old salt in his beard. She tenses, the knife hard against her thigh. "Did you have something to do with the body that came from the wreck?"

"Something to do with the body? What exactly do you mean by that? Did I dive onto the wreck and pull it from the ocean floor? Or did I plant it?"

Her skin is hot and sticky beneath her bodice. "Did you kill him?"

Leach puts down his pipe. "And if I did? You expect me to just admit to it? Absolve my sins by confessing to a little hawker?"

She flushes. "Why not? What power do I have? What authority?"

Leach jabs a finger under her nose. "You've a certain friendship with one of this town's preventative men. That's what power you have."

"I don't know what you're talking about."

Leach gives her a crooked smile. "Miss Bailey. You know how things are among us traders. We tell the truth. There needs to be trust among us. Or else where we be?" He takes a gulp of his ale and holds it out to her.

She shakes her head stiffly.

"A revenue officer on our side is of value to all of us. There need not be a rivalry between your brother's ring and my own. Why can't we work together?"

Scarlett laughs coldly. "You sent a bullet across our bow for the sake of a little silk. And now you want to work together?" She moves to stand, but Leach clamps a hand around her wrist.

"Accusing a man of murder is a serious thing. I don't appreciate it."

She clenches her teeth. "If you behave like a dog it's how you will be treated."

His grip tightens. "One day that tongue of your is going to get you into trouble."

"Scarlett."

She turns at the sound of Asher's voice.

"Let's go. Come on."

Leach releases her arm. "Is this the mysterious man from the wreck? Everyone is speaking of you. Been press-ganged into Isaac Bailey's miserable cause, have you?"

Asher says nothing. He catches Scarlett's eye.

"I'm not going anywhere," she hisses. She turns to Leach. "Tell me why you're here. Why were you in Talland when that body was found?"

"Think on it, Miss Bailey. That body was washed up from the wreck. Even if I had killed the man, how was I to know he would be coughed up by the tide today?" He smiles faintly. "You're so eager to be of value, aren't you. You want to be the one to run back to your brother with all the answers." He laughs to himself. "There's nothing quite so pathetic as a maid desperate to please."

Scarlett snatches her knife and leaps to her feet. In a second, Leach is out of his chair, grabbing her wrists and whirling her around. The blade hovers in her fist inches from his face.

Leach leans close. "I've struck a nerve, I see." His breath is stale and smoky. Threads of his beard tickle her skin.

She clenches her teeth.

He eyes the knife. "You know how to use that?"

"Ayes," she hisses. "Under the ribs. Good and fast. You'd be dead in an instant."

He chuckles. "Then it's a good thing your blade is nowhere near my ribs."

"Let go of me!" She kicks against him. Leach slams her back hard against the wall. Pain jolts through her. The knife clatters to the floor. Asher snatches it before the other men reach it.

"Perhaps I ought to be the one questioning you over this man on the beach," Leach tells Scarlett. "Who do you think you are, going about with a blade in your skirts?"

Asher holds out the knife. "Let her go, Leach. She's nothing to you."

Scarlett glances at Asher. There is a tremble in his fist.

Leach shoves her away. Asher grabs her hand hurriedly and pulls her from the inn. They walk in silence towards the cliff path.

They climb steadily, the darkness thickening. Scarlett is jittery, her skin damp with sweat. She hates that Leach can see into her so easily. Hates that Asher has seen her failings. She charges up the path, seeking the calming dark of the clifftop.

Asher hurries after her. "Let me go first."

"Don't be foolish. You don't know the path like I do."

The trail narrows. Careful steps. She runs a hand over the scrub to keep her bearings. A turn to the left here. Now the right. Below her, the sea thunders.

She glances over her shoulder at Asher. She can see only shadows of his face in the moonlight.

"You are a fool," he hisses. "I told you not to go after those men. They could easily have killed you. And then where would I be?"

For a long time, Scarlett says nothing. There is anger in Asher's voice. Is he rattled at the thought of losing her? Or losing a means to his fortune? He is still in Talland for a reason. Perhaps there is more to his search than he is letting on.

She pushes away her distrust. He has risked his life to save her.

"Thank you," she mumbles finally. "For coming for me. I know you were afraid."

"Afraid?" His voice sparks. "You think me afraid?"

She keeps walking.

"Leach is right, isn't he." Asher is close behind. "You want answers so you can go to Isaac and be of worth. So you can be more than just a chain around his neck."

Scarlett grits her teeth. "Leach isn't right about anything."

"Why does it matter so much? You said yourself, your brother is a liar and a thief. Why do you care what he thinks?"

Her throat tightens. "I'm tired of being a burden."

Asher grabs her suddenly. "You don't want to be a burden? Then stop chasing dangerous men in the night."

"I need to find the killers."

He whirls her around until she stands at the edge of the cliff.

Her heart shoots into her throat. "What are you doing?"

Asher hesitates, his fingers digging into the tops of her arms. Wind rushes up from the sea. Finally, he says: "Can I trust you?" His voice is a harsh whisper.

She nods faintly.

"And do you trust me? Because if I share this with you, it's important that we trust each other."

She nods again.

"Do you?" he says. "Truly?"

The wind thunders, whipping her skirts around her legs. She grapples at Asher's forearms, her heart speeding. "Yes." Her voice is thin, trapped in her throat.

"Show me."

She leans forward. Pecks his stony lips.

"No. Show me you really trust me. Take a step back. I'll not let you fall."

She hesitates. Shakes her head stiffly.

"I have most important things I need to share with you. But I need to know we trust each other."

She swallows hard. She is light, optimism, trust. She will see the best in Asher Hales. She will trust him with her life.

Will not let the darkness win.

Slowly, she shuffles backwards. The earth disappears from beneath her heels. Her toes cling to the edge of the path. Below her; air and sea.

She feels her weight teeter. Her fingers dig into Asher's arms. She blinks hard, fighting off a wave of dizziness.

"Are you afraid?" he asks.

"No." She tries to force the tremor from her voice. "You'll not let me fall."

A smile creeps across his face; his eyes warming suddenly. He steps back from the cliff edge, tugging her forward. She stumbles, gulping down her breath. Drops to her knees. Asher sits beside her. He kisses her forehead, her cheek, the edge of her lips. Scarlett tenses. Her breath is hard and fast.

Light, she tells herself. *Optimism. Trust.*

"You'll not find the killers," Asher says, looking out over the water. "The men of the *Avalon* were not killed by free traders. They were killed by me."

UNREASON

Dizziness washes over her. She scrambles away from Asher on hands and knees, afraid to stand in case she pitches into the sea.

Is this to be her reward for fighting the Wild? For daring to trust? To be thrown from the cliffs by a butcher?

He hurries after her. Braces his arms either side of her and presses his chest against her back. She hears herself cry out.

Asher wraps his arm around her middle. "It's all right." His mouth is close to her ear. "It's all right."

Scarlett gulps down her breath.

"Sometimes a man has no choice but to kill," he says, his breath hot against her cheek. "Sometimes his life depends on it." He pulls her into sitting. "Look at me."

She doesn't turn.

"I told you this because we trust each other," he says. "Because I thought you would understand. You know what it's like to need to protect yourself with force. I've seen it."

He runs a hand through her hair. His fingers catch in the tangles and send a jolt through her.

"And I told you this because I don't want you to go looking for the killers again. You'll end up dead. And I couldn't bear that."

Finally, Scarlett turns. His nose is inches from hers. She says: "Tell me what happened."

Asher keeps his hand pressed to her arm. "The *Avalon's* first mate died soon after we left London. A sudden death." In the faint moonlight, Scarlett can see his eyes glowing. "Death is a fascinating thing, don't you agree? The first mate sat among us at supper and the next morning he was gone forever. Where is a dead man's consciousness? What is this force that determines whether a man lives or dies?" A pale smile lightens his face. "It is the greatest of mysteries."

Scarlett shifts uncomfortably. "I have seen too much death to be fascinated by such a thing."

"Is there no curiosity in you? No interest in science?"

"Science? No, Asher, I've no interest in science right now!"

He smiles to himself. "I suppose that's to be expected. From a woman."

Tell me what happened on your ship!" cries Scarlett.

His nose wrinkles with annoyance. After a moment, he says: "The men wanted the first mate's body disposed of hurriedly."

"Why?"

He pushes past her question. "The ceremony was rushed and incomplete. And, well, I'm sure a Cornish girl like

137

yourself knows what they say about sailors who've not been buried properly."

Scarlett's throat is dry. "Their ghosts will walk."

Asher chuckles. "Their ghosts will walk. And superstitious men are immune to reason."

"Your crew saw your first mate's ghost?"

"Your curiosity is here, I see. In your fairy tales."

"They are not fairy tales." She cradles her knees. "If your mind is closed you'll never see the world for what it truly is."

Asher smiles faintly. "You are right, of course. In a strange sort of way, you and I, we believe the same thing."

No, her world is full of different mysteries.

When she was five years old, she had stood on the moor and watched a man disappear. She had gone to her father. Told him of the coldness in the air.

Yes, my girl. Sometimes the dead remain.

And so it has always been.

Asher tilts his head. "The same mysteries perhaps. Viewed through different eyes." He leans close. "There are strange noises on a ship at night. You know that. Shadows move. Sounds distort. It's easy to imagine things that aren't there. Yes, my crew believed they saw the ghost of our first mate. But that was nothing but unreason."

"Unreason."

"Yes. It spreads like plague. Men lose their ability to think rationally. People behave like fools. Like animals. It's a dangerous thing."

Scarlett thinks of the frenzied voices crowding the body on the beach. An odd shiver slides through her. Would unreason carry the villagers as far as it had carried the crew of the *Avalon*?

"The crew convinced themselves the ship was haunted. They were nervous. On edge. They began to speak of demons and dark things. Carried pistols in their belts.

'When I saw the smuggling craft approach, I told the other men to turn around. Told them not to engage with the traders. I found myself being fired upon. Two near misses. The men were manic; their shots wild. I had little choice but to fire back."

He lowers his eyes. "I hoped the shooting would stop after the first death. But it was not to be. I had little choice but to keep firing. I know how lucky I was to escape with my life."

Scarlett knots her fingers. "How many men?"

"Five. Five men. I'm not proud of such a thing. But sometimes we must kill to survive. Sometimes we have no choice."

Her thoughts knock together. "And the smugglers?"

"I stood on deck and told them we no longer wanted to trade. The gun in my hand was enough to convince them. I was left alone on the ship. Nothing to do but dispose of the bodies and try and make port. An impossible thing for a man to do alone, of course. In my panic, I must have left one of the men aboard. The body on the beach."

The story is terrifying. Dramatic. Torn from the pages of an adventure novel. But why lie to her now? Why tell her only half-truths?

She will trust. She will believe. She will have faith in the man who had risked his life to save hers, as she had risked hers to save him. She will not let herself believe the foolish talk of the villagers. Will not believe she has dragged a demon onto their shore.

Unreason. It spreads like plague.

He stands close. "I'm no coward, Scarlett. You can see that, can't you."

"I can see that, Asher. You're no coward." She stares over the edge of the cliff. White water glows in the darkness. "Why are you still here? No one can help you find the haul. There's nothing in this place for you but bad memories."

"That's not true." He traces a finger lightly across the back of her neck. Presses a cold kiss into her shoulder.

She shivers. Begins to walk slowly back to Talland. "Tomorrow Dodge will bury the body of your crewmate. Perhaps you ought to be there. Perhaps it might help you move on."

BURIAL

In the morning, Asher goes to the church. The body lies before the altar beneath its unceremonious sheath. Asher stands at the bottom of the aisle.

It has been several years since he has set foot in a church. Hasn't ventured inside a house of the Lord since his release from servitude. He has no desire to praise God for the rough hand he has been dealt.

Dodge appears behind him. "You."

"I need to see the body," says Asher. "I need to know which of my crewmates has been found."

Dodge hesitates, then nods. Leads him to the altar and pulls back the hessian pall.

As he expected; Peter Barrett, that bastard of a quartermaster. His skin is colourless and waxy, ravaged by undersea claws and mouths.

He lifts the remains of the man's shirt. Bullet wound in the chest. The poor, crazed fool.

The sea-soaked mind, Asher had realised during his days on the *Avalon*, works this way:

A death on board results in a haunted ship.

Men see ghosts in the shadows.

The men talk, tell stories and the tales take on a life of their own.

Ghosts become demons. A ship becomes cursed.

And reason founders. Panic tears through the crew and leads them towards death.

The *Avalon's* first mate was dead before London had slipped over the horizon. A tragedy, of course. But Asher had seen an opportunity to learn. The soul; he knew it responsible for every working of the body. Fever, convulsions, disease; all the result of an overactive life force. And when the soul abandons the body? Would it leave a trail on the affected organs?

If Asher were to look at a lifeless body, would he be able to determine how death had arrived?

A decade of exile had left him hungry for knowledge and learning. Released into the wilds of the New England colonies, he ached for his cultured homeland.

For three years, he lent his mind to growing New Hampshire. There were bridges to build. Inns, boats, schools. Mills to run and farms to tend to. Three years of back breaking, menial work. But enough to fill his pockets with a fare back to England.

And he was home. His sentence complete. His past beginning to fade.

He left his old, crime-stained name in New Hampshire with his old, crime-stained self. A new name for a new beginning. Asher; his grandfather. Hales; borrowed from the great English scientist.

This new man, Asher Hales, walked the streets of London with his shoulders back and head held high. He frequented the coffeehouses, filling his mind with the new ideas he had been so starved of. He used what little money he had to buy second hand books and the finest clothes he could find at the charity stalls. The shirts were discoloured and the coats worn at the elbows, but it was enough to give him a glimpse of the man he would soon be. A glimpse of the life that awaited him once he found Henry Avery's haul.

He secured a berth on a merchant ship. London to Penzance.

The day before the *Avalon*'s voyage, he stole into the Barber Surgeons' Hall and watched a man dissect a human corpse. He had spent countless hours poring over anatomy plates and drawings, yet the sight of a real body took his breath away. From the back of the theatre, he could see little, but it was enough to make his heart speed.

In contrast to his own racing pulse, the dead man's heart lay still and colourless. Asher craned his neck, trying to see lungs, stomach, bones, skin. Trying to see what clues the departing soul had left behind.

These surgeons would scoff at the animists' ideas, Asher was sure. But the controversy only added to its allure.

There was so much to learn. He needed to see more. Needed to be the man with the scalpel in his hand.

The dead first mate in the *Avalon's* sick bay. A body waiting to be wrapped for burial. Surgeon's tools. Endless hours of ocean.

He would be a fool if he did not grasp this opportunity.

He hunched over a candle. Slid a knife down the man's chest with precision. He felt a shiver of excitement.

There was a faint warmth to the body. Blood beaded on his knife.

Intestines. Lungs. Still heart.

All as he had seen that day in the Barber Surgeons' Hall. All as he had seen in his books. But look at these things he had not seen. These tiny veins and arteries, fine like a web. The puzzle of bones in the man's hand. Fibres of knotted muscle.

There was a beauty to it. A complex machine. But what was this magical element that brought the body to life? Where was the first mate's soul now?

Asher stood in the cabin beside that open body and let the mystery engulf him. Two men. One alive, one dead. What was it that made it so?

Footsteps yanked him from his thoughts. Quartermaster Barrett stood in the doorway, eyes wide. He crossed himself. Cursed and spat. Then he disappeared onto the deck, his footfalls thundering above Asher's head.

And the rest of the men arrived.

Filth, they called Asher as their eyes fell to the gaping body. Wild arms shoved him from the sick bay. The close-minded fools, unable to see beyond the blood to the mysteries begging to be unravelled. Could they not see how lucky they were to be living in this century where scientific discoveries waited around every corner? Could they not see how lucky they were to be living at all?

They wrapped the first mate's body, his insides gaping. Carried him through the dark ship.

Asher chased them through the passage, out onto the deck. There was still so much to discover. So much to learn.

The body left beads of blood across the deck and terror in

the men's eyes. They heaved the corpse over the gunwale and watched as it sank, devoid of prayer or ceremony.

Asher turned to leave. He would return to the sick bay. Ponder the things he had learnt before the body had been so rudely been torn away. Dive deeper into the mysteries of life and death that lay before him.

Barrett snatched his collar. Hauled him backwards. His spine slammed against the gunwale.

Filth, the men repeated. *Mad filth.*

"Did you hear me?" said Barrett. "You're mad filth. Nothing more. We ought to throw you off too."

Fear weakened Asher's legs. Barrett was a head taller than him, shoulders far wider. And he had four other men crowded behind him.

In his head, Asher played out the action. Fist to the side of Barrett's face. The man crumpling, blood streaming.

But Asher Hales was not that kind of man. He was a great mind, not a bully, or a criminal. Not mad filth. He would not allow small-minded men to drag him down to their level.

"What do you say?" hissed Barrett. "Ought we throw you over?"

Asher shook his head, his voice caught in his throat. Sweat trickled down the back of his neck.

Barrett released him suddenly and he stumbled towards the pilot house. Asher threw open the hatch and hurried below. He heard the distant voices of the crew.

"A prayer, quickly."

Say a prayer. Hurry now.

"We've done our first mate wrong. Now the poor man's soul will never be at rest."

He hears footsteps behind him.

"Better way you stay in the church, Asher," Scarlett says, entwining her fingers in her shawl. "The villagers have come to witness the burial. I didn't expect it."

He can hear voices in the graveyard. Many voices. A sign of respect? A desperate attempt to soothe their own fears, more likely. See their ill-luck buried along with the dead.

Asher looks back at Barrett's body. He needs to see this man buried. It will be a victory to watch the bastard disappear into the earth. He strides from the church. The villagers' eyes fix on him.

A demon, spat from their bell house.

Yes, he's real.

Scarlett stands close as the cursory service begins. Despite all he has told her, she is here by his side, her arm pressing against his. They will criticise her for it, Asher is sure. He feels an unexpected rush of gratitude.

It had been a risk of course, telling her of the killings. But Scarlett has bravery in her. Look at her, stumbling backwards on the cliff edge to prove herself a trusting soul. Plenty of bravery, no matter how misdirected. He needs her to see that he is just as brave. Needs her to see he is powerful. Needs her to see that when men like Quartermaster Barrett threaten him, they end up with a bullet in their chest. And he needs to keep seeing himself through her admiring eyes.

The body is lowered into a hurriedly dug grave. Earth tossed over it. The slosh of shovels is loud amongst the wordlessness.

Where are these people's superstitions now? Where are their bells and burial songs? This is no funeral. It's nothing but a disposal of rubbish.

The vicar bows his head. A hurried prayer as the body begins its descent into the earth.

A murmur ripples through the crowd. Now there is just one man left from the ghost ship.

George Gibson stares at the grave as though he is afraid the dead man will break free. He scans the crowd with shadowy eyes. "Where is Flora Kelly? Would she rather play her heathen's games than farewell a murdered man?"

Flora wrenches open the window and lets a salty breeze flutter the curtains. From the second storey of the inn, she can see the crowd in the cemetery.

No, my darling, we will not be going to the church.

She will not subject her daughter to the mania brought about by the burial.

Instead, she has spent the morning among dusty, herb-scented memories, as she cleans out her mother's room. She has been unable to part with much. Has tossed the moth-eaten bedsheets in the fire. Scant pieces of wearable clothing folded up for the charity collection.

In the corner of the room is the wooden chest. She has tucked it away. Unneeded. Unwanted.

But now, with Dodge hollering on the hilltops, the chest does not feel quite so unwanted. Flora opens the lid. Lines up its contents on the floor in front of her.

Pouches and glass vials. Bone rings and a length of hangman's rope. In one jar sits a preserved animal heart. She holds it up to the light, drawn to its grotesque black shape.

She remembers her mother using the heart as a counter spell to darkness.

Pierce the heart with pins and draw out the dark.

She allows herself a smile.

Camomile flowers, for aching joints.

Mugwort for a head cold.

Bullock's heart to combat ill-wishing.

Where is the line between nature and the unearthly?

Ground ivy has the power to heal a man's wounds, Flora has seen it many times. Mallow leaves to lighten bruises.

Magic?

And if camomile can ease a man's joints, can a blackened heart ease his terrors?

Healing herbs grow everywhere. A gift from God? Or the lure of the devil?

Flora rubs her eyes. She doesn't want this to be her world. She wants solidity. The clink of glasses and the burn of brandy.

And yet, what gratitude she had seen in Martha Francis's eyes when she had offered a simple herbal remedy.

Had the vicar ever threatened her mother the way he had threatened her? Had she too felt the unreason of the God-fearing?

Flora feels sure of it. And yet her mother had kept on sharing what little knowledge she'd had, kept on trying to bring hope to the desolate. She feels a sudden surge of pride.

Voices filter in the open window as the villagers leave the church. The murdered man is buried. What ghoulish theories has Dodge filled his parishioners' heads with today?

A sudden shattering of glass from downstairs. Flora leaps to her feet.

"Mammik?" Bessie's footsteps thud down the passage.

Flora snatches the fire poker from the parlour. "Stay here."

The stairs creak beneath her feet. Long shadows lie over the bar. Glass crunches beneath her boots. The front window has been shattered, broken edges jutting like teeth.

"Is someone here?"

Silence.

She feels something solid beneath her boot. Looks down. At her feet, a thick wooden cross.

Flora drags Bessie down the street and pounds on Isaac's front door. "You need to stop using the church," she tells him breathlessly. "Stop using Dodge. He can't be trusted."

"What are you talking about? What's happened?"

She shoves the cross beneath his nose. "Someone threw this through my window."

Isaac glances over his shoulder. Caroline and the children sit at the table, bent over steaming soup bowls. He takes Flora's arm and ushers her outside. Pulls the door closed behind them.

"You think this was Dodge?" he asks. "He may be mad, but I've never known him to be violent."

"Dodge threatened me last night," Flora tells him. "He's upset because I'll not follow him blindly any longer. And then he heard me offer an herbal cure to Martha Francis. He thinks I'm going to turn the village away from God. Looks at me like I'm the devil himself."

"You're giving out herbal cures?"

Flora folds her arms. "Is that how you see me too, Isaac? Like the devil himself?"

He touches her elbow. "Show me what happened."

Isaac follows her into the bar. A stream of cold air blows through the gaping window. Shards of glass are strewn across the floor.

Flora nods at Bessie. "Upstairs, *cheel-vean*." She turns to Isaac. "The cross was thrown after the burial. Perhaps Dodge felt I ought to have been there."

"You weren't there?"

"Nor were you, I see."

"There's madness in the town. I've no desire to surround myself with it." No desire to surround himself with talk of the wreck or the dead man spat from it. No desire to surround himself with childish talk of demons and curses.

He'd sat by the fire and played checkers with Gabriel while nervous chatter from the village floated beneath the door. Had hoped all talk of the *Avalon* might be buried with the dead man.

Flora tosses the crucifix into the fire grate. "You can't have the vicar involved in your operation. He's not trustworthy."

"You've no proof it was Dodge," Isaac says gently.

"Dodge or his supporters. They are one and the same."

"How are we to operate without him? We need the lane clear to bring the goods from the beach. And we need the bell house to store them."

Flora looks down. Her eyes on the floor, she says: "The tunnel."

Isaac's stomach knots. "No."

She clutches his arm. "You and Jack, you were almost through. You can land on the eastern beach. Bring the goods through the tunnel and store them in my cellar. You need not go near Bridles Lane, or the church. You'd not need Dodge." Her fingers knead his bare wrist. "I'd not think of doing it if I weren't desperate. But this frightened me. It frightened my daughter." She sits at a table and squeezes her hands together. "Jack always said there was something not right about the vicar. I know if he were here, he'd not want Dodge involved any longer."

"If he were here? And why is Jack not here, Flora? Because we were foolish enough to try and dig that tunnel." He hears his voice waver with emotion. "I watched him die. And now you're asking me to go back down there? I can't believe you of all people is asking!"

"The cross was a warning, Isaac. A threat. How do you think that makes me feel? I've a daughter to protect! You know exactly what that's like."

"Because of that tunnel, Bess is growing up without a father. Do you want Gabriel and Mary to as well?"

Flora squeezes her eyes closed. She kneels and begins to gather up the broken glass.

Isaac watches her without speaking. Though he's sure she'd be appalled by his pity, he has felt a need to watch out for her since Jack's death. A lifetime of friendship has taught him that her façade of strength is easily chipped. She has buried her grief deeply and he's sure it will one day resurface. The thought of her alone in the inn makes something tighten in his chest.

He kneels beside her. "I thought you wanted nothing to do with your mother's craft. I thought you didn't believe in such things."

She doesn't look at him. "All I did was offer a woman relief from her aching joints. Is that so terrible?"

151

"Of course not." He puts a hand to her wrist. "But, Flora, I can see where the vicar is coming from. People are frightened after this wreck. They see death and demons around every corner. Perhaps Dodge is right. Perhaps a little faith in God will do them good."

"The people are afraid because Dodge wants them to be! Each time you use the bell house, he stirs up the village with one of his sham exorcisms. You saw the way things were at the fair. These people are scared. I fear where it will lead."

Isaac sighs. "Opening the tunnel is not the answer."

"Perhaps it is."

He rubs his eyes. Lets his gaze settle on the cellar door. Sweat prickles the back of his neck. "Please don't ask me to do this."

DELIVERY

Isaac sits by the window of the Mariner's Arms, watching rain slap the glass. The fire crackles. The inn is warm with the smell of wood smoke.

A delivery tonight. Contraband transported to buyers. A late-night parade of candlelight and covered wagons.

The inn is quiet. Isaac is glad of a little stillness.

He has spent the day finding buyers for Caroline's tea. Her tainted brew is convincing, in looks at least. He is not sure how far the ruse will last once the west country's gentry start filling their cups. Still, the sales will make a start towards those elusive tickets out of Reuben's life. Tickets that have been far too many years coming.

He hears footsteps behind him. Flora takes his empty glass and replaces it with a fresh one.

She presses a hand to his shoulder. "Slower this time, ayes? Keep up at that rate and they'll have you in the stocks for drunkenness."

He smiles. She has said no more on the tunnel and Isaac is grateful.

She watches Asher and Scarlett pass the window. "Tell her to be careful. Hales shared his ship with a murdered man. I'm not sure we ought to trust him."

Isaac nods. "I'll tell her."

In truth, he has spoken little to Scarlett since she'd come home to find the house strung with tainted tea. The disappointment in her eyes had been glaring. He has found it hard to face her.

She has always looked up to him. Seen nothing but good in him, even when his arms have been full of smuggled liquor. Is this to be the cost of breaking free of Reuben? The loss of his sister's respect?

Heavy breathing behind him. George Gibson's eyes are underlined with deep shadows. Shoulders hunched as though he is trying to disappear into the earth.

"You look like hell," says Isaac.

Gibson crumples onto a stool beside him. "I heard them. Voices in the storm winds. Heard them hailing my name, clear as day. I'm going to be the next to die." He grabs fistfuls of his snarling grey hair. "I can't get the image of the dead man out of my head. His face all eaten up like that... I keep imagining it's me rotting there on the sand." He looks at Isaac with watery eyes. "The devil, he keeps us fixated on our mistakes, don't he. I am a good man, Isaac. I've always tried to be a good man."

"Ayes, George. I know." Isaac claps him on the shoulder. "You need a good sleep, is all."

"Sleep? How can I sleep? I'll be gone by week's end, I know it."

"This business with the *Avalon* has been no good for anyone. But we're all best off forgetting it. The man's been buried. It's time to move past it."

"Move past it? You've the sailor from the wreck staying with you."

"What choice have you given me? He's the only man willing to come to sea."

Gibson wrings his hands together. "Coming to shore alone on an abandoned ship. Do you think it's true what they're saying?"

Isaac chuckles. "Do I believe the man is a demon? No. I don't."

Gibson stares at the candle flickering in the centre of the table. Shadows move across his cheeks.

Isaac empties his glass and stands abruptly. "I'm doing my best to forget that ship, George. You ought to do the same."

Scarlett sits beside Asher at the bar of the Three Pilchards. A cloth bag has been placed in the corner of the counter. Asher peers inside.

Scarlett slaps his hand away. "Don't touch that."

"It's full of dirt."

"Earth from a man's grave. A charm against ill luck."

Asher chuckles to himself. The bartender eyes him warily.

"The innkeeper is fearful," says Scarlett. "Ever since Leach paid him a visit he's been convinced trouble is coming." She glances edgily over her shoulder as the door creaks open. "You'll stay here, ayes? Until the delivery is complete?"

Asher smiles wryly. "You don't want me in the cottage with the children. Is this your wish or your brother's?"

She says nothing.

"I'll need coin. I can hardly sit here all night without buying a drink."

Scarlett pulls a penny from her pocket and hands it to him.

"Give me another."

She does, reluctantly. Picks at her fingernails. "If we are to continue our search," she says carefully, "I need to know more. I know nothing of who you are beyond this place."

He has been waiting for this. Can't pretend to be surprised it has come now, after the monstrous revelation he had dropped at her feet the night after the fair.

How to play it?

He could tell her lies of a privileged, law-abiding upbringing. No. She will see through them to the truth of his tattered clothes and empty pockets. Instead, play on her pity. After all, isn't that what this twisted tryst is based on? She sees him as the debonair man who needs her help and at the thought of being useful, she has her skirts around her hips.

And useful she is. Useful for his fragile ego. Useful for his search. Soon Scarlett Bailey will see just how damn useful she is.

Asher waves for the bartender and orders an ale. "Life dealt me a rough hand," he tells Scarlett, wrapping his fingers around the tankard. "One I didn't deserve."

"A rough hand?"

He tells her of his life in broad, undetailed strokes.

A poor upbringing, his years of servitude. All because he'd been deceived by a man he had been foolish enough to trust.

"Which man?"

A nameless man, of course.

She asks about his exile.

He tells her of the orange leaves of New Hampshire and the bridges he'd built with his bare hands. No mention of the attack on the dragoons that had seen him carted from England in chains. And then to claw back any trust he may have lost, he tells his sorry tale of trying to land the empty *Avalon.*

Blackness around him. Creaks and groans and the rumble of the sea. Blood running into his eyes. The wretchedness of it is enough to wipe any scrap of doubt from Scarlett's face.

He had seen the jagged headland in the last of the purple light.

This coast he knew with a sickening familiarity. Sickening, yes, but he'd climbed aboard the *Avalon* in London so he might set foot here again.

He would reach that headland. Reach those stifling villages that dripped with secrets and superstition. The villages hiding Henry Avery's riches.

"You tried to sail the ship alone?" says Scarlett. "Why didn't you come ashore in the lifeboat?"

"How was I to manage the davits singlehandedly? I knew the ship would wreck close to Talland Bay. Exactly where I needed to be. How could that be anything other than providence at work? How could I not have trusted in fate and stayed aboard the ship?"

"You are a man of science," says Scarlett. "A man like you does not believe in fate. A man like you makes his own fate."

He says nothing. Lets her words fall into place.

She twists a coil of hair around her finger. "You could have died."

"Yes. But I didn't. Because of you." This is the way to placate her, of course. Acknowledge her most heroic of deeds. He touches her cheek. She stiffens, but doesn't pull away.

"You would risk your life to find this haul. You must truly believe in it."

"Of course. I've seen it."

"You've seen one coin. For a man who believes in science so, you are relying on faith an awful lot when it comes to Avery's haul."

She is right, of course. There is an element of faith. But one black night on the landing beach, he had seen a smile creep across Jacob Bailey's face. The smile of a man who had uncovered valuable information. The smile of a man who *knew*.

"I need to believe," he says. "I need that money so I can be the person I was always meant to be."

"And who is that?"

A better person than this wreck who sits before her, dressed in a dead man's clothes. A person with his hands in far more noble things than free trade.

Scarlett knots her fingers together. "You know something. Something that tells you the haul is real when everyone around us is convinced it's a myth."

"It's as you said. Faith."

Her eyes harden. "What are you keeping from me?"

"Nothing." He reaches out, covers her hand with his. "Look at me."

She does, reluctantly.

"I've told you what happened on the *Avalon*. I told you I killed those five men. Why would I keep things from you now?"

Close to midnight. The churchyard is lamp-lit, streaked with silver plumes of breath. Isaac feels Flora's brandy warm his insides.

Ankers are passed down a chain of men from the vestry to the wagon by the gate. Scarlett watches them hide the ankers beneath a layer of kelp, arms wrapped around herself to keep out the bitter cold.

"Where's Hales?" Isaac asks her. "Is he out of the cottage?"

"Ayes. He tells me he has no interest in adulterating tea." She catches his eye, trying for a rise from him.

Isaac hands her a package. "Leather gloves and tobacco. Smith has agreed to give you three shillings for it."

She slides the package into the pocket stitched in the lining of her cloak. Pulls the hood up over her dark hair.

"Be careful," says Isaac. Fourteen years have not made it easier to send his sister into the night.

She nods.

He grabs her wrist as she turns to leave. "Be careful with Hales too, Scarlett. Please."

She twitches her lips, considering. "You don't trust him. You're just like Caroline."

159

"And you? Do you trust him?"

She falters. "Of course." She takes a lantern from beside the gravestones. "I've got to go."

The delivery wagon rattles past her as she begins the walk towards Talland Hill.

Isaac checks the door of the vestry. Locked. He nods at the vicar. Makes his way towards the lane. The clatter of the wagon fades. But something is not right. The sound of hooves is coming towards him as well. Three horses? Perhaps four?

The urgency of the hoof-falls tells Isaac *soldiers. Riding officers.*

Impossible. They have the protection of Bobby Carter. Their runs are scheduled to align with his working hours. Reuben's fortune makes sure of it.

Isaac peers down the dark road. He looks back at Dodge and the other men. "Douse the lights."

Blackness falls over the churchyard.

Isaac hurries to his cottage. Caroline sits by the fire with a mug in her hand, Mary asleep on her shoulder.

"The tea. We need to hide it." He scoops up the bags from beneath the table.

She follows him into the bedroom. "What's happening?"

"Riding officers." He shoves two bags beneath their mattress, the third into the cradle.

Caroline lies the baby in the crib, pulling the blanket over her and the satchel of tea. "Do you think Bobby has betrayed us?"

"I don't know." Isaac goes to the door and peers into the street.

Caroline stands beside him. "Is the church empty?"

He nods. "Gibson has the brandy. He ought to have made it to Polperro by now." He folds his hands behind his head. "Scarlett is out there."

"Scarlett knows what she's doing."

Isaac hears Dodge's voice, faint. "How dare you suggest such a thing! This is a house of God!"

He pulls the door closed. What had he been thinking, allowing Caroline to steal the tea? Allowing her to risk their safety like this? He feels a flush of anger. At her. At himself.

He waits. Her hand tenses around his arm. Neither of them speak. He hears voices from the street. House to house go the officers. Questioning. Searching.

And then a knock at the door.

The two men are dressed in the blue and brass of the preventative service. Bobby Carter is not among them.

"We've received information about a smuggling operation taking place in this village tonight," says one of the officers, striding into the house.

"Mammik?" Gabriel stumbles from the bedroom, his hair tousled and eyes wide. Caroline pulls him into her hip. Wraps her arms around him tightly.

The officers tear through the house; emptying cupboards and chests. Searching the fireplace, the oven, inside pots and pans.

Gabriel watches silently. Knows better than to say a word, Isaac is sure.

Still eyes and silent mouths. He had repeated the same words to his son he'd grown up hearing his parents recite.

Still eyes.

Silent mouths.

"You'll find nothing here," Isaac says darkly. His heart speeds.

"Check the cradle," says one of the officers.

Caroline steps in front of the crib. "Don't you even think about waking my baby." She reaches a protective arm over Mary's body. "You've found nothing. Leave us in peace."

The officer meets her glare. "There are smugglers in this village."

Caroline narrows her eyes. "You've not found them."

Scarlett paces up the lane, her path lit only by the faint circle of light from her lantern. A hand from behind snatches her wrist.

"Asher!" she hisses. "What in hell?" She gulps down her breath. "You followed me?"

"What you're doing is dangerous."

"Dangerous? I've been doing it since I were seven years old."

"That doesn't make it any safer. Where are you going?"

"Talland Hill. I've a package for Elias Smith."

"I'm coming with you."

She eyes him. "All right. But stay out of the way when we reach Smith's house. He's suspicious of his own cat. It's taken years for him to trust me. He'll not like the look of you."

They walk steadily up the hill; the sound of their footsteps lost as wind thrashes the trees.

Scarlett hears a high-pitched grunt. An animal?

She shines her lantern over the edge of the incline. At the bottom, a horse writhes.

"Is anyone there?" She pans the light through the inky shapes of the trees. The beam falls across a crumpled body.

Her breath catches. "Someone's down there." She swings her legs over the edge.

Asher pulls her back. "What are you doing? It's too steep."

"We have to help them!"

She hears the steady thunder of hooves. She blows out the candle, plunging them into blackness. Lies on her front among the knotted undergrowth, the package of tobacco heavy at the bottom of her cloak. Beneath them, the horse bellows. Her stomach tightens.

Yellow light spills over the road as the riding officers round the corner. She presses a hand to her mouth to quiet her noisy breathing.

The horses thunder past and disappear up the lane. Scarlett scrambles to her feet.

Asher peers over the edge into the darkness. "You can't go down there."

"I have to."

She slides over the edge of the incline, her boots scrabbling. She grabs at the twisted tree roots that curl through the earth. Moves with careful, sightless movements.

She hears Asher above her, climbing onto the slope. Streams of earth shoot out from beneath his boots and rain down beside her.

She lands heavily at the bottom and hurries to the body. Kneels at the man's side. She leans over him, making out his face in the muted moonlight. Tears tighten her throat. "Perhaps that explains the riding officers," she coughs. "This is Bobby Carter."

TELL ME ABOUT YOUR FATHER

Scarlett kneels over the body. "He's still alive. Help me, Asher. We have to get him back up the cliff."

Asher squints at Bobby's broken figure. Blood is gushing from the back of his head. One of his legs is twisted beneath him. His eyelids are fluttering. Soul close to escape.

"I'm sorry, Scarlett. There's nothing we can do."

She covers her mouth, choking back a sob.

The horse groans loudly. Scarlett reaches beneath her skirt and pulls a knife from her garter. "The horse," she coughs. "Kill it."

Asher wraps his fingers around the handle. Stands over the animal's body. Its legs writhe beneath him. He presses a hand to the horse's head. Feels its heat, its life. He holds the knife against the thick pulsing neck. His own heart is racing, he realises. What power he has right now, holding this great beast's life in his hands. What power to control life and death. He feels a tremor go through him.

The horse is quiet now, as if waiting, submitting.

Asher swallows hard. He drives the knife into its neck. A final cry from the horse. Blood runs hot over his hands. He feels the animal still. Feels himself shudder with the power of it.

Yes, there is a strange beauty in death.

He looks back at Scarlett. She is hunched over the man's body, murmuring words of comfort. Bobby's hand is clasped in both of hers.

He has been where she is, crouching over a dying man, listening to his last groans and confessions.

He pushes away the memory. Can't let himself go back there.

Scarlett's voice is a lullaby: *tell me about your mother. Your father. Tell me about home.*

Bobby's voice is faint. Unintelligible. Scarlett's shoulders shake with tears.

What if it were himself lying broken on the undergrowth, Asher wonders? Would she cry as the life slipped out of him? Would anyone cry? Or has he gone too far into the darkness for that?

He hovers behind her, clutching the bloodied knife. Wants to step closer to the dying man. Observe that precious moment when the soul slips away. But he feels an intruder.

What had he been thinking, following her out here, digging deeper into her world of free trade? Scarlett Bailey ought to have been nothing but a means to an end. Gaining her trust no more than a necessary— if enjoyable— step towards finding that haul.

But as he had sat in the tavern and watched her disappear onto the cliffs, he had been gripped with apprehension.

He'd felt the need to follow. Chase the woman who sees him as a brave, bright man. Keep her safe. Close.

A sudden cry from Scarlett. She lays her head against Bobby's still chest.

A globe of light at the top of the cliff illuminates the night.

Riding officers: "Stay where you are."

Asher doesn't move. His shirt and breeches are soaked with the horse's blood. Wet linen clings to his skin.

Two officers make their way down the incline. One shines the light in Scarlett's watery eyes, then over Bobby's body. "What happened?"

She sniffs. "He fell… The horse… I saw them from the road."

"Why were you on the road?"

"Is such a thing a crime?" She meets the officer's eyes challengingly.

"On your feet."

She stands, swallowing her tears.

"We know Bobby Carter was working for Charles Reuben. That's why he left Polperro in such a hurry. I daresay that's why he fell."

More light. More voices. Asher looks up. Isaac Bailey and a cluster of men stand at the top of the cliff. His cowardly crew, no doubt.

"Scarlett?" calls Isaac. He and several of the men begin to climb down the slope.

The first officer pulls his pistol. "Stay where you are, all of you."

The men continue to scramble down the cliff.

Isaac looks at the body, at Asher's bloodstained clothes. He turns to his sister. "Are you hurt?"

No.

The first officer looks to the second. He nods towards Scarlett and Asher. "Search them."

Asher stands motionless as the man's hands work across his chest, into his pockets, feel for hidden treasures inside his boots. The officer moves onto Scarlett. He pulls the cloak from her shoulders. Kneels at her feet. His hands slide up her legs, over her bodice, around her waist.

Finally, she slaps him away. "May we go now?"

"No," says the first officer. "I'm no fool. I know well we've interrupted a smuggling run."

"You've found nothing," says Isaac. "You've no grounds to make an arrest."

"We've found a man covered in blood."

"It's the horse's blood!" cries Scarlett. "Can't you see that? He had to put the poor animal out of its misery!"

Isaac steps close to the officer. "Bobby and the horse fell. Any fool can see that. And you've no proof of this smuggling run you're so convinced is taking place. Let them go."

They walk back to the cottage in silence. Scarlett knots her fingers in her cloak and stares at her feet. She hears shouted instructions as the riding officers haul Bobby's body back up the slope.

"I ought to take the tobacco to Mr Smith," she mumbles.

"Not tonight." Isaac ushers them inside the cottage. "The man can wait." He produces a clean shirt and breeches from his bedroom. Tosses them at Asher and nods to the wash stand in the corner of the kitchen. "Clean yourself."

Scarlett sits at the table, staring into the lantern.

Isaac murmurs to Caroline, his words distant.

Bobby dead. A leak. Cover blown.

Scarlett wipes her eyes. "Tom Leach and his men saw me with Bobby at the fair. They know he was working for us." She coughs down a fresh flood of tears. "They did this. I know it. They tipped off the revenue men. Told them about Bobby."

Caroline looks at Asher. "How do you know your shipwrecked sailor wasn't involved?"

He laughs coldly. Sits at the table in her husband's shirt, pale curls of hair escaping out the open neck. "Is there a basis for these wild accusations, Mrs Bailey?"

"Asher had every chance to turn me over to the riding officers," Scarlett hisses. "I trust him." She says it again, to push away her doubts, Isaac's doubts. *I trust him.*

"I don't," says Caroline. "And after all that's happened, a little distrust may well be a good thing. Isn't that right, Isaac?"

Isaac rubs his eyes. "Leave us," he tells Asher.

"As you wish." He disappears from the table, letting the bedroom door slam.

"You're far too trusting, Scarlett. It will be the end of you." A faint tremor in Caroline's voice.

Pots have been flung across the kitchen, Scarlett realises. The tea hidden. Riding officers have been here.

Isaac pulls a bottle of brandy from the shelf. Three glasses. He empties his own in a mouthful. "Customs knows we're using the bell house. There'll be eyes on the lane next time we take the lugger out, you can be sure of it."

Scarlett pulls at the dirt beneath her fingernails. "Flora asked you to open the tunnel."

Isaac doesn't reply.

"You're thinking of it, ayes."

He lowers his eyes. "I saw Jack die in there."

Caroline reaches over and squeezes his hand. Isaac tenses visibly.

"You'll not let anything like that happen again," she says. "You'll take your time. Shore the walls properly. Take enough men." When he doesn't reply, she says: "I don't see what choice you have. You can't use the church now customs are on your trail."

He pulls away. Weighted silence hangs between the two of them. Scarlett keeps her eyes down.

Finally, Caroline stands. "You will come to bed soon?"

A nod.

She disappears into their bedroom.

Isaac hovers beside Scarlett, his empty glass in his hand.

She waits for a word from him. Waits for a hand against her shoulder. Waits for anything to show her that she does not have to carry her grief alone.

But he disappears into the bedroom without speaking.

Her throat tightens.

She has brought this distance on herself, she knows it. She has been critical and cold towards her brother since discovering the stolen tea. But she can't bear this iciness between them. She wants nothing more than to bury her head in his shoulder and disappear from the world, the way she had when she was a child.

He has always been able to fix things.

Lace from Saint Peter Port for her court doll's torn dress.

A tale of magic lands to keep the ghosts away.

A dimming of the lamp when anger takes her over.

She had spent two years in the Polperro children's home. There was a brother, she knew, out there somewhere, with tar on his hands and salt in his hair. She had no recollection of him, but made her own image, brought to life by her parents' stories.

Isaac, who sailed to faraway places. Who would one day come for her with his salty hair and take her back to that cottage on the hill.

Perhaps, they had told her at the home. For it was a dangerous thing to dream too hard in this world.

And what excitement she had felt the day he had appeared to collect her. Excitement she had been too afraid to express in case her brother vanished the way her parents had.

He and Caroline speak of escape; a conversation that is reignited every few years. But this time feels different. Isaac has a new desperation in him. A desperation that has him stealing from the bell house for his own gain. He is reaching the end of his patience; Scarlett can feel it.

And what is this bubbling beneath her own skin? The rage that lives inside her is simmering in her stomach, set alight by her fury at Tom Leach. She feels it build. Feels her breathing quicken. Feels sweat prickle her neck. Again, she sees herself with a pistol in her hand. Sees Leach crumple in his own blood.

The lamp hisses.

Turn it off.

A dark room will calm her, will send these murderous thoughts fleeing. But she stares into the flame and feels her anger burn.

She thinks of Bobby. His laughter, his sparkling eyes. Their childhood adventures, his loving words.

He wouldn't want this. No anger. No retribution. He'd just want to be remembered.

She turns off the lamp and empties her glass, her throat burning as the dark engulfs her.

Isaac tugs off his coat and shirt and slides tensely into bed. He stares at the rugged beams across the ceiling.

"I'm sorry," Caroline murmurs. "For the tea."

Isaac can't look at her. He feels an invisible barrier between them in the bed. He folds his arms across his chest. "Do you know how hard I've fought to keep the trade out of our home?"

Caroline covers her eyes. "I'm sorry. I wasn't to know the revenue men would storm the place."

"Of course you weren't! How can we ever know? And yet here we are lining our children's beds with stolen tea."

What would they have done had the riding officers lifted Mary's mattress? He'd have been hauled away and impressed into service. Thrown into naval slops and been shipped off to fight the Spanish.

"You're right," Caroline says huskily. "Everything you've said is right. Punish me, husband."

"I don't want to punish you." For all her misjudgements, she has done more to get them out of this life than he has.

Caroline sits up on her knees. "Look at me, Isaac." Her face is lined and shadowy in the candlelight. "I'm sorry.

Truly." She presses a hand to his stubbly cheek. His anger fades slightly.

She runs her finger through the beginnings of his beard. "I'll destroy the tea."

He closes his eyes. The tea. Caroline's desperate attempt at freedom. How can he take it from her?

"No," he says. "We'll gain nothing from that. But I don't want it in the house."

After a moment, Caroline mumbles: "Buyers?"

"It's arranged," he says. "We can sell it to the wink in Falmouth."

She keeps stroking. Her hands in his hair now. There is desperation in her touch. As though she is trying to push away her mistakes. Her fingers are hard and fast against his scalp. He reaches up and grabs her hand.

Stop.

She bends over him. The gold flecks in her eyes glisten with tears.

Isaac can't remember when he had last seen her cry. Something tightens in his chest. He pushes away the sweep of brown hair that has fallen across her face. "We were lucky this time. A reprieve."

Her tears spill. "I'm so sorry. For everything."

He nods slightly.

She straddles him suddenly, pressing her lips hard against his.

Isaac hears himself groan. Christ, how he's missed this. How he's missed *her*. But he feels her shaking in his arms. Feels her tears slide over his cheeks.

He turns his head, breaking her deep, desperate kiss. "There's something more. Tell me."

She shakes her head. Slides her shift over her head and presses her bare chest hard against his. "There's nothing more," she breathes. "Nothing more."

THE HEALING WOMAN'S DAUGHTER

Isaac heaves his axe into the wooden planks at the entrance of the tunnel. He had hammered these beams into place himself, the day they'd hauled Jack's body from the rubble.

Ahead of him, the tunnel gapes, black and lightless. He lifts his lamp. The passage is crooked, walls shored with bricks. All as he had left it two years ago. The smell of the earth is painfully familiar.

Flora watches from the cellar stairs. Isaac can't look at her.

The plan had been his from the beginning. Dig a tunnel from the tavern's cellar through to the eastern beach. No more carting barrels up the hill to the church. No more dealings with mad Dodge. The vicar's cut of the takings in their own pockets.

Jack had clapped him on the back. *The men will love it,* he'd said. *We'll be heroes.*

To be hero was a foreign thing to Isaac. He was a criminal, a petty smuggler under the thumb of Charles Reuben. He longed to be a hero. And so off they went with picks and shovels, carving into the earth beneath the Mariner's Arms. Brimming with confidence and knowledge they didn't have.

Jack had gone ahead, leaving Isaac to shore up the walls. An unexplained weakness in the rock. Isaac had heard the sound in his sleep for months. The rumble and roar of collapsing earth. Jack's screams. And worst, the deathly silence that hung in the tunnel once it was over.

Still, they can't risk using the church again. And he'll not risk water damage by hiding the goods in the caves. Now the revenue men or on their trail, they will need to be smarter than ever.

And so Isaac marches into the tunnel, trailed by John Baker and the men from the landing party. Men with shovels, bricks, hammers. They will do things right this time.

Isaac heaves his pick into the rock. Feels the vibration charge through his body.

Flora climbs from the cellar. Her throat is tight.

She had wanted this, she reminds herself. Had practically forced the pick into Isaac's hand. And yet the emotion of it simmers beneath the surface, threatening to break free.

She can't shake the tension in her shoulders. Can't shake the sense of things shifting, unravelling.

An hour before Isaac had prised open the tunnel, there had been revenue men at the inn. They'd stood with untaxed brandy to their right and a trading tunnel beneath their feet. Pressed her for information on the smuggling run they'd been unable to prove. Information on the dead man, Bobby Carter.

"I barely knew him," Flora had said, sure they could hear the thud of her heart. "Where was I the night of the delivery? Why, here of course, running my inn."

The night of Bobby's death, she had emptied the liquor kettle and lined the brandy ankers up behind the bar. If revenue men came searching, they'd take one look at the kettle and know she was unlicensed. Displaying the liquor is a risk, but it gives her at least the appearance of legality.

The officers stalked through the tavern. Flora felt a line of sweat run down her back.

"You have a licence for the sale of your liquor?"

"Of course." She forced her most law-abiding smile. "But that would be the business of the excisemen, would it not? And when they pay me a visit, I will be happy to show them my paperwork."

She'd bought herself a little time, perhaps.

She takes herself to the parlour and begins unhemming the skirts Bessie has outgrown. Even from the second storey, she can hear the thud of picks and hammers echoing beneath her feet. Had she sat listening to the earth splinter like this the day Jack had died? Had she been alone in the inn, the way she is now?

Her memories of that awful day are hazy. But *thud, thud* and the recollections return in pieces.

The thumping of Jack's pick replaced by the thunder of rock. Cries; Isaac's cries. She had run to the cellar. Found the room swirling with dust. Isaac had stumbled out of the tunnel and grabbed her tightly. Fallen to his knees.

Flora throws down her sewing; her hands trembling and ineffective. She walks down the hallway. Presses her hand to the door of the room containing Jack's things. For a moment, she considers stepping inside. Losing herself among his dust covered clothing.

No. Not today. The ache in her chest is already too intense.

She lets herself into her mother's room. She sits on the bed, pulling her knees to her chest. There is something calming about being here among the memories of her mother. This is where she needs to be while the men carve the tunnel beneath her.

She shivers. Lights the fire in the grate and stares into it, letting her mind still.

And then she has the black mirror in her hands.

She is hearing her mother's voice.

Hold the glass still.

Watch, cheel-vean. *Be patient.*

The black surface is swirling. Her eyes have lost focus, says her rational mind. But just for now, she wants to hear nothing from her rational mind. Her rational mind is the one who thought it best to open the tunnel.

And so she watches the swirling glass. Watches as flames dance across its surface.

She starts at a knock on the door. Throws down the mirror.

A reflection of the fire, of course. Nothing more.

She finds Martha Francis on her doorstep, huddled in a heavy brown cloak.

"Flora. Please. You need to do something to stop the darkness that has fallen over this village. The wreck and that dreadful body… And poor Bobby Carter… How can we deny we have been ill-wished?"

"Bobby Carter was involved in free trade. In all likelihood, the wrecked ship was too. It's a dangerous life. There will always be casualties."

Martha winds the strings of her bonnet around her hand. "There have been corpse candles on our horizon. Storm winds. A tip-off and two dead men. All since that ship was wrecked. Are we truly to put it down to coincidence?" The old woman shivers. A dreary, wet day. Flora thinks to let her inside. But she is sure the hammering will do nothing for Martha's fragile state.

She tugs her shawl tight around her shoulders and steps out into the street.

"My son won't go to sea," Martha tells her.

"No. He's left Isaac in quite the position."

"He'll not fish. He'll not trade. How are we to get by?" She wrings her hands together. "Not that I blame the boy, of course. The vicar's talk of ghosts and demons is very unsettling."

"The vicar's tales are intended to frighten you. Please don't believe everything he says. Man of God or no."

"If he means to frighten us, he is succeeding. It's why I've come to you." Martha's voice softens. "Your mother, she knew what to do at times like this. When you gave me that remedy for my joints, it brought me such joy to know you're choosing to follow in her path."

This had been her mother's skill, Flora realises. Not magic, or prophecy but providing comfort and peace to those around her. Providing a little assurance when the wind blew too hard or the sea surged.

She presses a hand to Martha's arm. "Wait here."

She runs upstairs and rifles through the chest. Finds two black feathers. She has vague memories of her mother using such things as a charm against disease. Perhaps if she speaks with enough conviction, they might also become a charm against fear.

She hurries back to the street and hands them to Martha. "Protection," she says loudly, clearly. "Carry this with you and no ill-luck will find you."

The old woman can see through her lies, surely. She is as much of a fraud as Reverend Dodge.

But Martha's face breaks into a relieved smile.

"And one for your son," says Flora. "Perhaps he might find the courage to return to sea and help Isaac."

"Thank you." Martha squeezes Flora's hand. "Please stop hiding, my dear girl. We need you."

They heave and dig and shore for four hours or more, finally stumbling back to the bar with aching arms and dusty skin. The inn is quiet. Dust dances in the shafts of pearly light. The Mariner's Arms will remain closed tonight, as it has each day since the revenue men had stormed the village.

Isaac feels for Flora. Her joy at finally opening the bar had been short-lived. But with a cellar full of unlicensed liquor, she has little choice but to keep the doors bolted. With the riding officers' eyes fixed to the town, the excisemen will not be far behind.

She comes downstairs at the sound of their footsteps and places a bowl of water on the table. "Clean yourself, Isaac. You're a mess."

The water is cold and bracing. He runs the cloth over his face and neck, washing away the grime, the unease. He steps back from the basin to let the other men wash.

"Are you all right?" Flora asks softly.

He nods. "And you?"

"Opening the tunnel was my idea."

"Still. I know it can't be easy for you."

She looks away. "No," she says finally. "It's not easy. But I'm not about to fall to pieces."

Isaac glances at the men. When they are looking the other way, he stands close to Flora and presses his hand over hers. "No one would blame you if you did."

She gives a faint smile, meeting his eyes. "My husband died a long time ago. I've moved on."

LEGAL STOCK

Reuben smiles when he sees Flora in his parlour. "Mrs Kelly. You are well, I hope?" He gestures to the armchair.

She remains standing. "I'm well. Despite a visit from the revenue men."

Reuben sits. Opens a tobacco box and fills his pipe. "Did they cause you trouble?"

"No trouble. Not yet. Though I fear the excisemen will be on their tail."

"You ought to hide your liquor. If you need help, I could—"

"I don't need your help. Thank you."

Reuben hums. "I've noticed that about you. Never willing to accept a helping hand. No matter how well-intentioned." He takes a long draw on the pipe and blows a line of smoke towards her. "You want to prove yourself independent, I suppose. Prove yourself a survivor, even without your husband. Show everyone you're not a weakling."

"What is wrong with that?"

"Nothing. But accepting help is not a sign of weakness. Especially when you've a young daughter to protect."

Flora presses her shoulders back. "There is something I need. A copy of a liquor licence."

"Why?"

"You know why."

"You plan to forge it."

She nods.

Reuben sighs heavily. "This is very dangerous. If you're caught, you'll be punished far more severely than if you were merely found to be selling unlicensed liquor."

"I'll not be caught."

Another draw of the pipe. "Run the Mariner's Arms as an alehouse. I will buy the brandy back from you."

"And how long do you think my business will last if I'm selling nothing but lambswool? The inns in Polperro will run me into the ground." She looks Reuben in the eye. "You want to help me. This is what you can do."

He leans back in his armchair. "You've put me in quite the position, Mrs Kelly. Yes, I can get you what you need. But by giving it to you, I would be putting you in serious danger."

"That is not your problem."

"Do you truly think I could wash my hands of your plight so easily?"

"The Mariner's Arms is my life. And until I can afford to run it legally, I'm willing to take my chances." She forces steadiness into her voice. Ignores the thudding of her heart, the trickle of sweat running down her back.

"The preventative service has their eyes on our village," says Reuben.

"Which is why I need the documents." She looks him in the eye. "Do you intend to stop your illegal activities, Mr Reuben?"

"No. But—"

"So why should I?"

"I can see there's no point in arguing."

"You are right. There is no point."

A temporary solution, she tells herself. As soon as she has the money, she will purchase the correct licences. Purchase only legal stock. And once Isaac has broken free of Reuben, she will block up the tunnel. The Mariner's Arms will be a law-abiding place she and her daughter can be proud of.

Reuben sits his pipe in a pewter ashtray and eases himself from the chair. "The licence is typeset. You'll need to find a printer willing to help you."

"I can do that."

He sighs. "Come back and see me this evening. I'll have what you need."

Scarlett pushes open the bedroom door. Asher looks up from the bed. He can see her silhouette in the glowing remains of the fire. Her shoulders are hunched. Hair hangs loose and tangled. She is wearing only her shift; a frayed tartan blanket around her shoulders. She hovers in the doorway like a ghost.

Asher's heart quickens. He had felt her trust slipping, but here she is in her underclothes, stealing towards his bed. Perhaps drawing her close will be easy after all. Perhaps all his work so far has not been a waste after all.

"You can't be in here," he says. "Your brother will kill us both if he catches you."

"I don't care." Her voice is thick with tears. "I don't want to be alone."

She climbs beneath the blankets. "They've opened the tunnel." Her voice is muffled.

"I heard."

"It's no good for them," she sniffs. "For Isaac and Flora. How it must be to go down there after what happened to poor Jack." She presses herself hard against Asher's chest and buries her eyes in his shoulder. "Still, they have no choice I suppose. Not after Bobby."

He feels her tears against his bare shoulder. With Scarlett clinging to him, he feels a bigger, better man. A man of coffeehouses and lecture halls.

It has been many years since he has felt a woman's skin against his own. For the last sixteen years, his life has been lonely one. His drive to succeed has left little room for love.

How different things might have been if he had walked away from Jacob on the beach that night. If he had been happy with all he'd had.

There had been coins in his pocket; a meagre sum, but enough to get by. There had been had a woman who had loved him. Had he walked away from the beach, he might be waking each morning to a woman's smile, gentle hands, loving words.

He can feel the heat of Scarlett's body through her thin sleeve. For a fleeting moment, his control leaves him. For a moment, he doesn't want wealth, or acknowledgement, or success. He just wants gentle hands. Loving words. The affection he has been starved of. And it matters little if it come from Jacob Bailey's daughter.

His hand slides up Scarlett's arm to the bare skin on her collarbone. He hears her breath catch in her throat.

It would be all too easy to draw her towards him and feel her skin against his. Feel, just for a few moments, a ghost of that life he could have chosen. He feels his blood heat. His hand slides under her nightshift and finds the hot skin on her thigh.

She shifts suddenly. "Asher, please. I've just lost Bobby." Her voice is thick with tears. "Be the decent man I know you are."

He rolls onto his back. Mumbles an apology. He feels his heart beat through his whole body; vibrating with desire, with humiliation.

But: *a decent man?* He has been a lowly slave, smuggling scum, mad filth. But now; a decent man?

He turns onto his knees and leans over Scarlett's curled body. He grips her wrists tightly. "You think me a decent man? Even after what I did to those men on the ship?"

She opens her eyes. Murmurs: "Sometimes you have no choice but to kill."

Asher smiles to himself. Yes. No choice but to kill a horse writhing in pain at the bottom of a cliff. No choice but to kill the men who have lost all reason and seek to take your life.

Bless this girl who is so easy to sway. Her thoughts so easy to manipulate. Bless her need to see the best in even the most miserable of men.

He kisses her impulsively. She stays motionless for a moment before softening, letting his tongue slide between her lips.

Good. Why not pretend this thing is real? Just for now. Real romance, real affection. It's what they both need, isn't it?

"What I did on the *Avalon*..." Asher says, his nose grazing hers, "the terrible thing I was forced to do... Do you think it courageous?"

Scarlett doesn't answer at once. Asher realises he is holding his breath.

"Courageous," she says finally. "Yes, I'm sure it was courageous."

He rolls onto his side, pushing his head against hers. He needs to be near her; this woman who sees him the way he has always longed to been seen. This child of Jacob's who makes him believe his desperate dreams are in reach.

He holds his lips against her neck. Closes his eyes. Allows himself to forget who she is, whose blood is coursing through her, how deep she is in the trade he so despises.

Her body tenses against his. She digs her fingers into his arm. Grips tighter and tighter until her nails leave flecks of blood on his skin.

POLRUAN

A gathering at the Three Pilchards.

Glasses raised.

To Bobby.

Scarlett sits with her back to the bar, red-rimmed eyes gazing out across the tavern. Isaac had tried to talk her out of coming. Wouldn't hear of it, of course.

He stands at her side, feeling useless. What can he say that might bring a little comfort? Words have never been his strength. He hesitates. "Scarlett—"

She looks at him expectantly.

The door creaks. Leach and his men.

Scarlett leaps from her stool, eyes flashing.

Isaac snatches her arm. "Don't."

She struggles against him. "Let go of me."

He wraps an arm around her waist and pulls her close.

Leach approaches with a faint smile. "We've just come to pay our respects, Miss Bailey. No need to be so aggressive."

"Ignore him," Isaac says, close to her ear. "Don't give him what he wants." He feels her trembling with anger.

Leach and his men make their way to the bar through a gauntlet of wild eyes and cursing. Someone hawks a glob of spittle onto his collar.

"Are you calm?" Isaac murmurs. Scarlett nods faintly. He releases his hold on her and pushes his way to the bar. "Get the hell out of here," he tells Leach. "You've caused enough trouble."

Leach chuckles. "You're damn quick to lay blame."

"We're not fools," says Isaac. "Leave us."

And finally they do, emptying their glasses and walking back through the tavern to the same icy silence they had entered to.

George Gibson appears at Isaac's side. "You've opened the tunnel?"

"Christ, George. Not now."

"Are you mad? Have you learned nothing after Jack? And to do such a thing with a curse upon us…"

Isaac lowers his voice. "We can't use the bell house, ayes. Customs have their eyes on it. And I'm losing whatever fragile faith I had in the vicar."

Gibson snorts. "It's that witch in the inn we can't trust. Is she the one telling you Dodge is untrustworthy?"

"You then was it? The bastard who threw the cross through her window?"

Gibson straightens his shoulders. "A warning, is all. At times like this, we don't need her kind inviting the devil along for the ride."

Isaac glares. "Stay away from her."

"What's it to you?"

Heat prickles his neck. He looks up. "Hell. Where's Scarlett?" He pushes his way through the crowded tavern. Shoves open the door and steps out into the icy night.

He finds her by the side of the building, untying one of the horses drinking from the water trough. "What are you doing?"

She glances at him, then swings herself into the saddle. Isaac snatches the reins. "This is theft."

"I don't care. I have to go after Leach."

"Go after him? And do what?"

"I don't know. But I can't just let him ride away. Bobby is dead because of him."

"Come on," he says. "Get off the horse."

But she pulls the reins from his hand and disappears up the dark street.

Isaac curses under his breath. He unties the second horse and leaps into the saddle. Unhooks a lantern from the inn's awnings.

He catches up with her on the edge of town. Ahead of the them, the road vanishes into blackness.

Scarlett looks over her shoulder at him. "Go away." Her voice is throaty.

"You know I'm not going to do that." He holds up the lantern. "Besides, you'll need the light."

Polruan is still. The streets are empty, bathed in shadow. The river slaps rhythmically against the harbour walls.

Scarlett asks after Leach at the inn. The bartender eyes them with suspicion, but points them towards a small stone cottage behind the blockhouse.

Isaac climbs from his horse and peers through the window. Leach sits at the table with a red-haired woman.

They scoop handfuls of pie from the same dish, laughing in the lamplight.

Isaac feels a strange flush of jealousy.

"That bastard," Scarlett hisses. "Going about his life as if nothing at all has happened." She reaches into her cloak. And Isaac sees it.

A pistol in her belt. His pistol. She must have been carrying it all evening. And for how long before that? He feels the same wrench in his stomach he had hearing Gabriel brag about stealing the tea.

Look at what his family is becoming.

"Give me the gun," he says huskily.

Scarlett slides from her horse.

He blocks her way to the door. "What are you planning to do? Just waltz in there and shoot the man?"

"Why shouldn't I?"

"Because you'll be strung up for murder!"

She opens her mouth to reply, then stops. Begins to pace. "He'll never be punished. The authorities see Bobby's death as an accident. But that's not what it was! He was fleeing Polperro because Leach turned him in."

"I know. Leach is a dog. But if you go in there and shoot him you'll hang for it. And he's sure as hell not worth that."

Scarlett blinks back tears. "It's my fault Bobby's dead."

What can he offer but dull words of comfort? *It's not your fault. Don't blame yourself.*

Once, he'd been able to make things better for her. Frighten away the monsters that hid in the shadows.

Now what? Now the monsters have faces, weapons, brass-buttoned uniforms and deceitful plots.

Now the darkness that has flickered in her since childhood is threatening to force its way out.

He holds out his hand. "Give me my gun." His voice hardens. "Do it. Now."

She shakes her head.

"You're not this person, Scarlett. I know it. Whatever Leach has done, it doesn't matter. You're better than this."

She squeezes her eyes closed. Hands him the pistol. The metal is warm in his hands.

Whatever Leach has done, it doesn't matter.

Ride away.

No. A man is dead. Their informant. Their friend. The safety of his family has been compromised.

He hands Scarlett his horses' reins.

"What are you doing?"

"Leach knew about the delivery. I need to know who told him."

He thumps on the door, hand wrapped around the pistol.

Leach's face breaks into a grin as he answers. Isaac grabs his collar and pulls him into the street. Shoves him hard against the wall of the house.

"How did you do it?" he hisses. "How did you know about the run?"

Leach chuckles. "I've no idea what you're talking about."

Isaac shoves the nose of his pistol into Leach's stomach.

"Tom?" The woman pokes her head out the door, starting at the sight of Isaac and Scarlett. She darts inside and returns brandishing a kitchen knife.

Leach glances at her. "Go inside, Jane. These people aren't worth the time of day. They're just smuggling scum from Talland."

Isaac shoves the pistol harder into Leach's flesh.

He groans. "We tipped off the revenue men. Is that what you wanted to hear? You've an innkeeper in Polperro who can't keep quiet when there's a gun pointed at him. Told us the day of the delivery."

"What were you doing in Talland the day of the fair?"

Leach sucks in his breath. "We had eyes on the Mariner's Arms. But the innkeeper is far too tight with your lot. I knew we'd get nothing out of her." He smiles. "What will you do now, Bailey? What will you do with this knowledge? Shoot me in front of my wife?"

"I ought to," hisses Isaac. "A man is dead because of you."

The faint grin doesn't leave Leach's face.

And suddenly Isaac feels that same rage he had seen in Scarlett's eyes. His finger trembles on the trigger.

You're not this man.

Isn't he?

He has been a man with morals. And what has it gotten him? Unpayable debt. A wife who longs for another existence. Children to which he can offer nothing but this life of servitude he'd been gifted by his own father.

He flings the gun away before he is tempted to use it.

Scarlett snatches it from the cobblestones. She holds it out in front of her, fingers clasped tightly around the grip. Fire behind her eyes. She walks slowly towards Leach. "Bastard," she hisses.

Isaac watches the gun tremble in her hand. Her eyes are coal. Face stony. He knows this look. Knows there is no reaching her. Knows her rage is winning.

He steps in front of the pistol.

"Get out of the way, Isaac!" she cries. "Now! Or I'll bloody well shoot you!"

"No you won't." He grits his teeth. Hopes he is right.

Leach laughs and disappears inside the house.

Scarlett lets out a cry of frustration and fires into the wall of the cottage. She grabs a stone from the side of the road and hurls it through Leach's window. Isaac snatches her wrist and drags her away from the cottage, down into a shadowy alley. Down into the dark. He pushes her back against the wall of a house. "Calm down now."

She closes her eyes. And the fire is gone. Replaced by a flood of tears. She throws her arms around his neck. "I'm sorry," she sobs. "I'm sorry. I can't control it."

"It's all right, ayes?" He holds her until her tears ease. He steps back. "It's all right."

Scarlett sinks to the ground. "It's not all right."

He sits beside her.

"I didn't want you to come here tonight," she says. "I didn't want you to be burdened by me. This is my fight with Leach. I started it by accusing him of killing that man from the wreck."

"You didn't start it, Scarlett. Leach and his men have been looking for a fight for as long as I've known them. They like the thrill of it I suppose."

"They're dogs," she mumbles.

"Ayes. And we'll not lower ourselves to their level, do you understand me?" He is trying to convince himself as much as he is her, Isaac realises.

Scarlett rubs her eyes. "It's my fault you're caught up in this life. You're right to want to get out."

He turns to face her. Her eyes glisten in the faint light. "You think this your fault?"

"Of course. If it weren't for me, you'd never have stayed in Talland. You'd have signed on another merchant voyage and you'd have been free. It's what you ought to have done. Reuben would never have found you."

"I don't regret coming for you, Scarlett. I wouldn't change any of it."

She laughs incredulously.

Isaac puts a hand to her arm. "Listen to me. If I'd left Talland, I'd have no one. But I have you. My children. I have Caroline."

"Caroline?" Scarlett snorts. "I'm no fool, Isaac. Men in happy marriages don't have wandering eyes."

He drops her wrist. Stands. "I've to go for the horses," he says tautly.

Frustration and anger simmer inside him. He feels a need to make someone pay for this twisted slope their lives have begun to career down.

For a fleeting moment, he wishes he had let Scarlett pull the trigger.

For a fleeting moment he wishes he had pulled the trigger.

He collects the horses and leads them back towards the alley. They climb into the saddles and pace without speaking.

Isaac looks out over the harbour. Leach's cutter rocks on the dark surface of the river. And as he watches that boat sway, he is suddenly done with this doomed attempt at decency. Done with trying to shoehorn his life of free trading into a moral existence.

He dismounts and unties a dinghy roped to the moorings.

"What are you doing?"

"Keep watch for the harbour master." He climbs into the boat and pushes away from the moorings. The oars sigh in the water.

His common sense says this will do nothing but cause more trouble.

But he is done listening.

Done listening to Caroline's disapproval and the men's foolish fears. Done following Charles Reuben's orders.

His own inaction sickens him. What intense, crushing uselessness he'd felt when he'd stood beside Scarlett at Bobby's wake. Her grief and guilt had been glaring, and what had he been able to offer her but a miserable glass of brandy?

Now what? He will sink a ship out of retribution and say *here, Bobby's death avenged?*

Don't cry, Leach's cutter is at the bottom of the river.

Sinking Leach's boat will not help Scarlett, of course. But perhaps it might still the restlessness inside him, if only for a moment.

He climbs aboard the cutter and carries his lamp below deck.

There is little in the hold but piles of canvas and old lines.

He takes the rope. Holds it to the lamp until it flares. He lets the flame flicker against the hull. The fire snakes along the coiled rope, blackening, weakening the wood. He kicks hard. The hull cracks, splinters. In comes the first trickle of sea, dousing the smouldering rope. Isaac kicks again. Dark water swells around his boots. With each kick, he feels a dam break inside him.

No longer will he sit by and let Reuben take everything. No longer will he live in fear of the life he will leave his children. To hell with his hapless attempt at decency.

He climbs from the hold, heart thumping with a new, violent enthusiasm.

Water swells around the bottom of the ladder.

Let the river flow in.

A MYTH

Flora pulls open the door of the inn. "Thank you for coming."

Scarlett smiles faintly. "Of course."

Flora pulls her into a tight embrace. "I'm sorry. I know how dear Bobby was to you."

Scarlett plays with the hem of her shawl. She is still humming with nervous energy from the previous night in Polruan. Still feels the pistol in her hand.

The Wild has always been with her. A shadow she has learned to live with. A shadow she has always been afraid to explore. Where does it come from? Why has it chosen her?

The anger steals her reason and, sometimes, her memories. Often, she'll crawl out from behind the shadow and have no recollection of what had triggered it, or what it had made her do.

But there is no haziness to her memories of Polruan.

She had scared herself. What would she have done had Isaac not stepped in front of Leach? For all the wildness that plagues her, she had never truly considered herself capable of murder. Never considered herself capable of the urge to kill that had seized her when she'd stood with a gun pointed at Tom Leach's chest.

"The place needs a sweep and polish," Flora says, leading her into the bar. "I want to reopen as soon as possible, but the place is a mess and Bessie's not well."

Scarlett takes off her cloak and shawl. Reaches for the broom. "You're reopening now? Is that wise?"

"Perhaps not. But I have protection in place. Best if you know no more."

Yes. Best. Scarlett can't fill her head with Flora's troubles too. "Go to Bessie," she says. "I'll see to things down here."

She sweeps and polishes and remains in an ignorance to the workings of the inn that is both necessary and pleasant. Lamplight flickers over the bar and slowly wears away her tension. She feels a little of her warmth creep back.

She thinks of Leach's cutter, lying at the bottom of the river. Fish in the pilot house and weed hanging from the gunwale. She allows herself a faint smile.

Isaac had surprised her. In their fourteen years together, she had never seen him act out in such a way. That night there had been a new fire behind his eyes.

A part of her is glad of it. Glad to see him breaking free of his henpecked existence. But a part of her is wary. Leach will come again, for certain, once he discovers his sunken ship.

Isaac had climbed from the dinghy, his clothes thick with the smell of smoke. He slid the pistol into his belt. "Scarlett," he said, not looking at her, "we'll speak of tonight to no one."

When the shelf is lined with glasses and the counter shines, she trudges upstairs to see Flora.

A faint lullaby comes from Bessie's room.

Over thee I keep my lonely watch
Intent thy lightest breath to catch
Oh when thou wakes to see thee smile
And thus my sorrow to beguile

Scarlett goes to the parlour. The fire crackles and casts dancing shadows. On the table lies a black glass mirror.

This mirror, she knows it. She had watched Flora's mother stare into it and pull out pieces of tomorrow.

She picks it up curiously.

She has heard the talk, of course. Flora and her healing herbs. Antidotes for the vicar's tales.

Scarlett stares at her distorted reflection. What have Flora's farsighted eyes seen in this? Can they pull the truth of Avery's haul from a tangle of myths and fairy tales? She longs for a distraction from the constant ache of Bobby's death.

"What are you doing in here?" Flora's voice makes her start.

Scarlett holds out the mirror. "Can you use it?"

Flora takes the glass and places it back on the table.

"Can you find things? Things that are lost?"

"What do you mean? What are you looking for?"

She hesitates. "Mr Hales is looking for Henry Avery's haul."

Flora lets out her breath. "Scarlett—"

"Everyone says it's a myth but—"

"Everyone is right."

"How can you be so sure? Asher knew a man who sailed with Avery when he raided the Moghul fleet. He's seen a coin that came from the haul." Scarlett lifts the mirror again. "Please. I need the distraction. Just let me bring Mr Hales here. You can speak to him about it. And perhaps something may show itself in that mirror."

Flora nods finally. "Very well. Bring him here."

"A mirror?" Asher snorts. "That's ridiculous." He rams his shovel into the earth and leaves it standing up beside the carrot patch.

"Didn't expect to find you in our garden." Scarlett smiles crookedly. "Hoping to impress Caroline were you?"

Asher gives an unenthused laugh. He'd found himself craving the physicality. Craving anything to alleviate his boredom.

Scarlett touches his elbow. "Come and see Flora. She can help with our search. I know it."

He wipes his muddy hands on his breeches. "Men have been searching for this haul for decades. You'll not find it by resorting to cheap parlour tricks."

Scarlett folds her arms. "I respect your beliefs, Asher. Perhaps you ought to do the same for me."

"You will hound me until I agree to go along with your games."

"Ayes."

"Very well." He sighs dramatically, marching from the vegetable patch. "Take me to your witch."

His memories of the inn are hazy. He remembers the cold floor of the cellar, the boarded tunnel, the pain in his head. Remembers waking intermittently with Scarlett watching over him.

Flora leads them up the stairs into the parlour. She looks at Asher with cold blue eyes. "Scarlett," she says, "I will take Mr Hales into my mother's room. I will try with the mirror in there."

Scarlett nods; her disappointment at being left out thinly veiled.

Flora gestures for Asher to follow her down the hall. Her footsteps click rhythmically on the floorboards. She pushes open a door and leads him inside. Thin curtains hang over the windows, allowing the last threads of daylight inside. On the bed lies the black mirror.

Flora nods to a chair beside the washstand. *Sit.*

She stands over him. "You'll not find that haul. My family has been in this village for generations. If Avery was ever here, I'd have heard about it. The story is a myth."

"All myths are born from a grain of truth."

Delirious in the cellar, he had been unable to place this woman. But of course. The charmer's daughter.

He dares to look into her eyes. Recognition there too. "You remember me," he says.

Flora nods.

He will not panic. She will remember him as no more than a foolish sailor caught up in free trade. Surely, she knows nothing about what had happened that dreadful night on the landing beach. Asher had been hauled out of the place by dragoons while the moon was still high. Any knowledge the villagers have can be based on nothing more than gossip.

His hand shoots out to cover the mirror. "Don't."

Flora turns the looking glass over so its black surface lies against the bed.

"I don't know how to use that mirror, Mr Hales. You know that, I'm sure. You'd not have come otherwise. Honestly, I don't know if the mirror is anything more than a game." She leans forward. "But I can tell there is fear in you. You're afraid of what I might discover."

Asher's heart quickens. "You're a fraud. You're just trying to scare me."

"For what purpose?"

"Perhaps you know more of Avery than you are letting on."

Flora laughs. "Avery. Forget that myth and leave our village in peace. There is nothing to find."

"I know better than to trust a woman in league with free traders."

Flora raises her eyebrows. "Perhaps that is something you ought to tell Scarlett."

He feels her eyes burn into him.

"You were in league with the Talland free traders once, were you not?" she says.

"Yes. My greatest mistake. And from it, I learned never to trust any of you."

"Well, Mr Hales, I can assure you the feeling of distrust is more than mutual. Scarlett is young and impulsive. She sees the best in people, which is both a blessing and a curse. But there are many of us who will do all they can to protect her."

"I care for Scarlett. I would never see harm come to her."

"Does she know you sailed with her father?"

Asher snorts. "Did you see that in your mirror?"

Flora says nothing.

"I had little to do with the man. I understand he is long dead."

She smiles wryly. "I may not have the abilities this village believes I have, but I can tell when a man is lying." She sits on the bed and folds her hands. "I couldn't place you at first. But now I remember. You made trading voyages with Jacob Bailey. Around the time he became obsessed with Avery's lost wealth."

Asher stares her down.

"Scarlett and Isaac know nothing about what happened with their father that night on the beach. And there is no reason for them to find out, do you understand?"

"That night on the beach," Asher spits. "I've no idea what you're talking about."

Flora doesn't speak, infuriating him. Does she believe him? Impossible to tell.

"This mess over Avery's fortune," she says finally, icily, "it's in the past. Leave it there. For the sake of Jacob's children."

Scarlett hears footsteps thud down the stairs. She races after Asher. He throws open the door and disappears into the purple dusk.

"Let him go," says Flora.

Scarlett whirls around in the doorway. "What happened? Did you see something about the haul?"

Flora sighs. "There is no haul, Scarlett. Please believe me."

"You didn't see that. That's just what you want me to believe."

"Ayes." Flora reaches for her arm. "It's what I want you to believe, because I don't want it to consume you, the way it consumed your father."

Scarlett peers into the dark street. "What did you say to Asher?"

"The same thing I just told you."

"Don't lie to me! Whatever you said has sent him running into the night."

Flora sighs. "Mr Hales is keeping things from you. You ought to involve yourself with him no longer."

For a long time, Scarlett says nothing. "How do you know that?" she mumbles finally.

"It doesn't matter how I know."

Scarlett glares. "He's keeping things from me? Just as you're doing?"

"I'm sorry. It's not my place to tell you any of this." Flora tries to usher her inside, but Scarlett stays planted in the doorway.

"Any of what?" she says icily.

"I'm sorry. I shouldn't have said a thing. But please, just believe me. You can't trust Asher Hales."

Scarlett clenches her teeth. Wind tunnels through the open door and makes the lamp above the stairs flicker.

Flora plants her hands on her hips. "You know I'm right. It's why you brought Mr Hales to me, ayes? Because you're not sure you can trust him?"

"Of course not! I brought him to you to help find Avery's haul." Scarlett looks at her feet, her stomach knotting. She swallows heavily. "I trust Asher. I do. He's not hiding anything."

"You asked me for help because you believe I can see things," says Flora. "This is what I can see."

SEA CHANTEYS AND SHOULDER RIDES

Scarlett sleeps little. She had returned home from the inn and lain awake by the fire, waiting for Asher to return.

He is keeping things from you.

Anything that comes from Flora is difficult to disregard.

When Asher had slipped through the door in the early hours of the morning, Scarlett had been unable to confront him.

She will not let Flora plant doubts. She has lived her life seeing the best in people and that is what she will do for Asher. See good in the world and keep the Wild at bay.

Her sleep had been punctuated with dreams of falling horses and Bobby's lifeless eyes. She wakes to the sinking feeling of reality being as bleak as dreaming.

She leaves for the fishing port without a word. The pilchard palace is quiet without the men at sea, but she busies herself with a mop and polishing rag. Anything to calm the doubts tearing through her mind.

In the evening, she goes to Martha Francis. "Why did you warn me to stop looking for Avery's haul?"

Martha sighs and ushers her inside. "Look at you. You're a mess."

Half her hair has blown loose from her plait and her boots are caked in mud. She is still wearing her fish-stained apron beneath her cloak.

Martha wraps her arms around her anyway. "After what happened to poor Bobby, I can't blame you."

"You told me not to dig up the past. What were you afraid I would find?"

"Scarlett, please. Let's not talk about this now. Not after all that's happened."

"Tell me!"

Martha sinks into a chair at the table. "Sit down."

Scarlett begins to pace. "I'd rather stand."

The old woman sighs. Wrings her hands together. "A man was shot on the landing beach many years ago. Back when you were just a child. When the soldiers arrived, they found a young man crouched over the body. The victim was killed over Avery's haul, this man said." She opens her mouth to say more, then stops.

"What?" Scarlett pushes. "Tell me."

Martha avoids her eyes. "He claimed your father was the killer."

Scarlett's stomach turns over. She feels suddenly hot. Angry. At who?

"It was all lies, of course," Martha says hurriedly. "Your father was no killer. You know that."

"Of course." Her father was sea chanteys and bedtime stories and shoulder rides. And yet the world feels suddenly colourless and unsteady.

Martha bustles to the range and pours a cup of tea from the kettle. She places it on the table and ushers Scarlett into a chair. "Drink this. It'll do you good."

She stares into it, unable to lift it to her lips.

All the people who must know of this. Flora. Dodge. Gibson.

Isaac? He had been away at sea. Has the village let him live in ignorance or has he kept things from her too?

The Wild stirs inside her. She clenches her fist until her hand begins to shake. She cannot let her anger out. Not here, not now.

Her hand flies out and knocks the cup from the table. It shatters on the flagstones, tea splattering up the table legs.

Martha whirls around.

"I'm sorry." Scarlett drops to the floor and gathers up the broken pieces. "I'm so sorry." Her cheeks flush with shame.

Martha bends stiffly and takes Scarlett's arm, ushering her back to her chair. "It's all right, *cheel-vean*. It was just an accident. No bother." She stands over her, holding her tightly. Scarlett lets her head rest against Martha's heaving chest. The old woman smells of musk and baking. Comforting smells. Smells from her childhood. Scarlett closes her eyes and tries to breathe deeply. Lets Martha run a hand through her tangled hair.

At the back of her mind, Scarlett finds a faint memory. Soldiers at the door. Her mother crying, father comforting. *All a mistake. I'm innocent.*

"What happened?" she asks finally.

"Jacob was freed, of course. They found no evidence connecting him to the murder. Your father was a good man, Scarlett. I know you remember that."

"Who was the other man?"

Martha sighs. "A stranger. No one I ever knew."

Scarlett's heart speeds. "Was he found guilty?"

Martha shakes her head faintly. "Of the murder, no. But they say he attacked the officers who came after him. Sent to the colonies. After that we never had word from him again."

DEAD MEN'S CANDLES

Bessie curls up in a corner of her bed, hair clinging to her damp cheeks. Her forehead burns. And then that horrid, growl of a cough that wracks her tiny body.

Flora sits at the bedside, drizzling elderflower tea down her daughter's throat.

A powerful, otherworldly odour.

The scent of the tea draws out her memories.

Flora; seven years old, the age Bessie is now. Sick in bed, feverish and weak. The world tossed upside-down by fever. Her mother had bent over her and whispered an incantation.

In the name of the Father, the Son and the Holy Ghost...

Within two days, Flora had been out of bed and running in the street.

She had become well because she had believed.

And this, Flora thinks sadly, wiping a damp cloth over Bessie's forehead, this is why she will never truly follow her mother down the path of the charmer.

Yes, she can bring hope. Help others believe. But she herself cannot see magic. Cannot see healing in a desperately whispered rhyme.

Magic. Another word for trickery. Deception. The vicar's flailing arms to hide a bell house full of liquor.

She bends to kiss Bessie's damp forehead. Leaves her daughter breathing raspily and sets her lamp on the table in the parlour.

Rain pelts the windows. Flora throws a log on the fire. She looks at the pages spread across the table.

Licence for the retailers of spirituous liquors…

The printing is neat, professional, the seal a close replica. Surely only the most alert of excisemen will be able to tell it a fake.

What would Jack make of all this? He had been a free trader to the bottom of his soul, so perhaps he'd have loved the thrill of it. Or perhaps it would sicken him to see the danger Flora is putting herself and their daughter in.

She pulls a flask of brandy from the shelf and pours herself a shallow glass. She sips slowly, feeling it slide hot down her throat. Her heart refuses to slow. Is it the counterfeit licence on her table, or that shipwrecked sailor heaving up the past? Perhaps the growing tunnel that snakes through the earth, clutching the last memories of her husband.

Grief wells inside her. She forces her tears away. How can she hope to show strength in front of others if she cannot even show it to herself?

She finds herself standing at the mouth of the tunnel; the lamp in her hand casting shadows into the gloom.

She has not stepped inside since the day Jack had been killed. Isaac had boarded up the entrance and Flora had done her best to forget the dark chasm that lay beneath her feet.

But tonight she feels drawn inside. Feels the need to be close to her husband. What a cursed thing, that it's here Jack feels closest. Here, where his life had come to a sudden and horrific end. Not beneath the sheets of the bed they had curled up in together during their nine years of marriage.

She steps into the tunnel, trailing a finger along the cold walls. Her footsteps echo. She hears herself say: "Jack?"

Silence, of course.

Her tears resurface and spill.

She has prided herself on holding her life together. On being strong for Bessie. No weakness. No neediness.

She drops to her knees. She longs for him. Longs for his tuneless whistle, his guttural laugh, his hands, his beard, his mouth, his skin.

She has never let herself think *if only*. What good will *if only* do? But now the words churn through her head as though they've spent the past two years gaining momentum.

If only they'd taken their time. If only Jack had been happy with all they had had. For underneath it all, Flora knows the uncomfortable truth: Isaac is a free trader out of necessity. Jack had been one out of greed. And for his greed he had paid dearly.

What is she doing staying here in Talland, ensnaring herself deeper in free trade? Pressing Isaac to reopen the tunnel? Why not just take Bessie and disappear east? Start a new life.

Fine, flighty ideas. But opening the inn has consumed her every thought for the last three years. How can she walk away?

She presses her eyes against her knees. There is more to it, she knows. Hiding in the back of her mind is the fear that perhaps Jack's soul lingers in this place. As much as she longs to believe he is at peace, she fears a man killed in such a terrible accident would rarely be so lucky.

Their souls will walk, her mother had told her when she was a child.

How hard she has tried to silence these ideas. Tried to let her rational mind win. These childish thoughts of ghosts go hand in hand with tales of blackened bullock hearts and blood magic. Things she does not believe in.

But what if she is wrong? What if she has been wrong about all of it?

How can she leave the Mariner's Arms if Jack will be forever unable? How can she leave the Mariner's Arms if there is even a scrap of possibility that her husband is still here?

The idea brings a fresh flood of tears. These are thoughts she has never allowed to take shape. She has gone about her life speaking with Jack since his death— casual asides to allay her loneliness– but she has never allowed herself to truly consider that he might be in the inn with her.

"Jack," she whispers, her voice disappearing. She waits in the silence. Leaps to her feet and hurries back to the land of the living.

Isaac makes his way home from the harbour along the cliff path. Rain pours in runnels down his tarred greatcoat. The path slides beneath his boots.

He is grateful when the earth begins to slope towards the village. Lights from the scattering of houses glow through the mist. And there, at the bend in the road, is an orange glow from the top floor of the Mariner's Arms.

He follows the light; a moth towards a flame.

A rough arm seizes his neck. He swings wildly. Contact. Fist to—what? A man's face? Yes, Tom Leach, spitting, hauling his arm back, ready for the retaliation.

Leach's men surround him. Isaac ducks a wild fist. The second blow makes contact, splitting the skin above his eye.

He'll take a blow to the head for a lost cutter. Dizziness swirls through him, along with a frisson of exhilaration.

He wants to fight.

The men grab his arms. He thrashes against them, outnumbered. The punch to his stomach is hard and fast. Blood runs into his eye. A second blow. He gasps for breath.

Flora throws open the door and charges into the street, something twisted and black in her hand.

"Get away from my inn," she hisses. "I wish to God that good luck never comes to your door." She shoves a needle into the charred ball in her fist. Isaac feels the hands fall from around the tops of his arms.

"Witch," Leach hisses. "We'll see you hanged."

Flora gives a short laugh. "Hanged?" She steps close, holding the black ball to his face. "These are enlightened times, Mr Leach. It is a crime to accuse a woman of witchcraft. This is, after all, nothing but a bullock's heart."

Leach's eyes flash. He and his men turn and hurry up the lane, disappearing into the darkness.

Isaac wipes the blood trickling down the side of his face. "A bullock's heart?"

She laughs. "A rotten potato. But it seems superstitious men will believe anything." She tosses it into the street and takes his arm. "You're soaked through. Come inside and let me fix that cut."

She leads him up to the parlour. Isaac drops onto the rug by the hearth and slides off his sodden coat. He edges close to the flames. After a moment, Flora returns with a basin in her hands. She kneels opposite him, her knees pressing against his. He can see the pale freckles scattered across her nose. She holds a cloth to the cut on his cheek. Her fingers to his skin. Heat courses through him.

"They were the traders from Polruan," she says.

He nods.

"Why did they attack you?"

"I sunk Leach's cutter. Payback for Bobby."

Flora sighs. "Oh Isaac. Please be careful. You're behaving rashly. It's not like you. You're going to get yourself killed." She plunges the cloth back into the bowl and wrings it out. Holds it to his cheek again. "You've always been so careful."

"And what has being careful brought me? I've spent fourteen years being loyal to Reuben. Trying to do things the right way. And I'm no closer to a free man. Every day I look at my son and think of what kind of life he'll have when I'm gone. I have to start taking risks. Do something to get my family out of this life."

"Ayes," says Flora. "You do. But you need to do things wisely. You can't go about sinking ships out of retribution. It's foolish."

"I know. I've just grown tired of decency. Of morality."

She tosses the cloth back into the pink water. "Perhaps you cannot be so moral when you're caught up in this world."

Isaac touches the swelling at the side of his face. "No. Perhaps not."

"Just be careful," she says. "Please. I can't lose you too."

Her eyes are red-rimmed, he notices, feeling his heart lurch. A heaviness had fallen about her the moment he had prised the tunnel open. He reaches out impulsively and clutches her hand.

Flora glances down at their intertwined fingers. "Isn't it Caroline you ought to be speaking to about all this?"

"You're right. I'm sorry." He pulls away. "I shouldn't have burdened you."

"That's not what I meant. I..." She digs a hand into her apron pocket and produces a vial of liquor. Uncorks it and hands it to Isaac.

"What's got you carrying brandy in your pocket?"

Flora snorts. "Fear of the devil. Or the vicar."

Isaac tosses back a mouthful, his throat heating. "Dodge? Is he still threatening you?"

"He has the villagers worked up. He's feeding them these stories so they'll cling tightly to God. I fear where this will lead."

"I hear there are some that are clinging tightly to you. Following in your mother's path, they say. Cursing men with rotten potatoes." He gives her a half smile. "I thought this was no more than offering a woman a remedy for her joints."

"The people need comfort. Dodge is not providing it. Perhaps I can."

Isaac hums noncommittally. He glances at the papers on the table. He stands, looks over them. "A liquor licence?

You're reopening the inn?"

She nods.

"Is it—"

"Forged? Ayes. And before you say it, I know it's dangerous. But I have no choice."

Isaac looks at her pointedly. "I'm the one who ought to be telling you to be careful."

Flora hugs her knees and stares into the flames. "This man from the wreck, Asher Hales. Please don't take him to Guernsey with you. I don't trust him."

"I have to take him. I've no one else."

"Aren't you bothered that his crewmate was found with a bullet in his chest?"

"Hales didn't kill that man. I'm sure of it."

"How are you so sure?" She squeezes his arm. "Tell Reuben you can't make the run. He'll understand, surely. After all that's happened."

"Understand? Are we speaking of the same man?"

"Just tell him, Isaac. Please. I don't want you at sea with Hales. Especially not on such a perilous journey."

He hesitates. Sits with his shoulder pressed against Flora's and watches steam rise from his wet shirt. The fire pops suddenly and he leaps to his feet.

"What is it?" She grabs the lamp and chases him downstairs. "What are you doing?"

"I'm going to finish this bloody tunnel." He charges through the dark bar and heaves open the cellar door. "The final beams are in place. I just wanted to wait until dark to break through to the beach." He grabs his pick. "Give me the lamp."

Flora grips the lantern. "I want to come."

"Are you sure?"

She nods. Wraps her long fingers around the handle of the shovel and follows Isaac into the dark passage.

Their footsteps are steady, rhythmic. Isaac's heart is fast, as it has been each time he has stepped into the tunnel. But the agitation in him has stilled.

Flora sets the lamp down at the end of the tunnel.

"Listen." Isaac reaches blindly for her wrist.

A sighing. Whispering. The sea.

He sees a faint smile on Flora's face. He runs a hand over the beams he and Baker had pounded into the earth the day before. Sturdy. Solid.

He heaves the pick into the earth, his beaten muscles groaning in protest. His wet shirt clings to his shoulders. Fragments of rock prickle his skin.

Suddenly, a thread of cold air. He swings the pick again and the blade bursts through the surface. Another swing.

As the rock gives way, the tension in his chest shatters. He begins to laugh. Showers of dirt rain over them. Isaac tosses down the pick and crawls through the hole. The rain has eased to a fine drizzle. His boots sink into the sand.

Flora wipes the dirt from her face and follows him onto the beach. Faint blue lights glow on the horizon.

Isaac takes a long, slow breath. These lights will spark a fresh wave of chaos. But just for now, there is stillness. There is just he and Flora and the constant ocean.

This hidden eastern beach, accessible only by sea. And now by the secret tunnel he has carved through the rock.

Flora looks out at the corpse candles. She tilts her head, considering.

Isaac watches her out of the corner of his eye. He wants to step closer. Wants to touch that white skin on her neck.

Wants to feel her breath against his ear. His heart thuds at the thought of it.

As he shifts his feet, Flora turns to look back at the tunnel. She reaches for his forearm and squeezes tightly. "You did it."

THE GHOST OF ALBERT DAVEY

'Avery came and said, "I am a man of fortune, and must seek my fortune."'

Testimony of David Creagh,
Crewman of Henry Avery
1696

"I've been waiting for you," Asher says, when Scarlett finally returns to the cottage. It's late and cold; the sky dotted with corpse candles. "Where have you been?"

She unlaces her cloak and flings it over the back of a chair. Beneath it, her apron and skirts are grimy. "I thought you'd be asleep." She goes to the kitchen and hacks at a loaf of bread.

Asher hovers. He regrets running from the witch's house. Regrets his anger. Asher Hales is poised and polished; not a fool who tears into the night, mad with rage. What conclusions must Scarlett have drawn?

She pulls the crust from the bread, refusing to look at him. He feels a weight in his stomach. Where is Scarlett who makes him feel a worthy man? When he catches his reflection through these new, cold eyes of hers, he doesn't like what he sees.

He takes the bread from her hand. "Walk with me."

She watches his fingers trying to needle their way between hers. Chews slowly. "Very well. We will walk."

She takes the lead. Straight for the landing beach. And Asher feels his stomach clench.

She knows.

They stand beside each other, eyes fixed to the ghostly blue lights. Scarlett wraps her arms around herself. She has left the house without her cloak and she shivers slightly as wind whips up the sand.

The sea is white and restless. The cliffs make shadows. Splintered moonlight falls across the wreck.

The beach is empty. No one will venture here at night now. No one will dare look at the ribs of the *Avalon* emerging with the low tide.

A haunted beach, they say. Plagued by the souls of his lost crew.

The people are right. The past has a way of lasting.

There by the cliff is the patch of sand on which the quartermaster's body had been found. That gift from the twisted wreck of the *Avalon*.

And there, by the river? There is the invisible ghost of Albert Davey, the man who had brought the Moguls' treasure to Talland.

"A man was once killed here over Avery's haul," Scarlett says to the sea. "Did you know of it?"

Asher shakes his head.

"I know you're lying." She breathes heavily. "They found a man on the beach with the body. Was it you? Were you the man who accused my father?"

Asher pauses.

"Yes," says Scarlett. "Just say it Asher. Yes. Tell me the truth."

So he says: "yes."

He waits for the eruption. Waits for her anger to tear itself free.

There was to be a time for these revelations. A time to tell Scarlett of his relationship with her father. She would be trusting, loving. And when the truth knocked her down, she would let him catch her. To hell with that witch in the inn, prying and planting doubts.

But there is no eruption. Scarlett's voice is controlled, even. Sends a chill through him.

"Is that why you didn't tell me you knew him? Because you were afraid I would find out what happened here?"

"Your father is your hero. I can see that. How could I ruin your memories of him?"

Look at her; dishevelled and dirty, her eyes wide and glistening. If he shakes her foundations further, how hard will she fall?

"Please. I'm sure my memories are of little bother to you." She shivers. "Who killed that man, Asher? You or my father?"

He exhales sharply. "How can I answer that? Whatever I say will destroy you."

"How do you answer it? You answer it with the truth!"

The truth.

Jacob Bailey had tried to double-cross Charles Reuben. His penance; an unpayable debt.

To many, Avery's haul was a myth. To Jacob, it was a life raft. One he would pursue by whatever means necessary.

Since the trip to Guernsey when Albert Davey had produced the coin, Jacob had trailed the man like a shadow. Under the guise of friendship, of course, but Asher was sure no one was fooled. Jacob's friendship with Albert was two-faced and laced with threat. Full of questions.

What happened to the rest of Avery's crew?

How much coin was distributed?

Show me more. I want to see more.

Albert was lonely and desperate for friends. Desperate for acceptance. But he was no fool. "I have that money well hidden, Bailey. I'd die before I let you get your hands on it."

A threat Jacob was willing to test. He trailed Albert home from Polperro. Asher followed.

He was in too deep, he knew. What had been a drunken tall tale had become a thing of guns and knives and threats. He wanted to leave. But Jacob was sure Albert would crumble under the pressure of two men. He had promised Asher a share of whatever was uncovered if he would be that second, ruthless man.

Asher had never been a ruthless man. He had been walked over by life, dragged through the mud. But if Albert's stories were true, his share of the haul would be enough to buy the life he longed for. And so he stayed on the beach.

Jacob put forth his case. Albert was an old man with no friends or family. Jacob had a wife and children and a debt hanging over him that darkened their lives. What use did an old man have for a haul of foreign riches?

Albert laughed coldly. "So I ought to hand it over to you so it can line Charles Reuben's pockets? You made your own mistakes, Bailey. Fix them yourself."

More heated words. Asher watched without speaking. Couldn't hear what was being said. Jacob drew a pistol and held it to Albert's chest. More words. And a smile on Jacob's lips.

In that moment, Asher knew. Jacob had information. On the threat of death, Albert Davey had given up the location of the fortune.

Asher let himself think of the learning. The people he would meet. The luxurious life he would build.

And then a pistol shot. Albert Davey fell to the sand. Jacob ran.

Asher dropped to his knees beside the dying man. Pulled off his neck cloth and pressed it uselessly to the bloom of blood creeping across Albert's stomach.

Albert motioned to the knife in his belt. "Kill me."

Asher's stomach tightened. He slid the knife from its holster. A violent tremor struck up in his hand. The man's face was contorted, his cold fingers gripping Asher's forearm. Blood ran from his body, into the stream, into the sea.

And then Albert Davey said no more. His breathing grew shorter, shallow. His eyes glazed.

Asher realised he was watching death. Watching the soul escape. This was the crucial moment. The moment with the answers. He sat the knife beside Albert's head and leant close to the body. He heard the distant clatter of horses. Didn't take his eyes from Albert Davey's quaking chest.

"On your feet."

And only then did Asher look up. Dragoons. They hovered over him on their horses, pistols in hand.

Again: "Stand."

No. Not until the man was dead. Then they could haul him away. But at that moment, following Albert Davey's soul was the only thing that mattered.

The soldiers yanked him to his feet. Asher fought against them, struggled to get back to the body. He pulled an arm free. Snatched Albert's knife from the sand. And with a wild swing, the blade sliced through a coat, through a soldier's forearm.

A pistol was pulled. Asher's hands tied. He was leashed to the back of a horse and marched from the beach before Albert Davey was dead. The priceless opportunity lost.

Asher protested his innocence. The dragoons had been aggressive, he claimed. The attack had been provoked. A misunderstood fisherman, yes. A killer, no.

He named names, of course— what loyalty did he have to the man who had left him on the beach with a murder victim?— but he had nothing linking Jacob to the crime. A Cornish jury would always protect their own.

Asher was an outsider. A foreigner.

Hang by the neck until you are dead.

In the end, the absence of a murder weapon saved him from the scaffold. But his attack on the soldier saw him labelled a criminal. His sentence; half a lifetime of exile in the blazing and bloodstained New England colonies.

But he is a free man now. A new man. And whatever secrets Albert Davey had whispered to Jacob, he will uncover. Wherever that haul hides, he will find it.

"Tell me who killed that man." Scarlett's eyes are critical, cold. He had seen the same look from the men of the *Avalon* when they had found him bloodied beside the first mate's body.

Who is she to look at him this way? How dare she? His anger gives way to self-loathing. She has made him feel worthless. Small. Things he never wanted to feel again. So he will gift her with the truth.

"Your father," he says. "Your father killed that man."

THE MAN WHO SHONE LIKE A STAR

"I must confess the parishioners do not send their children and servants to be instructed in the Catechism as your Lordship expects they would."

From a return made by Rev. Richard Dodge,
Vicar of Talland
1745

Polperro Harbour is strung with mist. The corpse candles have vanished with the dawn. Isaac scrubs, polishes, loads ankers of water and loaves of bread, readying the lugger for tomorrow's voyage.

Caroline wipes the windows of the pilot house, Mary clamped to her hip. Gabriel lies on his stomach across the deck and lines his soldiers up for impending battle.

Caroline speaks in jaded half-sentences as she works. *Apples from the market, your son needs new boots, be careful, be watchful.*

Isaac's responses are habitual, unthinking. Once, these mundane words between he and his wife had been enough. But this talk of escape has made him restless.

Sink the cutter. Break through the cliff. Steal and lie and see the faint, glittering potential of a better life.

He glances sideways at Caroline. Her skirts are grey, cloak grey. Her hair in a lifeless plait down her back. So often these days, she seems devoid of colour. He thinks of her in the Ship Inn so many years ago, dressed in yellow with a white ribbon in her hair. He tries to conjure up that old desire. Tries to find the passion he'd felt when they had curled up in his cabin while the sea writhed beneath them. All he can manage is a kind of muted tolerance.

He disappears below and returns with a packet of finely embroidered lace. A souvenir from a trading run.

He has been waiting for the right time to give it to Caroline. Has come to the conclusion there will not be one.

He hands it to her without speaking.

She sits beside the pilot house and opens the cloth wrapping. "Where did this come from?"

He smiles stiffly. "Never you mind."

She runs her finger over its delicate gold embroidery. "It's beautiful. Thank you."

"You'll wear it at your collar," he says throatily. "In our new life."

A smile flickers in the corner of her mouth.

He kneels over her suddenly. Presses a palm to her cheek. He wants the girl with the white ribbon. "Sleep on the ship tonight."

"What?" She gives a short laugh.

"As we used to." He kisses her neck. Feels her soften slightly.

She hesitates. "What of the children?"

"We'll put Mary in her basket with us. Gabriel can have a hammock in the saloon. He'll think it an adventure." His lips work their way along her jawline. "What do you say?"

Caroline lifts Mary onto her shoulder as she begins to whine. "What's gotten into you, Isaac?"

"I thought it was what you wanted. Things to change."

She smiles faintly. Stands. "Your daughter's hungry," she says, pulling on the hatch.

Isaac grabs her elbow before she disappears. "Sleep on the ship tonight. Please."

"In that cramped little bunk?"

"Ayes. In that cramped little bunk with Mary on the floor beside us."

She sighs, but there is light behind her eyes. "Very well, husband. You want to sleep on your ship, we will sleep on your ship."

Asher wakes from a broken sleep. The house is still. Is he alone? He has not seen Scarlett since she ran from the beach last night.

He pushes open the bedroom door. The kitchen is empty, the fire cold.

He is afraid of her, Asher realises. She has Jacob's blood in her. What is she capable of? How much has the truth of her father shaken her?

He slides on his coat and laces his boots. Fills his pockets with bread and cheese. Takes the handful of coins that sit on the kitchen shelf.

He'll head east. Find work. Reassess and plan where his search goes from here. His head will be clearer once he is free of this place.

He steps into the street. Hears angry voices. A crowd is gathering on the landing beach.

Another body? He finds himself hurrying towards them.

Men and women wade in the shallow water, clambering over rocks like frenzied beasts. They attack the skeleton of the Avalon with axes and hammers, frantic hands. Pieces of charred wood, sunken ropes and gnarled iron are carried back to shore. A pile of debris sits on the sand. Children run across the beach with armfuls of bracken and fling them onto the pile.

The vicar stands on the sand, the thin thread of the river running over his boots.

"What's happening?"

Dodge glances at Asher, then looks back at the crowd. "The people think to burn what's left of your ship. Burn out the spirits that haunt them. They believe it will free them of this curse. The corpse candles were on our horizon again last night."

Eyes are on him, Asher realises. Women frozen at the water's edge. Children whispering. Men with axes.

"You," says George Gibson.

Dodge clears his throat. "As you were, my son."

Gibson hesitates. His body tenses as he stares at Asher. Around him, the procession continues. The pile of debris grows.

Asher turns to leave. An arm is around him suddenly, hurling him backwards. He falls to his knees.

Gibson shoves him onto his back. "What are you then? A demon? You can't be no man to have come from that ship!"

Asher tries to push him away, but Gibson's thick arms pin his shoulders to the sand.

"Ought we throw you to the fire too?"

Asher's heart speeds. "Bloody fools," he spits. These witless men. He has seen their kind before. Seen them walking the decks of the Avalon.

The crowd closes in. Small-minded men with hate in their eyes He feels suddenly hot. The world seems to contort and contract around him.

He hears the voice of Barrett, the quartermaster.

Ought we throw you over?

"Violence will not solve your problem, Mr Gibson," says the vicar.

"And what would you have us do, Father? Sit by and wait for your empty promises to be fulfilled? Sit by and wait to die?" He stands, letting Asher scramble to his feet.

"What do you expect to befall a village who has turned to black magic to cure their ills?" Dodge looks out over the crowd, the wind whipping his white wig. "Yes, I know where your faith is. With the trickery pedalled by Flora Kelly. Do you truly expect the Lord to do your work, when you show faith in nothing but a witch's charms?"

"I had faith in you, Father," Gibson hisses. "But the lights in the sky are still with us. And so is he." He points a grimy finger at Asher. "How can we believe him a normal man when he came to us alone on that cursed wreck? How can we believe him anything but a demon?"

Dodge looks at Asher; his eyes glowing beneath ragged brows. "You are right to fear the demons around us, Mr Gibson. And in such times, only a fool would turn from God."

Asher sees a sudden flash of light. Gibson swings a flaming branch towards his head. He ducks, falls to his knees. He scrambles to his feet, dizzy with fear.

And he runs.

He runs until his lungs blaze. Where is he? Trees fill the land below him, hiding the village. A wild expanse of moorland behind, ocean beyond.

He stumbles out onto the moor.

Space. Openness.

Wind scuds through the grass and the ancient hills look to be breathing. The sky is white and endless. After crawling through the cramped villages, the moor is a deep inhalation.

How beautiful the silence is. How terrifying.

But it isn't really silence, is it. Even on this empty plain, there's the twitter of birdsong, the hiss of the wind.

Emptiness does not mean silence. On an abandoned ship, there is the creaking of spars, waves against the hull, the thunder of sails catching the wind.

Real silence is as rare as gold.

Asher lies on his back. The grass is damp and cold through his coat. He seethes with anger, hatred. For this place. For superstitious men.

Why was he returning to the west country, he had wondered, the night Quartermaster Barrett had threatened to throw him from the ship. What would he find there, but heathens and a land seeped in ancient ways? Why not stay in London among minds lofty like his own? Among people who would see beauty in the human body and the secrets it held.

The thought had been fleeting. Because what choice had he had but to return to Cornwall? Finding that haul is his key to bringing him the life he longs for.

He climbs to his feet. Begins to walk. He needs this openness. This breathing room. He walks across paddocks and unclaimed plains. Through winding villages and over tiny glittering streams. He walks away the day. Walks until his feet ache and the bread in his pocket is gone.

He looks out over the carpet of shadowed green. Boulders are silhouetted in the fading light.

Remnants of the giants' battles. He's heard the tales.

He hears himself laugh, cold and humourless.

Giants. Ghost ships. Curses.

Buried gold.

The realisation swings at him suddenly. Is he the most foolish of the superstitious men? Has he spent his life chasing a myth? Fallen for the bedtime stories Jacob Bailey had told his daughter?

No. He had seen that coin glittering between Albert Davey's wrinkled fingers.

All myths are born of truth.

But truths the size of coins become myths that can consume a desperate man. He thinks of the broken cottage that had housed Albert Davey. The home of a pauper, not a man rich with foreign silver.

That elusive haul, it had been a light in the darkness. He'd seen Jacob Bailey chase those coins to make his life better and to hell if Asher is not doing exactly that.

Sweat prickles his neck. His cheeks burn, then sting with cold.

These fools, he'd thought, clinging to fairy tales that make their dark world glitter. But now he sees with sickening clarity. He has fallen for the myth he had been so desperate to believe.

This is the secret Albert Davey had whispered to Jacob as he'd stood with a pistol pressed to his chest. Asher is certain of it. This is the secret that had made Jacob angry enough to kill.

All a lie. All a myth.

A story poor men clutch at so they might know greatness.

Once he had found Avery's money, Asher had told himself, then the world would come to know him and his great mind. He would travel. London, Paris, Rome. He would learn more, share his ideas. Chase the elusive soul.

Look, the world would say. *Look at this man born with nothing. Look at the way he crawled from the wreckage of his life and shone like a star.*

WHEN GOD STOPS LISTENING

Flora paces. Countless sick children had been brought through these doors while her mother was alive.

Give me hope. A miracle.

Flowers boiled, leaves crushed, spells whispered.

But Flora can see behind the magic. Sees there are no miracles on offer. And yet she feels the desperation shared by so many of the mothers who had carried their children into the Mariner's Arms.

She goes to the parlour and opens the chest.

Herbs have done nothing. She has flooded Bessie with healing teas and elderflower baths. Still her skin burns and her body is wracked with violent coughing.

At the bottom of the chest are the tufts of animal hair, the jars of nail clippings. That grotesque, blackened heart that had inspired her deception of Tom Leach.

Sorcery.

What good will it do? She doesn't believe. Power lies nowhere but with a God she cannot reach.

Illness a trial from the Lord, says Dodge. A thing to be endured. And for days, Flora has prayed and hoped, while Bessie groans and writhes in her bed.

But what happens, she thinks, when God stops listening? Ought they then turn elsewhere for answers?

A memory comes to her.

A charm against the child's-cough.

Spar stones from a running stream. Collect the water. Heat the stones. Brew a healing infusion that will silence the cough.

Flora grabs a jug from the kitchen. A lamp. She runs outside before she changes her mind. The night is cold and solid. She stumbles around the back of the inn to where the stream trickles towards the sea. She fills the jug. Plucks stones from the icy water and shoves them into the pocket of her apron.

She lights the fire in the bar. Lines the stones up along the great black hearth. Holds her numb fingers to the flames to warm them.

A knock at the door. She ignores it.

Again, louder. Insistent.

Go away.

A third knock.

The shipwrecked sailor leans wearily against the doorframe, shivering, despite wearing Jack's greatcoat. His cheeks are flushed and his hair is tangled about his shoulders.

"The inn is closed," says Flora. "I'm sorry."

He holds out a hand, preventing her from closing the door. "It's not real, is it."

"I don't know what you're talking about. Please, just leave, Mr Hales. My daughter is unwell."

"Just tell me. Avery's haul. Is it all a lie?"

"I've no idea."

"You spoke of it before. Tell me what you know!" He slams his hand hard against the door.

Flora glares. "It's a myth, ayes. A story. People cling to it because they need hope."

Asher looks over her shoulder to the stones lined up along the hearth. "Healing stones. Is that what you cling to? I thought you more intelligent than that."

She feels heat rising in her cheeks. "My daughter is very ill. I'm desperate."

"What is wrong with her?"

"The child's-cough. The herbal remedies are not working."

"Hot stones won't cure her. But salted water may."

"Salted water?"

"Yes. There is a new school of thought that believes illness is caused by an overactive soul." His voices catches slightly, then grows louder, imbued with sudden confidence. "The cure, many believe, is to cleanse the body with salted water."

Flora hesitates. This man is a liar. She knows it. But for the first time since he stumbled bloodied into her inn, she sees a sincerity in his eyes.

This is his passion. His life.

She steps back, pulling open the door. "Mr Hales. Please. Will you help my daughter?"

"Is she going to die?" Flora asks Asher.

The girl has kicked off her blankets in her sleep. Her nightgown is tangled around skeletal white legs, blonde hair clinging to her flushed cheeks. Her breathing is shallow and husky.

Asher takes the jug of salted water and drizzles it down her throat. "You'll not cure her with magic stones."

He sees the irony. These scornful words coming from the man who has sailed across the world in search of a fairy tale. And why not? Look at this dying child. This ruined man. This sad, creaking tavern, haunted by lost love. Reality is cold and unforgiving.

"The salted water," says Flora, lacing her fingers through the girl's. "Will it work?"

Truly, he has no idea. His knowledge is built on borrowed books and theory. All his life will allow. He longs to be able to offer cures with conviction.

"Yes," he says. "It will work."

She nods faintly. Looks up at him. "Thank you."

What is that in the witch's eyes? Gratitude. Respect.

Where is the suspicion, the distrust?

For a fleeting moment, Asher catches a glimpse of the man he longs to be. The man with power. Knowledge. Wealth.

The man he will never be.

He lets himself out of the inn. Sees an orange glow from the bonfire as the villagers play out their strange ritual.

A light shines in the church.

He climbs the hill and pushes open the gate. Finds himself wandering among the graves. Albert Davey; is he here? Where does a lonely, murdered man lie?

There; a memorial stone. Jacob Bailey, lost at sea. Asher snorts. Backs away from the marker. The wind whips through the graveyard. He shivers violently and pushes open the door of the vestry.

What is he doing here? He is wise and forward thinking. Not a man who cowers at a priest's feet. And yet, now he sees the haul for what it is, he feels himself unravelling. Begins to see himself for who he truly is.

Begins to see that bold, brave Asher Hales is also a myth.

Dodge looks up from the book in his hand. Squints. "The shipwrecked sailor."

Asher shivers. "Why are you here, Father? It's the middle of the night."

"It seems these villagers could use a watchful eye. Even if it's the eye of a man they no longer trust." He hauls himself to his feet and retrieves a greying blanket from the cupboard. Hands it to Asher. "Sit down, boy."

Asher sits, pulling the blanket around his shoulders.

"You are troubled," says Dodge. "Perhaps you might unburden yourself before God."

Asher tries to slow his breathing.

Unburden yourself.

Yes. He feels the weight of it all; his past, his lies, his secrets. Feels the weight of being so far from the man he ought to be.

"I am lost," he tells Dodge. "I feel as though my world has crumbled beneath me."

The vicar says nothing. Allows Asher to continue.

"I want to be a great man, Father. I have spent my life in pursuit of knowledge. Medicine. The work of the animists. I tell myself I will one day have the greatness I deserve."

"The animists," says Dodge. "You chase the soul."

"Yes. The soul is responsible for all the workings of the body."

"Many would say these are theologian's ideas. Not the ideas of a scientist."

"And why must these two views be exclusive? Why can they not exist in harmony?"

Dodge murmurs indistinctly. His gaze drifts out the window into the lightless churchyard.

Asher sighs. "Men are so terrified of new ideas. So afraid to see the world in a different light. I never understood why. But now I do. Now I see how your entire existence is upturned when you realise you've been believing a lie." He rubs his eyes. "I'm a man of science. But I've spent my life searching for something that isn't real." He looks again at the vicar. Can he see the irony; this gnarled, faded man of God? Can he see they've both spent their lives chasing demons in the dark?

"Searching for what?" Dodge asks.

"A myth. I can tell you no more."

"How do you know it isn't real?"

"Because all the evidence points to the opposite. And a man of science looks to evidence."

"Must a man of science also be devoid of faith? You said yourself, science and religion ought to exist in harmony."

Asher pulls the blanket around himself tightly. Faith has led him to a dead end, he is sure of it. "I believed because I had to. I looked down on these people who hear the dead in a storm and believe themselves cursed. But what difference is there between I and them? I'm far more of a fool than any of the people on that beach. And this life I want, this life of greatness, I can see now it will never be more than an illusion."

He closes his eyes. Sees himself in embroidered waistcoats and monogrammed shirts, drinking wine with men whose work he admires.

Fiction, of course. He is penniless. Hopeless.

But then Asher Hales sees with sudden clarity. Scarlett has led him deep into their world. He knows of the tunnel, the church, the false bottom in the hold of Isaac Bailey's lugger.

He knows, of course, of their run to Guernsey tomorrow. And knows the man who had protected these free traders now lies lifeless in the earth.

Fifty pounds reward for the capture of smugglers.

Nothing on Avery's haul. But Avery's haul is a myth.

Asher leaps from his chair and runs from the church. Tears through the village until he reaches the flickering lights of Polperro. He is breathless when he reaches the customs station.

"A lugger will return to these parts tomorrow night," he says. "They will land a load of contraband in Talland Bay. Intercept them."

FRENCH LACE

Scarlett sits on the edge of the cliff and watches flames colour the sky. Behind her, a little to the right, stands the memorial stone to her father; a path worn through the grass towards it.

She feels its presence, as though Jacob is standing behind her. She can't bring herself to look at it.

Asher's story of the murder on the beach is just that; a story. One that, like tales of ghost ships and curses, she can choose to believe or discard.

Her father a killer? The thought is far more foolish than dead men's voices in the wind.

In truth, she has no knowledge with which to acquit him. She had been five years old when Jacob had died. She has no proof of her father's decency beyond garbled, tinted memories. But it is a matter of faith.

And so here is her choice: Asher Hales is a liar. Asher Hales had kissed her lips and whispered of trust and spoken to her in lies.

Her father had been found not guilty. Why should she believe the word of a convicted man?

Her muscles tighten and her skin prickles. She has always believed the Wild to be separate from her true self. An intruder. But perhaps she has been gifted this darkness by her father. Had Jacob truly stood on the landing beach with a gun in his hand? Had he felt the same anger Scarlett had felt when she'd pointed the pistol at Tom Leach? Had her father left her his darkness as well as his debt?

Asher Hales is a liar, she could say until the words lose their meaning. But the darkness inside her makes it frighteningly easy to picture her father pulling the trigger on a another man.

She stands abruptly. She can't be here beside his memorial any longer. She stumbles out of the churchyard. George Gibson is staggering towards the beach with his arms full of branches.

"You're right," Scarlett tells him. "That ship has cursed us."

Perhaps it has not bought ghosts and demons, but it has brought her Asher Hales. Those garbled memories of her father are all she has of him. How dare he chip away at them?

Gibson nods. "Ayes, maid. It will destroy us if we're not vigilant."

"I was a fool," she says. "I trusted him. The man from the wreck."

"Trust?" Gibson steps close, his cheeks streaked with ash. "Don't you know, a demon can work its way inside your head. And when they do that, you'll believe anything."

She lets herself into the cottage and lights the lamp. A scrawled note from Isaac sits on the table. Spending the night on the lugger. No sign of Asher. No doubt he has dropped his tales at her feet and disappeared.

Scarlett's head pounds. She feels like she has lost her father all over again. Has Isaac heard these stories about the murder on the beach? How can she ask? How can she risk darkening his memories of their father too? She feels rattled at her foundations.

What a fool she had been to trust Asher so willingly. She has always fought to see the best in people; her fight back against the anger inside her. But what has she done but open herself up to disappointment?

That night, she had sat at the edge of the churchyard and watched through the window as Asher whimpered before the priest.

Deceiver, she'd thought.

Dodge: *manipulator*.

Look down at the beach.

Gibson: *madman*.

Martha Francis: *secret keeper*.

She hates this bitterness that is taking root inside her. But perhaps it is safer. Perhaps it is closer to the truth. Perhaps bitterness is better than believing a lie.

She hopes Asher has left for good. Hopes there'll be no voyage to Guernsey tomorrow. The Wild is close to the surface. She doubts it will stay silent if they are flung across the sea together.

She moves to blow out the candle, seeking darkness.

She stops.

What is that on the table, beneath her brother's knitted cap? She'd not noticed it when she'd stumbled bleary-eyed into the cottage.

Lace.

She lifts its delicate threads; holds them close to the candle flame. Gold anchors glitter in the light.

Gold anchors.

She has heard Asher speak of this lace. Lace the *Avalon* had been transporting. Lace once carried by vanished men.

Lace that is now in her brother's possession.

Her breathing quickens.

Isaac had made a trading run the night of the wreck. And now she sees. He had been trading with the *Avalon*. Trading with the man who had turned up dead on their landing beach.

Scarlett feels hot and dizzy.

She will not believe it. After all she has learned these past days, she cannot follow this thread.

She looks down at the lace.

Evidence, says the Wild. She had pronounced her father guilty with far less.

Her father is nothing more than distant figure she had moulded into a hero. But Isaac is real. The love she has for him is far more solid than anything she has ever felt for Jacob. She longs for her sunny sham of a world where the men she cares for can do no wrong.

To hell with the *Avalon* and all the trouble that washed up with her. The villagers are right to burn her.

She grips the lace, her hand trembling. Is this where George Gibson's terror has come from? Guilt? Were he and Isaac the ones to put the bullet in the quartermaster's chest?

No. Not her decent, moral brother who had given up everything to raise her.

Her brother who had dug the pistol into Leach's stomach. Sent his ship to the bottom of the river.

She had never imagined her father capable of killing. But with each stir of the darkness inside her, the possibility seems more and more plausible. Is the Wild inside Isaac too?

It has her. It had her father. Why not her brother?

She shoves the lace into her pocket. Turns out the light.

VOYAGE

Scarlett stands at the edge of the harbour and stares at her brother's ship. The morning is pink and misty. Her eyes sting with sleeplessness and old smoke.

Through the window of the pilot house, she sees Isaac bending over his log.

How many times has she watched him do this? Ready his ship to be filled with smuggled goods? Land by moonlight, deceive the authorities. And what had she seen in him but decency? An honest man in a life he did not choose.

But she sees now there are pieces she has been missing. The night she had stood on the clifftop and watched the *Avalon* catapult into Talland Bay, Isaac and his men had been on the very same ship. Cleared her of her cargo.

And what of her crew?

She can't bear to confront him. Better to live in doubt. Better to cling to those last threads of optimism.

She glances over her shoulder into the empty street. No sign of Asher. She is glad of it.

If Isaac had been aboard the *Avalon*, Asher's tales of killing the crew are lies. *Sent the smugglers away*, he had told her. And yet her pocket is crammed with smuggled French lace.

Lies for what purpose? What kind of mind tells tales of murdering men?

Gabriel scrambles out of the hatch, trailed by Caroline and Mary. Isaac kisses each of them. One, two, three.

Do they know, Scarlett wonders? Does Caroline know her husband walked the decks of the wrecked ship? Has he seen the faces of the vanished men?

Isaac watches them leave. He leans over the gunwale and calls down to Scarlett. The side of his face is bruised and dark, a cut beside his eye. Reluctantly, she makes her way towards the ship. Reaches for the ladder and climbs aboard.

"Where's Hales?" asks Isaac.

She shrugs.

He nods at her mud-caked skirts. "You can't come to sea dressed like that. There are spare breeches in the cabin."

Scarlett glances down at her skirts. She'd left the house without thinking, dressed in her smoke-stained clothes. She trudges below deck and exchanges her petticoats for Isaac's shirt and breeches. Cinches the waist with a belt and pulls her cloak back over her shoulders.

"You've not slept," says Isaac, when she returns to the deck. "You're in a state. What's happened? Has Hales done something?"

She clenches her teeth. Refuses to look at him.

"I don't want you at sea like this. It's not safe for any of us. Tell me what's happened."

She turns away, her throat tightening. She will see the best in him. Find a forgiving explanation for that lace with gold anchors.

"I'm well," she says huskily.

She hears footsteps. Asher climbs onto the ship. His face is shadowed with sleeplessness, but his eyes are determined. Isaac nods to him wordlessly.

Underway.

Smoke curls through the churchyard.

The vicar trudges down to the beach. The bonfire roars, sparks shooting into the sky. The pile is far too big to be the ruins of the ship. Dodge had watched the fire throughout the night. Burning down, blazing, burning down, reborn. Now the flames lick at... what? Chairs? A table? Is that a man's bed? This fear, he realises has seeped into every part of their lives.

George Gibson watches the flames with wild eyes; his hair loose, shirtsleeves black with ash.

"Go home, Mr Gibson," says Dodge. "Sleep will do you good." He rubs his stinging eyes. "Sleep will do us all good."

"How can I sleep? I can think of nothing but when death will come for me. I'm afraid to close my eyes in case I never open them again."

Dodge presses a hand to the man's arm. Tries to steer him away from the fire. Perhaps with the leader gone, the rest might disperse.

But no, here come more men, trudging down Bridles Lane. Lord protect them. He knows these men. The free traders from Polruan.

"Burning the wreck won't solve your problems," Tom Leach spits. "You've a witch in your village." Such venom in his voice that Dodge feels a run chill through him. "I was cursed by your innkeeper."

The villagers' eyes flash and harden. Voices rise.

No. When we fear the devil, we turn to God. We don't become the very monsters we are running from.

Dodge hollers to the crowd, his words disappearing beneath the clamour. He has tried to create faithful, decent souls. And yet before him is a band of witch-hunters, arming themselves with flaming sticks and axes. George Gibson leads the charge towards the Mariner's Arms. And the vicar sees his own failure.

WITCH

Banging on the door. Violent. Insistent.

Flora peeks through the parlour window. The street is full of men with weapons in their hands. Behind them, smoke darkens the sky.

Her heart thuds. She locks Bessie's bedroom and throws the key in the drawer.

A weapon. She needs a weapon. Had Jack owned a pistol?

She snatches the fire poker. Stands with her back pressed against Bessie's door. She grips the wall to stop the trembling in her hands.

Glass shatters. "Witch!"

She squeezes her eyes closed. Mumbles a hurried prayer.

How many women before her, she wonders, had pleaded to God while *witch* floated through their broken windows?

She hears the thud of boots inside the tavern.

She will meet them. Face them. See they come nowhere near her daughter. Gripping the bannister, she edges downstairs, the poker held in front of her. Six, seven, eight men? Perhaps more. George Gibson at the front, his face flushed and wild. Beside him, Tom Leach.

The men circle her. Grab her arms. The poker clatters to the floor.

"Let go of me!"

They march her from the tavern, towards the funnel of smoke. The people shout all at once, their voices unintelligible. Martha stoops at the edge of the beach, tears rolling down her cheeks. There are those who support her, Flora realises. But the men who don't are stronger.

Gibson looms over her, his wild grey hair grazing her cheek. He smells of sweat and smoke. "You laid a curse on Tom Leach. Do you deny it?"

"It was a trick. Nothing more." Her words tangle with fear.

"A trick?" Leach spits.

"Yes. Nothing more. I swear it."

"Did you curse us by bringing that ship?" Gibson hisses.

"The ship? No! I—"

Leach produces a knife and holds it close to Flora's face. Dizziness courses through her.

"They say to break a curse, you must bleed the witch."

Her legs weaken. The hands around the tops of her arms yank her back to standing.

Leach presses the knife to her stomach. "Shall we cut the witch here?" Her throat. "Or here?"

"Please," Flora coughs. "My daughter. I'm all she has."

Her eyes fall to the gun in Leach's belt. He jerks suddenly and swipes the knife across her forearm. White-hot pain. She clenches her teeth. Will not give these people the satisfaction of hearing her scream.

The men holding her arm release their grip as blood runs over their fingers. She lurches forward, snatches Leach's pistol. Hands yank her hair, pulling her backwards. She falls on her side, not releasing the gun. The men circle her. Flora scrambles to her feet, holding out the pistol. Her blood beads on the sand. She backs away. Reaches the top of the beach. And she runs.

Where to go? Bessie is alone at the inn. But she cannot risk the men storming through her windows again.

Help. She needs help.

Isaac and Scarlett are at sea.

Reuben, perhaps, would help her, but she will never make it to Polperro without the men catching her.

Desperation has her knocking on Caroline's door.

Caroline's eyes fall to the blood tricking down Flora's arm. She pulls her inside and locks the door. "What happened?"

Flora gulps down her breath. "They blame me for the wreck. They believe I cursed them."

"Mad fools." Caroline pushes back her bloodstained sleeve. "The cut is deep. It will need stitching."

"Not now. I need you to go to Bessie. Please."

Caroline wraps a cloth tightly around Flora's forearm. "Where will you go?"

"I don't know. But I need to keep those men away from the inn."

"You've a gun," says Caroline. "You have power over them."

Yes. The pistol is solid in her hand. Real power. Not flimsy incantations whispered in desperation.

Caroline scoops her baby from the cradle, cocooning her in blankets. "We'll go to the inn together. Bessie needs her mother."

Flora glances out the window. Two hundred yards from the cottage to the inn. The street is empty. Perhaps the pistol has kept the crowd away. "We need to go now," she tells Caroline. "Quickly."

They hurry down the hill. The beach is still dotted with people, still murky with smoke.

The door of the tavern hangs open. Broken glass juts from the windows. Flora pushes the door tentatively. A dark figure stands in the bar. She raises the pistol, hands trembling. "Stay where you are."

"Please, Mrs Kelly," says Dodge. "I'm not here to hurt you."

She gulps down her breath. "What do you want?"

He shuffles towards her. Glances at the blood splattered down the front of her dress. "I'm sorry I couldn't keep those animals from coming after you."

Flora snorts. "Did you not send them?"

"I suppose it is to my shame that you would think such a thing."

She pushes past him and hurries upstairs towards Bessie's bedroom. Unlocks the door to find her daughter asleep on her side, her breathing rapid and raspy. Flora straightens the blankets and smooths Bessie's hair.

Dodge joins her, breathless. "Your daughter is unwell?"

Flora says nothing.

"Perhaps I might pray for her."

"You did not come to pray for my daughter. Tell me why you're here."

Dodge begins to pace, the floorboards creaking beneath his boots. "The people of this town are scared. They are divided between the way of God and the old ways your mother once followed. Ways you too have chosen to follow." He grips the foot of Bessie's bed. "Last night I was reminded that perhaps two ways can exist in harmony. Perhaps if the people see you and I working together to end the curse they believe has befallen them, it will restore a sense of peace."

"You expect me to go back out there? I was lucky they didn't kill me."

"You have set yourself up as a healer," says Dodge. "A figure of note. And now people will turn to you in good times and bad."

Flora rubs her eyes. "I just wanted to help them."

"Indeed. I have thought the same many times."

She runs a finger over Bessie's knuckles. "I know how you see me, Father. As a dark witch. And thanks to you, that's how much of the village sees me."

"Thanks to you, much of the village sees me as a fraud who has done nothing but stoke their nightmares." His voice softens slightly. "This town, these people, they cannot survive with such a divide. Look at them tearing themselves apart. They need to see you and I working together."

Flora closes her eyes. Her heart is still racing and the cut on her arm burns. She has no desire to face the crowd again. The hunched and fragile vicar can't protect her. He can barely protect himself. But what are her choices? Barricade herself in the inn until the fire and the fury has burned out? Let the village believe she is responsible for their ills?

She sucks in her breath. Looks up at the vicar. "Very well, Father. As you wish."

He eyes her bloodstained sleeve. "Forgive me. I ought to have done more to help you." He presses a paper-thin hand over hers. "I failed your mother, Mrs Kelly. I don't intend to fail you too."

Flora closes the door on Bessie and ushers Dodge into the parlour. "What do you wish me to do?"

He sits at the table and clasps his speckled hands. "For better or for worse, we have created a village of believers. And we must use that to our advantage."

Flora thinks of Tom Leach fleeing her rotten vegetables. Yes, people can be trained to believe anything.

Chaos and unreason have raged like a disease. She is not without blame. But perhaps now she might spread the antidote.

She carries her mother's chest into the centre of the room. Caroline watches from the doorway.

At the bottom of the trunk is the grotesque, blackened heart. Flora stares at it. It had been enough to strike terror into Tom Leach. Perhaps she can use that fear. Twist it. Convince these frightened people she is fighting a powerful curse with powerful magic.

Pierce the heart with pins and draw out the dark.

She lifts the jar from the chest.

Caroline's lip curls. "What is that?"

"A charm. To break a curse."

She gives a short laugh. "Do you believe in such things?"

"It doesn't matter what I believe. It matters what the people believe." Flora can see this through Caroline's eyes, of course. Can see it through the doubting eyes of a foreigner.

She holds her aching arm close to her body. There is no room for doubting eyes. She must dig into superstition, into faith. Dig into beliefs as old as the land. If she is to calm the unreason, she needs to convince them that she herself believes.

She turns abruptly as footsteps thunder on the stairs.

LETTER

Saint Peter Port is just as Asher remembers.

Brick houses line the waterfront, the anchorage a forest of masts. The afternoon sun shines off the water, making a silhouette of the castle.

Asher waits with Scarlett by the harbour. The streets are a wash of coloured gowns and carriages. Barefooted slaves trail men in velvet frock coats and sailors stumble bleary-eyed from harbour taverns. Anker-makers heave their wares into waiting coaches.

Scarlett paces the cobbled walkway in boots and breeches, oblivious to passing glances. Her brother has disappeared to the office of Reuben's agent. There is money changing hands, contraband being loaded onto wagons. In a few hours they will return to Talland Bay with a full ship and be swooped upon by revenue men. Revenue men who know the lugger's route, know of her false bulkhead.

Perhaps it will be a strange kind of revenge, to string up Jacob's children.

The lugger will be broken up; her parts sold at auction. Isaac will be thrown into naval slops. He will have a touch rod forced into his hand and he will be ordered to light the cannons against the Spanish.

And what of Scarlett? Perhaps a jail cell. Perhaps a lenient Cornish jury.

If the lugger is full enough, perhaps the hangman.

Will she walk calmly to her death? Or be hauled onto the scaffold a tearful mess?

Asher sees her with a rope around her neck, sees her patched woollen skirts bubble around her as she falls. Black hair a stark contrast to her lifeless white skin.

When would her soul leave her? When would she stop being that starry-eyed person that had seen the good in him?

What does it matter now? Dead or alive, she is no longer that person.

But then something twists inside him. He thinks of her, pink-cheeked upon the clifftops. Thinks of her hauling him from the drowning *Avalon.*

"You can't go back to Talland tonight," he says suddenly. "You can't be on the lugger."

She gives him little more than a passing glance. Keeps pacing. "What are you talking about?"

Here is what a good man would do; tell Scarlett about the revenue men. Tell her it was all a mistake. Have Isaac moor in Guernsey for the night and return to Talland in clear waters.

Scarlett will go free. But Asher will be poor. He will never have that elusive university degree. And he will never again see the gratitude he had seen from the witch when he had proffered a cure for her daughter.

Which man is he to be?

He takes her arm and pulls her from the walkway. Sits on the harbour wall. "It's not safe for you to be on that ship. Isaac and I will return to Talland without you. You'll find passage back on another vessel."

She stands over him and plants her hands on her hips. "Do you think me mad? Why should I trust a word that comes from you?"

Asher opens his mouth to speak. Finds nothing.

"You didn't kill your crew," Scarlett spits. "Your tale of being fired upon by madmen, it was all a lie."

He feels a sudden rush of anger, a sudden rush of fear. "Why do you think me lying?"

"I don't *think* you lying, Asher. I know it! What kind of madman would confess to murders he did not commit?"

He stands to face her. Stares her down. *Madman.* How dare she? He feels a sudden urge to strike her.

She rams her fists into his shoulders. "What happened aboard that ship, Asher? Tell me!"

He forces himself to breathe evenly, though his insides are rattling. "I have told you. I have told you everything."

"Everything you've told me is a lie. You didn't kill your crew. And my father did not kill anyone." She looks at her feet. "My father is a good man."

He hears the tremor in her voice.

Say it again. Convince yourself of its truth.

Asher reaches into the pocket of his coat. Pulls out the yellowing letter he has carried with him for the past sixteen years. "Jacob is a dog, Scarlett. He's deceived you as much as he did me."

She falters. Keeps staring at her boots. Finally, she dares to look up at him. "What did you say?"

He hands her the letter.

Jacob is no longer in Talland. He left this place in his fishing boat, the village believing him drowned. On your return to England, you will find him in Portreath. He has taken a small cottage on the edge of town.

The words swim in front of Scarlett's eyes.

She glances at the date. 1724. The year her father had disappeared.

Her throat tightens. "Who wrote this?"

"No one you know."

"This person is lying. My father didn't go to Portreath. My father drowned at sea."

"Did they find his boat? His body?"

She feels a sudden weakness in her legs. "There is never a body. The sea makes sure of it." Yes, it is easy to mould the truth. Make it fit. Make it easy to swallow. If Asher can do it, so can she. "My father is dead. His grave is in our churchyard."

"His grave?"

No. His memorial stone.

She had never questioned it. An honourable dead father, she realises, is so much better than a living man who has abandoned his family in the face of his debts. The world feels colourless. "Whoever wrote this letter is making things up."

"What reason would they have to do that?"

"I don't know, Asher! But you have plenty! That much is obvious!" She screws up the page. But then shoves it into her pocket.

She sees her own foolishness. Trusting, naïve Scarlett who sees the sun before the clouds. Who sees good in the world around her. Sees only what she wants to see.

Bitterness rises in her throat. She drops to her knees at the harbour edge and retches into the water. Nothing comes up. She reaches into the sea and splashes her hot cheeks.

Asher stands behind her. "You were to be my key. I was to take you to Portreath. You would bring Jacob out of hiding for me."

She sits with her back to him, letting droplets of water slide from her chin. She feels the Wild heat her heart, tighten her muscles. "That's why you're here? That's what I am to you? Your key to finding my father?"

For a while, he says nothing. "You were more once," he tells her finally. "You made me believe I could be the man I long to be."

Scarlett turns to look at him. For a long time, she stares at him without speaking.

Deceiver.

Manipulator.

Madman.

Secret keeper.

She lets this new, accurate view of him wash away the last of her love-struck blindness.

She turns suddenly as Isaac leaps from a wagon stacked with crates and barrels. The dinghy bumps against the harbour wall, ready to be loaded and rowed back to the lugger.

Asher climbs into the boat to take the ankers from Isaac.

Scarlett kneels on the wall and looks down at him. His eyes are red and shadowy, his shoulders sunken. A shadow of his polished self. "You planned to take me to Portreath?" she hisses.

"Yes." Asher waits until Isaac has returned to the wagon. "Perhaps your father would tell you his secrets. Tell you all he knows of that haul. But I see now that all Jacob knows is that Avery's haul is a myth."

"A myth," she says. "After all this, you believe it a myth?"

Asher glances at her, then looks away hurriedly. Is that fear in his eyes? Can he see how close the darkness is to the surface? He takes a crate from Isaac and stacks it into the corner of the boat.

"Eventually," he says slowly, "everyone stops believing."

TO THE FIRE

'A public path leads by at no great distance from the spot and on diverse occasions has the labourer returning from his works been scared nigh into lunacy by sights and sounds of a very dreadful character.'

Taken from a letter to Rev. Richard Dodge from Mr Gryllis,
Rector of Lanreath
1725

Flora snatches the gun from the table. She rushes to the drawer and hands Caroline the key. "Lock Mary in my mother's room."

Men charge into the parlour. Leach grabs the chest and upends it over the floor. He hurls a vial of nail clippings into the cold fire grate. Spins around to face the other men. "You question why you're ill-wished? How can you be otherwise when you've black magic in the village tavern?"

"Ignorant fool," spits Flora.

Gibson points a grimy finger at Dodge. "You expect loyalty, Father? When we find you here?"

Leach lurches towards Flora. "Give me my gun, witch. What need do you have for such earthly things?" He makes a grab for it, but she darts backwards, clattering into the table.

Dodge shuffles towards them, hand outstretched. "Put the gun down, Mrs Kelly. Please. Before someone is hurt."

Men rifle through the spilled contents of the chest. Glass shatters as jars are flung into the fireplace. Bunches of herbs are kicked across the floor.

"Stop this second!" cries Dodge. "Look at yourselves! Look at what you're becoming!"

A wild arm catches him on the side of the head and he stumbles, landing hard against the sideboard. Flora grabs his arm, the gun spilling. She kicks it across the room. Caroline darts in from the hallway and snatches it from the floor.

Into the fireplace go feathers and flowers. Gibson reaches for the jar containing the blackened bullock heart.

"Stop," Flora cries, suddenly, instinctively. "Destroy that and you'll have no way of ridding us of this curse."

He lowers the jar. "Are you lying to us, witch?"

She gulps down her breath. "No. I can use the heart to draw out the curse. It's a charm of my mother's. She did such a thing many times."

He steps towards her, his breath hot and stale. "If you have the power to end this, why have you not done it already? Why let that body wash up on our beach? Why let Bobby Carter die?"

Flora looks past Gibson at Leach. "You wish to blame someone for Bobby's death, you ought not be looking at me."

Dodge stands shakily and holds out his hand for the jar. "Give it to me, Mr Gibson. This town has been divided for long enough."

Hesitantly, Gibson hands Dodge the jar. Flora takes it, shoves it into the pocket of her apron.

"We will go now to the beach," says the vicar. "We will see an end to this darkness. This madness." He glances at Flora. "Mrs Kelly?"

She nods. Picks up a crumpled parchment of incantations, scrawled in her mother's flowery hand. She shoves it into her pocket beside the jar. Perhaps carrying a little of her mother's handwriting might help her carry a little of her mother's faith. "Get out of my house," she tells the men. "And then I will come."

The crowd snakes slowly from the parlour. Flora laces her cloak. Helps the vicar shuffle to the stair rail.

Caroline hands her the pistol. "Take it. Just in case."

Flora nods. Slides it into her cloak.

Caroline touches her wrist. "Be careful."

She manages a faint smile.

To the beach. To the fire.

Witch they had called her. So *witch* she will be.

BELIEVERS

They walk together to the beach, the witch and the vicar. Walk to the fire and the frenzied, smoke-stained villagers.

The sun is sinking; the sky orange behind the smoke haze.

"The churchyard," Dodge murmurs. "These people need to see this done beneath the eyes of God."

Flora leads the way, past her inn with its broken windows and snaking tunnel. Up Bridles Lane where the demons gather. Towards the creaking gate of the churchyard.

She hears voices behind her.

Where is she going?

To the bell house.

Sacred ground.

She keeps walking.

Witch. How dare she enter?

She glances over her shoulder.

George Gibson at the front of the crowd. Martha Francis huddled in her cloak. The men who had held her arms and dragged her from the inn. Tom Leach stands among them, her blood still staining his knife blade.

Flora stops at the edge of the cemetery. The sea stretches out behind her, grey and white and restless. How many times has she stood here, signalling to the traders at the end of Dodge's exorcisms? She has been as responsible as anyone for sparking the mania that has consumed the village.

"Let us pray." The vicar bows his head. Wind billows up from the sea and makes a cloud of his black robes. "Strengthen us in the power of your might, oh God. Dress us in your armour so we might stand firm against the schemes of the devil." He turns to Flora. "The heart," he murmurs.

She takes the jar from her pocket. A murmur ripples through the churchyard. She feels Tom Leach's eyes on her; dark and hard. Beside him, Gibson is edgy, peering over his shoulder into the shadows of Bridles Lane.

Flora holds the blackened heart in her palm.

"As I pierce this heart," she begins, forcing a steadiness into her voice, "the darkness will be drawn from this place."

Another murmur from the crowd. She can't make out their words.

Fraud? Charlatan?

Witch?

She speaks the incantation loudly, clearly.

In the name of the Father, the Son and the Holy Ghost.

Shoves the first pin into the blackened flesh.

Beside her, she hears Gibson's breathing quicken.

He cries out. "Stop her, Father! Don't you see them? The demons? Her black magic is bringing them to us!"

Dodge presses a hand to Gibson's arm. "Calm yourself, my son. The Lord is with us." He nods at Flora to continue.

Another pin. Another shout from Gibson. He grabs at Flora's elbow. "Stop! Please!" He drops to his knees, clutching fistfuls of her skirts.

She glances at Dodge.

"Keep going," he tells her.

Gibson howls. Points to the shadows in the corner of the churchyard.

His wild cry gives Flora a sudden, violent chill. She stops. Bends over him and looks into his feverish eyes. "This is nothing but a trick, do you understand me? Look." She flings the heart from the cliff. A murmur ripples through the villagers. A woman pushes forward and peers into the sea.

Gibson stumbles, backing towards the edge of the cliff. "Stop them, Father. Please. They're coming for me." Sweat trickles down the side of his face.

Flora grips his shoulders. Drops her voice. "There's nothing in the lane. There never was. You know that, ayes? Our exorcisms, they were just a cover."

Gibson shakes his head. He breathes short and fast. "No. You're wrong. You've closed your mind and now you can't see the world as it truly is." He drops to his knees, burying his eyes in her blood-splattered skirt. "But I can see. They're coming for me. Because of what I did aboard that ship."

And then Flora does see.

Hales didn't kill that man.

How are you so sure?

She pushes Gibson into sitting. Looks him in the eye. "You and Isaac were on the *Avalon*."

The cutter appears like a blot of ink against the sunset.

Asher lifts the spying glass.

Revenue men.

He says nothing.

Scarlett's hands are clenched, her shoulders back. Something is boiling inside her.

She reaches into her cloak. Pulls out a spool of lace and flings it at her brother's feet.

Asher has seen this lace before. He had carried it from the hold of the *Avalon* and stored it in the captain's cabin to protect it from bilge water.

And now it is on Isaac Bailey's ship.

Scarlett glares at her brother. "You were on the *Avalon*."

Asher's heart begins to speed. Isaac Bailey was on his ship. Isaac Bailey and his crew put a bullet in the quartermaster's chest. Somewhere, in a distant pocket of his mind, Asher is aware he ought to feel anger at this. Ought to feel to the need for retribution, the desire for justice on account of his murdered crewmate. But the only thoughts he can manage are these:

Isaac Bailey knows the truth of what happened that night. He knows the weak and miserable man Asher Hales truly is. Sickness rises in his throat.

Isaac says nothing. His eyes lift to the ship on the horizon. He snatches the spying glass.

Yes. Revenue men.

"Was this your doing?" Isaac demands.

His doing? Of course not. Asher knows better than to accept responsibility while Scarlett has such fire in her eyes. This will not be his doing until he is safely aboard the revenue cutter and the Baileys are in chains.

Isaac curses under his breath. "Bring her about," he calls sharply. "We'll try and lose them."

Scarlett stands on the foredeck, staring her brother down.

"Christ, Scarlett!" he cries. "Move! If they catch us, this bastard will tell them where the goods are hidden!"

She kicks the lace towards him.

Isaac charges past her. "I've no time to explain myself to you."

"Make time!"

"To convince you I didn't kill those men? Is that what you want? And why in hell should I have to do that? Why do you see good in everyone but the worst in me?"

Asher glances at Scarlett. Her brother is wrong. That girl who sees the good in everyone is gone.

Isaac turns to leave, then stops. He sees it too, Asher realises. Sees this new depth to his sister's anger.

She steps towards him, not taking her eyes from his. "Tell me what happened."

Isaac looks at the revenue ship. Looks back at his sister. "Reuben arranged a rendezvous with the *Avalon's* captain. We came aboard to buy a shipment of whisky. The crew was mad. Saw ghosts. Wanted to rid themselves of a ship they saw as cursed. They paid me in coin and lace to ferry them ashore."

"Ferry them ashore?" Scarlett's voice is clipped. Disbelieving.

"Yes."

Behind the lies, Asher has always known, of course. Knows the crew of the *Avalon* saw him as a monster. Mad filth, who cut up the body of a dead man.

He was knocked unconscious by his own crew before the smugglers had even boarded. A blow to the head and left to die. How could he have admitted such a thing?

A man abandoned on a plundered merchant ship is not who he wants Asher Hales to be. A man who fights off would-be murderers, yes. Who refuses to be sunk with a wreck, yes. Mad filth, no.

But when he looks up, Asher sees he has become invisible. Scarlett's eyes are flashing, fixed to her brother. "The crew are alive?"

"Does that surprise you, Scarlett?" Ice in Isaac's voice. "Did you have me pegged as a murderer?"

"You left Mr Hales to die."

The rest of the night Asher remembers only in fragments. Men leaning over him. *Madman.*

Men dragging his body into the cabin so he'd not be seen by the boarding smugglers. Footsteps thundering down the passage as the traders raided the ship. Men climbing onto the deck.

And then, when consciousness returned completely; the impenetrable darkness of an empty ship.

Left to die on account of his great mind.

And as he lay there feeling blood trickle down his neck, he'd had just one thought. No one could ever know of this. No one could know of such shame.

He climbed to his feet, dizzily searching the ship for any leftover life. He found Quartermaster Barrett in the hold. And the thought came to him. One man murdered? No, let the world believe there had been five men killed. Let them see Asher Hales as the brave man who had survived both a shipwreck and a shower of gunfire. Far more commendable than being left to die.

But in pliable, trusting Scarlett he had seen an opportunity to become more than just the man who had survived a murder. With her trust secured, he had become the killer. An act of necessity, of course. Necessity and great bravery. And through her eyes, Asher had seen himself as the man he'd always wanted to be.

But now Scarlett's optimistic eyes see nothing. The man who fought off his five killers is gone. Left to die.

The smugglers who had taken Asher's crew ashore had been nameless. Faceless. But now, when he pictures the men scrambling from the *Avalon* and leaving him to bleed and drown, it is Isaac Bailey at the helm of the rescue ship.

Confront him. Demand answers.

But Asher Hales says nothing. Because beneath the lies and the dreams, he knows he is nothing more than a coward.

Scarlett is watching herself from afar. The world feels hazy. Unfocused. A distant, detached part of her can see Isaac's innocence. But the rage taking her over wants him condemned. "The dead man on the beach. Who killed him?"

The sea streams over the gunwale, soaking her boots. The lugger flies, plunging violently into the waves.

The revenue cutter is faster.

Isaac pushes past her question. "We need to lose the cargo." He looks pointedly at Asher. "Help me."

Scarlett chases the men into the hold. She feels both heavy and alive with energy. Hears herself speak without the thoughts entering her head. "The dead man. Tell me."

And Isaac tells her.

As he hauls the ankers from the hold, he tells her of the fear he had sensed the moment he had stepped aboard the *Avalon*. Tells her of the scrawled crucifixes and the crew red-eyed with sleeplessness. As he heaves the crates through the hatch, he tells her of the current in the air. The way it prickled his skin. The way he had questioned, fleetingly, the solidity of his rational world.

He slams the hatch and tells her of the blood staining the deck of the *Avalon's* sick bay. Their first mate's body carved up by a madman.

Scarlett's thinks of Asher and his fascination with death. She sees him with a knife in his hand. Blood-stained skin.

Isaac tells her more. As they shove the contraband into the sea, he tells her of the unexplained shape passing through the hold.

Ghost, said the men. *Demon.*

And Isaac tells her how quickly fear spreads. He tells her of the panic that rippled through his own men.

The pistol in George Gibson's fist.

The shadow again.

Unreason, it spreads like plague.

Thirty years of Dodge's stories have worked their way beneath the men's skin. Thirty years of ghosts and demons and sea spirits.

Unreason makes it easy to see things on the edge of your vision. To see a ghost where there is only a shadow. To see a demon where there is only a man.

Gibson whirled around. Fired.

The quartermaster fell.

And there was silence.

A cursed ship, said the men of the *Avalon*. They loaded their cargo into the hold of Isaac's lugger. Emptied their cabins.

"Coin and lace. Ferry us ashore."

Let the ship wreck.

Scarlett looks into the sea. The barrels and cases vanish below the surface. Whisky. Tobacco. Wine. Enough to tie them to Reuben for another lifetime.

She doesn't care. The Wild tells her to leave this place, this life. Escape Talland and let her brother carry the debt. His story doesn't vindicate him. His story shows that *we don't tell secrets* is the biggest of lies. Shows that there is trust between them only when Isaac chooses.

Beneath them, the sea thunders. The sea that had brought the *Avalon* to Talland. The sea that has ill-wished them. The sea that brought them Asher Hales, the man who has shattered the pedestal on which she had placed her father, her brother. On which she had placed Asher himself.

Demon, say the villagers. Perhaps there is a little truth to it.

She reaches into her belt. Pulls out the pistol and holds it to Asher's chest.

"Get off the ship," she says.

Send him back to where he came from. To break a curse, a sacrifice must be made.

Gibson's breath is fast and ragged.

Ghosts, he'd told Flora. A bloodstained ship. A terrified crew.

Demons.

He stares into Bridles Lane, eyes glassy with fear.

What does he see? What form has he given these creatures crawled from his nightmares?

Flora squeezes his hands. "There's nothing there. I swear it." Her voice is muted. How can her mumbled words compete with a lifetime of belief?

"I killed that man," Gibson coughs. "And now the demons are coming for me." He pulls at her cloak. Finds the pistol in her pocket. He yanks it out and presses it into her hand. "Shoot me. Before they find me." He clamps his hands over hers, working her finger towards the trigger. She pulls free. Hurls the gun over the edge of the cliff. Gibson lurches towards her with a cry. His fingers dig into the cut on her arm. Pain shoots through her, blurring her vision.

And she sees the shadows move. Sees, what? A shifting of the darkness in the corner of the churchyard. Arms? Legs? Eyes?

No.

She looks again. The shape is still there, moving in the shadow. A strange, fluid, human form.

She feels suddenly hot. Her ears ring. The world loses colour.

Unreason. Spreads like plague. She will not let it catch her. Will not let Dodge's exorcisms be anything more than theatre. This is her eyes playing tricks, nothing more. This is flames reflecting in the black mirror. This is her stress, her fear, her pain, her grief. The opening of the tunnel, the counterfeit licence, the revenue men at her door. But for all the clamouring of her rational mind, she can't pull her eyes from that shape in the shadows.

Beside her, Gibson stills. He follows her gaze. Does he see what she sees?

He scrambles towards the cliff edge. With his sudden movement, Flora's world is solid again. She dives after him, clutches desperately at his coat hem. The worn fabric slides through her fingers as he jumps, flying from the edge of the churchyard into the waiting sea.

Scarlett backs Asher towards the gunwale until his spine is hard against the rail. "Get off the ship," she says again.

Isaac edges towards her, hand outstretched. "Scarlett—"

She glances at him. Is that fear in his eyes? What will you do now, Isaac? Turn out the lights? The sun is still sinking.

"Give me the gun," he says. "Please."

When Scarlett remembers her father, he has Isaac's face, Isaac's body. She is sure in reality, her brother is not such a copy of Jacob, but her memories are hazy and she fills the gaps as she can.

She looks at Isaac now and sees Jacob on the landing beach, pistol in hand. She sees a trail of men climb from the *Avalon*. Sees the ravaged body coughed from the wreck. "Why should I listen to you? You're as much of a liar as the others."

"The others? Who are the others?" Isaac steps closer. "Who are the others, Scarlett? Who else has been lying to you?" She hears the control into his voice, the forced composure, the thinly veiled fear.

She turns away. Stares instead at Asher. The man in front of her is dishevelled; his face colourless. His shoulders curl. Hands white around the gunwale.

How had she seen superiority in this pathetic creature? Is he a different man? Or is she seeing through different eyes?

She hears herself say: "Jump."

Asher's eyes flicker. "I can't swim."

Good. Then the sea spirits will take him. He will vanish into the depths and the darkness over the town will be lifted. Perhaps the darkness in herself might also be eased.

She cocks the trigger. A sacrifice to the sea spirits. A sacrifice to the wildness so desperate to see her kill. "Jump."

And Asher does.

The sea rises to meet him. Steals his breath. Cold water closes in over his head, pulling him down, down. Filling his boots, pulling at his coat, making his hair dance around his head. His muscles tighten with shock.

Fitting that he might die in Cornish waters. He has always reserved a special hatred for the place. And the place has reserved the same special hatred for him.

But then he finds himself kicking.

And he remembers himself.

Asher Hales is a man with ambition. Dreams. He will not become these foolish people's sacrifice. He will not drown to appease the dark thing Scarlett Bailey has become. Will not give her the satisfaction of seeing him die.

He opens his eyes beneath the water. Gains little light. He wriggles free of his coat, letting it float to the bottom with the barrels. He kicks again. Feels himself rise.

Kicks again. Again. This time, strong and sure.

Somehow, he will win against a world that has done nothing but beat him down. He will stand before a body with a scalpel in his hand and the crowd will hold their breath in anticipation of his brilliance.

For all his lies, he sees a sudden, brilliant truth. Asher Hales is a survivor. Exile, abandonment, shipwreck, drowning. The crushing reality of the haul's nonexistence.

Today, the revenue men will find an empty ship. But tomorrow he will lead them to the smuggling tunnel, to the landing beach, to the monstrous house in which Charles Reuben directs his troops. He will have customs chip away at the Talland ring until that reward money is safe in his hands.

After all life has thrown at him, he can still see the sun glowing through the surface of the water. He bursts through with a gasp, fills his lungs with frosty air. Asher Hales is a survivor. A great mind. The man who shines like the brightest of stars.

Scarlett watches from the afterdeck as Asher climbs from the sea. She sees him the way the villagers had; a curse casting its shadow over their lives.

This curse brought with the *Avalon*; she sees now it can't be broken. She can't unlearn the things she now knows.

The world feels darker. Heavier.

Clearer.

She pulls Asher's letter from her pocket and holds it over the gunwale. It flutters between her fingers like a flag. Something stops her from letting go. She screws it up. Shoves it back into her pocket.

Isaac watches. "What was that?"

"Nothing." He has kept things from her. And she will do the same.

She walks without speaking towards the hatch. Seeking out the dark.

It won't work, she thinks, feeling the Wild press against her heart. Dark can't bring her peace. How can she feel peace after all she has learned?

But she walks towards the hatch anyway. Perhaps she'll not find peace, but she will find solitude, if only for a moment.

The revenue cutter is growing larger. It will catch them. Board them. Tear through the ship.

Find us, she thinks. *Find us empty. Find us with our wealth at the bottom of the sea.*

Flora drops to her knees. She pulls the parchment from her pocket. Lets it flutter from her fingers and follow George Gibson over the cliff. She stares at the patch of dark sea where he had disappeared.

When such things go wrong, her mother would say, the charmer blames black magic.

What a relief it would be to share her mother's belief. To say, *no, I didn't fail that man.* The man's soul was darkened as he stepped aboard a cursed ship.

Black magic. Not her own failings. What a pleasure it would be to believe.

She glances over her shoulder to where she had seen the shadows move. Nothing, of course. Empty darkness. And yet there is a strange depth to it as though an unseen layer has opened up behind her world.

She feels the eyes of the villagers burning into the back of her. Her arm pulses with pain. Slowly, she climbs to her feet. Dares to face them. Will they see Gibson's death as her doing? Her failing?

But then she hears: "The spirits have been appeased." A small, trembling voice at the back of the churchyard. The words filter through the crowd.

The spirits have been appeased.

And what more powerful thing is there, Flora wonders, than to believe?

Dodge hovers on the edge of the cliff, a prayer for the dead man cast down into the blackness.

"Mrs Kelly?" says the voice. "Tell us the curse has been lifted."

Their eyes are on her. On this sceptical, charlatan of a woman who has done little more than recite incantations she does not believe. On this sceptical, charlatan of a woman who wanted nothing more but to help ease the fear in the air.

She swallows hard, forcing away the sickness in her belly. "Ayes. The curse has been lifted. You may safely return to sea." She fills her words with as much confidence as she can manage, the way she remembers her mother speaking.

Drink this, Flora. And you will be well.

John Baker turns to Dodge. "Father? Is she telling the truth? Will we see the corpse candles again?"

The vicar glances at the sea. "Perhaps the lights will come and go. Perhaps we ought not fear them, but pray for the souls caught between this world and the next."

Enough. Enough madness.

Flora walks towards the gate, weaving through the cluster of people.

Inside the inn, she takes the spar stones from beside the hearth and drops them into the jug of water. She climbs the stairs to Bessie's bedside. Pours a cup and shakes her daughter's shoulder.

Drink this, Bessie. And you will be well.

ANOTHER DAWN

Here is Polperro harbour; misty and still and blue as they had left it. Caroline waits at the docks, the children in her arms. She watches as customs boards the ship. Watches Isaac hand over the passenger list, watches them disappear into the hold.

They are hours late into port. The landing party will have dispersed with the dawn. The tunnel remains unused.

The cargo was lost, Isaac will tell his wife. Will tell her of how the revenue cutter had chased them down. Boarded them to find an empty ship. And perhaps she will say: *you're safe, at least.*

Or perhaps he will just see that familiar coldness in her eyes as she adds the sum of the lost cargo to the unclimbable pile of their debt.

No. Instead, he will tell her of the plans he had set in motion in Saint Peter Port. Plans he had made as he had slipped away from Asher and Scarlett to his new agent's office. Secret, underhand plans that will see them free of this life. An agent of his own. Runs of his own. The takings in his pocket.

Deceive Charles Reuben.

This world of free trade has dragged him far from the man he wants to be. Far from the life he wants for his wife and children. His sister. The only way to break free, he sees now, is to burrow down to the level of Leach and Reuben and the man he became the night he sank the cutter.

Burrow down to the level of his father.

He takes an oar to bring the lugger into her moorings. Scarlett stands over him. Her eyes are shadowed with exhaustion, her skin colourless.

"We don't keep secrets," she says coldly. "That's what you've always said."

He nods, avoiding her eyes. "Ayes. I'm sorry."

Her voice sparks. "Why didn't you tell me what happened on that ship?"

"Because I left a man to die, Scarlett! I left a man to die for a scrap of lace and a few miserable coins! How could I admit that to you?" The guilt flares inside him. "How could I admit that this is the man I am now?"

They had left the quartermaster's body in the hold where he had fallen, both crews desperate to leave the ship. They had loaded the lugger and formed a frantic parade up to the deck, past hurriedly scrawled crucifixes and a sick bay stained with blood.

What else could be done, Isaac had thought? The sea would take the body when the abandoned ship foundered.

How, he had thought later, as Scarlett brought a sailor from the *Avalon* through their door, was he to know they were leaving a second man to die?

She looks down at him. "If the ship's owner comes looking you'll likely hang for what you did."

"There'll be no investigation. The ship is burned. The crew has disappeared."

"Not all of them."

"Asher Hales has no proof of anything. The revenue men will have no choice but to throw out his stories."

Scarlett knits her fingers together. "Did you know he was aboard?"

Isaac's guilt gives way to anger. "Do you truly need to ask that?"

"Yes." Her eyes are coal. "Because I've spent my life being deceived. And I see now I can trust you no more than anyone else."

Isaac exhales sharply, suddenly hot with resentment.

And he lets himself reach the thought he has spent fourteen years avoiding.

What if he had left? What if he had walked past that children's home and sailed away from this place?

For a fleeting moment, he lets himself see that life, that freedom. And a fleeting moment is enough.

When he looks back at Scarlett, he is done with her. Done dimming the lights, done excusing her temper, her tantrums. Done pretending that wildness is the doing of anything other than herself. If his only thanks is to be accused of murder, she can find her own way in the world.

He pulls on the oar. Turns away from her bitter, ungrateful eyes. "Believe what you wish."

Asher stands at the edge of the harbour. Watches Isaac with his family. His son trails him like a shadow as he checks the moorings, scrawls his final entrance in the log. He lifts the baby above his head, making her squeal with laughter.

Asher feels something burn inside him as he watches.

Hatred? Strangely, no.

Jealousy? This is closer.

He watches Scarlett disappear towards the cliff path. Waits until Isaac has climbed back aboard the lugger. And Asher stands beside Caroline, close, his shoulder pressed to hers. Her baby stares up at him with her father's dark eyes.

Caroline doesn't turn. "Leave."

Standing so near her, Asher feels something faint stir inside him. He smiles. "How long are we to keep playing this game, Callie?"

"You think this a game?"

"Yes. And a fine one at that."

"If it's a game, I'll not be outplayed." Her eyes are on the lugger, ready to spring away from him if Isaac should reappear. "Leave," she says again. "Avery's haul is nothing but a fairy tale. Have you not you realised that by now?"

"I've realised it, yes. As have you, I see."

"I realised it a long time ago."

The details on her face are just as he remembers them. Freckle beside her nose. The faint cleft in her chin. The neat, expressive arch of her brows. There is something exhilarating about standing close and speaking after so many wordless days in the cottage.

He smiles faintly. "I missed you."

She gives a snort of humourless laughter.

"You think me lying? I thought of you endlessly."

285

"Well I thought nothing of you."

"That I know is not true."

"Stay away from me." Her eyes flash with an intensity Asher had once known well. "And stay away from Scarlett."

He raises his eyebrows. "I didn't imagine there was any love lost between you and Scarlett."

"Don't pretend to know me," she says bitterly. "Leave this place and don't come back."

Her demands are unsurprising, of course, yet the sting of them feels fresh. "Is that truly what you want, Caroline?"

She looks at him for the first time. "Do you honestly think I could want otherwise?"

He thinks to tell her of his plans to send customs rifling through the Baileys' life. Thinks to tell her of the greatness that awaits him once the money is in his hands. Thinks to say *come with me.*

But her iciness has halted any scrap of the love that had once existed between them.

"Very well," says Asher, his voice controlled and even. "Then I will leave."

Flora unlocks the inn and lets Isaac inside.

He cups her injured arm in his hand. "I heard what happened. Are you all right?"

"Ayes. I think so." She nods at the boarded windows. Needles of pale light hatch the floor. "The place is a mess, but it will be fixed." She speaks softly, the confidence gone from her voice.

"We will mend the windows," says Isaac. But he can tell this new unease comes from far more than broken glass.

She follows him to the fire. Crouches by the hearth, her blue skirts pooling around her. "I feel responsible for George. I know I ought to have left my mother's chest where I found it. But…" She wraps her arms around herself. "Bessie. Her fever … it's less. I don't know why."

Isaac smiles. "It doesn't matter why." He squeezes her shoulder.

"How did Reuben take the news about the goods?" Flora asks.

He exhales sharply. "I need a drink."

"That I can offer." She pours him a glass of brandy. "Why did you not tell me you were on the *Avalon*?" she asks, her back to him.

Isaac's stomach turns over. He'd thought of telling her. Had wanted to the night they'd finished the tunnel. "The men and I swore we'd tell no one. It was foolish, I know. Perhaps if he'd spoken of it, it wouldn't have haunted George as it did."

Flora hands him the glass. Her face gives nothing away.

"I'm sorry," he says.

He looks up as his wife and children enter. He catches a faint smile between Caroline and Flora.

And then the crew. John Baker and Martha Francis's son. Men from the landing party.

Gaping holes, thinks Isaac. George Gibson. Bobby Carter.

Scarlett.

Glasses filled, raised. Toasts to the dead.

Isaac sits with Caroline at a table close to the fire. He edges his chair closer to hers and lifts the baby from her arms. Mary's head feels downy and fragile against his chin. "I've made arrangements with an agent in Saint Peter Port," he says. "He's starting out in the business. I'll invest the money from the tea in a run of my own."

He sees a new light behind Caroline's eyes.

"Reuben will have your head if he catches you."

"Ayes." He is walking in his father's path, he knows. He thinks of the smugglers' banker who had stood on the landing beach and held the gun to his head so many years ago. And he thinks of the rush he'd felt when he had sent Leach's cutter to the bottom of the river. Immorality, he realises, makes him feel alive. "But I have to do it."

Caroline smiles. "Yes. You do. We do." She touches his wrist and tilts her head to catch his eye. "I do love you, Isaac. You know that, don't you?"

He loops his fingers through hers. "Of course."

A gentle squeeze. Caroline glances across the bar at Flora. "I hope you'll always remember it."

Asher trudges up the lane, his lungs hot and straining. Easier to escape this way, than to take the cliff path past the inn full of villagers. He will climb the hill into Killigarth and follow it into Polperro where the customs house waits.

Needles of light pierce the trees. He keeps walking. Higher, higher until the cottages and church have given way to green. His legs burn. The muscles in his arms ache from his battle with the sea. His heart thumps with determination.

Scarlett stands at the top of the lane. She wears a brown woollen dress and riding boots. A pack is tied to her back.

"I thought I would catch you here," she says. "Asher Hales, the greatest of liars." Her eyes are hard, underlined with shadow. She has clamped a fist around the strap of her pack.

Asher's mouth is suddenly dry. He keeps walking. "Let me leave. It's the best thing for both of us."

She snatches his arm. Digs her fingers in with a force that stills him. "You're coming with me. Now. We need to find a carriage."

"I've no money."

She pulls a tangle of white and gold lace from her pocket. "This will get us to Portreath."

Asher's chest tightens. "Portreath? No, Scarlett. I don't think that wise." He tries to shake his arm free.

She hitches her skirt to reveal the silver blade in her garter. "I will decide what's wise, Mr Hales. Take me to see my father."

Enjoyed *Bridles Lane?*

Find out where the story began in *Moonshine*, the free short story prequel to the West Country Trilogy.

ABOUT THE AUTHOR

Johanna Craven is an Australian-born writer, pianist and film composer. She loves travelling, meditative dance and playing the folk fiddle. Johanna divides her time between London and Melbourne, escaping to Cornwall— one of her favourite places in the world— as often as she can.

Find out more at www.johannacraven.com.

Printed by Amazon Italia Logistica S.r.l.
Torrazza Piemonte (TO), Italy

13082276R00176